TRACKED

HEATHER SUNSERI

Sun Publishing
VERSAILLES, KENTUCKY

Copyright © 2015 by Heather Sunseri.

All rights reserved. No part of this publication may be reproduced, distributed or transmitted in any form or by any means, including photocopying, recording, or other electronic or mechanical methods, without the prior written permission of the publisher, except in the case of brief quotations embodied in critical reviews and certain other noncommercial uses permitted by copyright law. For permission requests, write to the publisher, addressed "Attention: Permissions Coordinator," at the address below.

Heather Sunseri/Sun Publishing
PO Box 1264
Versailles, Kentucky 40383
http://heathersunseri.com

Publisher's Note: This is a work of fiction. Names, characters, places, and incidents are a product of the author's imagination. Locales and public names are sometimes used for atmospheric purposes. Any resemblance to actual people, living or dead, or to businesses, companies, events, institutions, or locales is completely coincidental.

Book Layout ©2014 BookDesignTemplates.com
Cover design by Mike Sunseri
Edited by David Gatewood

TRACKED/ Heather Sunseri. -- 1st ed.
ISBN 978-1-943165-03-2

*To the many people across the continents
who give their time and resources to those in need
and to the people of Costa Rica
who shared their beautiful country with me for a short
period of time.*

ONE

Raven

Barely clinging to consciousness, I rolled side to side. My temple burned, and a stabbing pain erupted behind my right eye. The moonlight revealed no more than silhouettes slashing through the shadows at the base of the trees. I flinched with their every movement.

The two men arguing twenty feet away drifted in and out of focus. Their muffled voices were a confusing crescendo of sound, their bodies merging into a single figure. Suddenly, one man separated from the other. He clutched his chest and collapsed backward against a tree before sliding down to rest at my eye level.

I raised a hand and pressed it against my aching temple, where my fingers met with sticky hair. When I pulled my hand away, it was dark and wet. I gagged at the metallic smell of blood.

I rolled onto my back. My body trembled. I wanted to get up, but the throbbing pain in my rib cage glued me to the thick foliage. I glanced down the length of my body. Fire ignited in places I hadn't thought possible. My eyes burned. Thoughts of Pascal kept me almost lucid. How would I tell him what I'd witnessed? Or what I'd heard?

The river rushed in the distance, just like the creek back home after a hard spring rain. Oh, how I wished I could flee toward the water's soothing song and float away.

The urgency to help Nicholas—Pascal's father—and a newfound strength pushed me to my hands and knees, but a fresh wave of pain stung my side, and I collapsed again beneath the rainforest canopy, my eyes closing.

Seconds, maybe minutes later, I smelled a new pungent odor. I tried in vain to turn away. When I couldn't escape the stench, my eyes fluttered open. A dark figure kneeled beside me, his face inches from mine. The stale tobacco on his breath made me gag.

Behind him, another man spoke in a whisper. I couldn't see his face. "Don't kill her. I'll do anything. Just don't kill her."

The man with the cigarette breath held a small metal object between his thumb and forefinger. The corners of his lips crept upward. His dark brown eyes danced like a trained German shepherd just before being ordered to attack.

Time seemed to pass, as one figure morphed into another.

He pulled a knife from a sheath at his ankle, then forced my head forward. As his fingers brushed my hair off the back of my neck, my body shook. I was defenseless. I felt a sudden pinch to the skin just below my hairline and above my spine, the coolness of metal—and then a searing pain and pressure I couldn't identify.

I wailed and gnashed my teeth, writhing from the burn of whatever he had just done.

He stood, and the pain subsided slightly. The metal object was gone from his hands, as was the mystery man whose face I never saw. I teetered on the edge of consciousness. The man

tracked

stared down at me with a chilling hatred, his cruel eyes burning into my memory. *You will return to California. Forget what you've seen.* His voice was inside my head, but his lips remained motionless. *I'll see you in your dreams.*

As those words chiseled their way into my mind, I lost consciousness.

~~~~~

One year later

I stuck a leg outside the covers; the air was unseasonably hot for central California. My body was tired, but my mind was restless. I tossed and turned until I discovered just the right position to sink into what I hoped would be a peaceful night's sleep. I squeezed my eyes tight, concentrating on the settling noises of my parents' old house—the house my parents were selling without even discussing it with me. I was nineteen, and they still treated me like I was a fragile child; they had done so ever since the "accident" a year ago.

Eventually, I relaxed and dozed off. Then my cell phone buzzed.

Of course it did, right? It was one a.m., and sleep had finally found me.

Letting out a heavy sigh, I patted around the nightstand with my eyes closed until I found the source of the noisy vibration. I threw an arm over my forehead in Scarlet O'Hara fashion and brought the phone to my ear with my other hand. "Hello."

"Amagita?"

I sat up, eyes wide, and shoved my hair from my face. My heart raced to twice its normal speed. Only one person had ever called me that Spanish name, and I hadn't heard from him since last summer. "Pascal?"

"Sí. ¿Cómo está?"

"Fine."

A long silence followed. My eyes darted around the room, adjusting to the limited light shining through the window from the street lamps outside. Pascal and I used to email every day, but since I'd left—more like fled—Costa Rica last June, we had stopped all correspondence. Well, *he* had stopped. At first, anyway.

Why was he calling now?

"Raven? Are you there?"

"Yeah. I'm just surprised to hear from you." I narrowed my gaze to a pile of stuffed animals and childhood toys my mom refused to throw out. Just hearing Pascal's voice made my room spin, knocking me off kilter. I focused on the large unicorn on top of the stack, anything that might still the out-of-control room. My hand shook, and I gripped the phone tighter. Bad memories of that night a year ago assaulted me. I raised a hand and ran a finger across the scar on my right temple. My breathing began to slow, and my thoughts turned to the months of psychiatrists poking around my head, the time I spent searching for that happy place where I was okay with leaving that night—the night when I witnessed a murder—where it belonged: in the past.

"I know. I'm sorry it's late." He spoke in English with a thick, Hispanic accent. "Something's happened. They're threatening to close Puro Cielo. I thought you would want to know."

tracked

A chilly sweat broke out across my neck. Pascal's voice represented something in my past I wasn't willing to face. Not yet, anyway. "Who wants to close Puro Cielo?"

"The camp's governing board. Several members came on the same flight with your parents last week. There have been a few break-ins at the camp, and with express kidnappings on the rise in La Fortuna..."

What was he talking about? Daniel and my parents wouldn't keep this information from me. Would they?

Of course they would. My parents were life-long humanitarians, and Puro Cielo, a camp for volunteers and humanitarians traveling to Costa Rica, had been our second home for as long as I could form memories. Daniel, who co-directed Puro Cielo with my dad, was like a second father to me. They didn't tell me about Puro Cielo's troubles because they wanted to protect me from the pain they knew I would feel if the camp was forced to close. They didn't tell me because I'd made it crystal clear I would never return to Puro Cielo again. Not after what happened last summer.

"What does this have to do with me?" I whispered. I searched the ceiling for answers but found nothing.

"I just thought..."

"What? What did you think, Pascal? That I would come running back to La Fortuna?" Did he think I'd race back to him? After twelve months of silence? What would I even be coming back to? "Daniel and my parents can handle whatever's going on. I can't go there."

I told him goodbye and let the phone drop into my lap. A knot bounced around in my stomach. I reached over to my nightstand and lifted a picture. My fingers traced the heads of

Pascal, his brother Miguel, and myself. Was it so wrong that I wanted to leave Puro Cielo in the past? To leave behind the memories of the night I'd crossed from sweet innocence into something else altogether?

Setting the frame down, I lifted the folded piece of paper that I'd not so gently placed on the nightstand the night before—the real reason for my restlessness.

There they still were in black and white: grades from my second semester at Stanford University. I, Raven MacMillan, was slowly flunking out of school. At the very least, I would lose the rest of my scholarships after this report card.

Minutes after informing Pascal that I had no intention of stepping foot near the rainforests of Costa Rica again this soon, I logged onto my laptop and pulled up the flight schedule to Liberia, Costa Rica.

Shifting from computer to closet while the airline website loaded, I threw clothes at my suitcase. I turned in circles, searching for my camera, my passport, and anything else I needed for an unplanned trip to join my parents.

So much for my last summer in my childhood home.

I toyed with calling my parents or Daniel. Make them confirm what Pascal had said. I picked up my cell phone three times, but tossed it back on the bed every time without pushing send. Since they hadn't informed me of the crimes Pascal had spoken about, I figured they were keeping information from me on purpose. Again. And that was okay with me. I had no one to blame but myself. They'd tried to convince me to join them for the summer season, and I had refused every time, making excuse after excuse. That was before I'd discovered that my parents were selling my childhood home; before a second

tracked

concussion had ended my college soccer career; before I'd received crappy grades from my second semester of college; and before Pascal had inserted himself into my life again after nearly a year of silence.

But if Pascal was right, I couldn't allow Puro Cielo's governing board to shut the camp down. Not if I could do something to help. Even if that meant returning to the place where I'd nearly died.

~~~~~

Darkness never used to bother me before. Now, well... I knew monsters really did come out at night—monsters with no face or name, hiding in the shadows and whispering inside my head. And sometimes no one was there to protect me.

Daniel and I bumped along the pothole-infested roads as the crescent moon slid in and out of view behind the lush forest. Three hours later Daniel turned down the driveway to Campamento Puro Cielo. It was after eleven p.m., and the camp's visiting guests would already be tucked into their beds for the night.

Once out of the truck, Daniel ducked inside the building that housed the kitchen and the camp's office. Other than a few small lights coming from the windows of some of the cabins, the camp was dark. The sounds of the rainforest rang out around me: the chirring call of the nightjar, the incessant racket of the cicadas, and the random hoot of a pygmy owl.

The security light by the dining pavilion flickered on, and a couple of lizards scurried along the outside wall of the neighboring kitchen.

I stood alone in the center of camp. An eerie breeze swirled around my skirt, and goose bumps spread up my legs. I crossed my arms and rubbed my hands from my shoulders to my elbows.

I walked out of the light surrounding the pavilion to survey the rest of the camp. The soothing sound of the river that flowed at the base of camp welcomed me to the home I'd grown to love over the previous eleven summers. The leaves on the trees rustled in the night breeze. Moonlight filtered through the foliage and cast scurrying shadows along the bank. I closed my eyes and basked in the sweet scent of the wild impatiens growing around the river, hoping that the scent and the sound of the gentle rapids would calm the blood that coursed through my veins. I was caught up in a deluge of senses, torn between ghosts of one horrible night and memories of a lovely childhood.

A cool hand brushed against my arm. My entire body tightened.

I spun around, stepped back, and felt relief rush over me when I saw Daniel.

"Hey. You okay?" His hands shot out to the side to show me he meant no harm.

"Yeah." I chuckled, feeling silly. "Just taking it all in. It's been a while. I wasn't here for long last summer."

Daniel looked like he wanted to say something, but held it in.

"My fondest childhood memories are of this place..." I looked toward the river again before turning back to Daniel. "Of being here with my parents and you."

Daniel's lips tugged downward. "It's a shame one terrible night cast such a dark shadow over those memories. It's good you're here, Mac. It's time to put that night behind you."

tracked

I nodded. What he said was much easier said than done. If six months spent on Dr. Anderson's couch for crazies hadn't cured me of repressed memories, what made him think I could lay my fears to rest just by being back in Costa Rica? I would try, though. I might have to in order to save Puro Cielo.

He led the way along a narrow path in front of a cluster of cabins. Though it had only been a year, Daniel had changed since I'd last seen him. More gray hair, maybe. His eyes drooped slightly. Although he was still a physically fit man, a certain energy was missing. I couldn't help but study the man who had helped raise me as he carried my suitcase and set it gently in front of my cabin door.

"Here you go, Mac. Home sweet home." He unlocked the door and gave it a shove with his foot.

"Thanks." I took the key from him. My pulse raced and my stomach tightened as I entered the cabin, hesitating just inside the door. Other visitors might eventually join me in this cabin, but I was alone for tonight.

The fresh scent of the rainforest blew through the open windows. That comforted me a little. I walked farther inside, then turned and threw my arms around Daniel.

"What's this?" he asked, giving me a squeeze. "You sure you're okay?"

"Yeah. Just happy to be here. And a little touchy I guess." I pulled away, attempting to swallow the emotions that betrayed me. I had to get a grip, be strong.

"All right..." He drew out each syllable. "As long as that's all it is."

"The stress of last week is catching up with me. You know, finals," I added when he raised a brow. "And can't a girl miss a man that's like a father to her?" I forced my lips into a smile.

"Of course you can." He tossed my suitcase on one of the bunk beds. "You sure you don't want to stay with your parents in their cabin? Or with Eva and me? You don't have to keep up this brave front you're trying so hard to pull off."

I tilted my head. A smile spread across my face more easily this time. "No, I'm good. Doc and Mom and Dad all agreed that I should come back here. It's just gonna take some time to block out old ghosts."

"Why don't you get some sleep. We'll talk in the morning. I'm glad you decided to join us. Even if it's only temporary."

"Yeah, me too." Although, I thought, my stay might become more permanent when the reality of my status at Stanford sank in.

"Your parents will be glad to see you, too."

"Where did you say they were?"

"Well, when you called, they had already left for the San Jose Airport to pick up a pre-med student coming to stay with us for the summer. They're going to be thrilled to see you when they get back. They've talked constantly of you since they got here." He punched her shoulder lightly. "You know? They worry too much."

I laughed. My parents did worry too much, and they were guaranteed to be concerned when I told them the many reasons I'd traveled to La Fortuna—the least of those reasons being that Pascal had informed me of the board's plan for Puro Cielo.

TWO

Kyle

"What the hell is this place?" I tried to keep my voice down while videoconferencing with Jonas on my phone.

It was three in the morning, and I had arrived at some sort of resort of small villas with no knowledge of why, other than a cryptic email from Jonas.

"It's supposed to be housing for groups like Doctors Without Borders and other volunteer organizations."

I glanced around the interior of the villa I had been assigned. It was minimally equipped with a set of bunk beds, a small dresser, and an attached private bathroom. I could still hear the roar of the rapids coming from a nearby river—a river I hadn't been able to see through the dense trees when I was led to my sleeping quarters for the night. It had been pitch black in the direction of the water.

"The couple who picked me up at the airport... they think I'm a med student." I couldn't hide the frustration in my voice or the desire to sucker punch Jonas through the small screen. I sat on the edge of a bunk bed and leaned my face into the palm of my hand.

"*Pre*-med. And you practically are. You just need to do the best you can to help with the camp while listening and looking out for anything suspicious."

"Suspicious... right. What kinds of things are we talking about? Like someone using supernatural powers they shouldn't even have? Someone with mind-controlling abilities?" I was only half-joking while thinking about Jonas and the rest of my friends back in Kentucky who could mind control, speak telepathically, and even heal with the use of their minds.

Jonas answered my last question with a roll of his eyes. "Apparently, one of the camp's main volunteers decided not to return this summer. A daughter of one of the owners or something. This gave us an 'in.' The camp administrators needed the help. They're American, and apparently they've lived there off and on for years, so they know many people in the area. That's how *you'll* get to know the area."

I rubbed my temple. "What the hell am I really doing here, Jonas?"

"Look, Kyle. No one forced you to take off on a plane to a foreign country. You could have come here, to Palmyra, instead. We could have talked about it first. But since you didn't, I found you a place to stay so you could get to know the area. Just say thank you."

"You wouldn't have sent me that video if you'd expected me to sit around and chat about it. You knew I wouldn't be able to stay away after seeing those kids being manipulated like that." I sighed while linking my hands behind my neck. "Those kids in the videos were being controlled. They had the same look in their eyes that—"

tracked

"I know. I saw the look. I thought of Dani, too." Jonas went silent for a couple of beats. "Man, I'm sorry. I know this brings up a lot of baggage, but you were the only one of us I could think of that could go to Costa Rica right now." Jonas stared at me. Even on the small screen, he appeared tired.

There were seven of us: seven original cloned humans who had spent nearly a year learning who we were and what we had been designed to do. Seven of us who were hell-bent on stopping insane scientists from cloning humans and performing experiments in attempts to control human minds.

Jonas had spent the last six months on an atoll in the middle of the Pacific Ocean where human clones had been created and grown inside incubators. If we hadn't stopped Dr. Sandra Whitmeyer and her minions, she'd still be experimenting on young clones and forcing some of us to help her in sick and twisted ways. Jonas, with the help of some others, was now trying to undo much of what the woman who'd created us had done the past eighteen years.

"So..." I began, calmer now. "Tell me what you know. You think there's another lab here? You think the International Intelligence Agency is behind it?"

"I'm not sure. All I know is that those videos were taken somewhere in the area of La Fortuna, Costa Rica."

"Why didn't you come here and check it out yourself?"

"I was needed here."

"You mean, Briana's coming to see you for the summer."

"That, and I have reason to believe my DNA donor is behind the shipment of trackers that went missing more than a year ago. Those trackers may have ended up there in Costa Rica. I couldn't risk being recognized."

I narrowed in on Jonas's face. "Are you saying that the person I'm looking for could be an older version of you?"

He nodded.

I closed my eyes. "Damn it, Jonas. What if this person recognizes me?" Anyone involved with the IIA or this cloning operation was bound to know what any one of us looked like.

"Well, you obviously need to be careful."

"If you weren't so far away, I'd force you to hit yourself right now."

Jonas laughed. "I'd like to see you try."

With another sigh, I glanced at the time. "It's three a.m. I'd better get some sleep. Apparently, I'm scheduled for some volunteer work first thing in the morning." Before I hung up, I added, "Lexi's pissed at you, by the way. She said you purposely sent me the email at a time you knew she wouldn't be able to come with me."

Jonas's smile faded. Despite Lexi being in love with Jack, who just happened to be Jonas's best friend, Jonas would never stop protecting her. "She needs to move on with her life—put the past in the past. You do, too. Try to look at this as a vacation. You most likely won't find anything there in Costa Rica. So take in some sights. Go ziplining. Soak in the hot springs. Just keep your eyes open and report back to me if you see anything that doesn't look right. I'll be on the first plane out if you do."

I hung up with Jonas and set my alarm for only a few hours later. The windows of my villa were made of glass slats that were turned open. Sheer curtains blew in the warm breeze. Without even changing out of my clothes, I leaned back against the headboard, knocking my head against the wood

tracked

before settling down into the less than comfortable pillow. Despite the troubling information from Jonas and the racket of cicadas outside my cabin, I managed to close my eyes and let sleep find me.

THREE

Raven

I woke just shy of five a.m. I was exhausted from a busy night of running from the evildoers who haunted my dreams; my eyelids were heavy and scraped like sandpaper with every blink. Most days I managed to push the dreams aside and smile anyway. An easy morning jog should help chase away the bad vibes left over from last night's nightmares.

I laced up my running shoes and glanced toward the window when a frog croaked outside. "How do you always seem to find me?" I chuckled at the reverberation of the most obnoxious amphibian in the rainforest. "At least you waited until I was already awake to start that noise."

I locked and checked the cabin door, then turned toward the river. The sun was barely up and a light fog hovered over the ground. I performed a set of lunges toward the neighboring cabin, stretching my legs.

"What is that? Make it stop!"

I spun toward the voice coming from the cabin beside mine.

Inching up to the open window, I peeked inside. The curtains were pulled back. A young man flailed around in the bottom bunk. His feet curled over the end of the mattress, and a sheet covered half his body. Nothing covered the top half, and

I couldn't help but stare at his broad shoulders and his well-defined pecs. Definitely the body of an athlete.

He stuffed a pillow over his head. I stifled a laugh, covering my mouth with my hand. The guy removed the pillow from his head, eyes still closed, and slammed it forward. I jumped back, stumbling. I glanced both ways down the sidewalk and behind me, suddenly aware that I was breaking all kinds of rules of decency. Finally I moved on, not wanting to get caught snooping, but I made a mental note to find out who was staying in the cabin next to mine.

Then I made another note to stay away from said person. The last thing I needed was another distraction.

I jogged toward Arenal Volcano, backdrop to La Fortuna and Puro Cielo. I wasn't sure how to categorize the emotions that churned in the pit of my stomach. My parents would be thrilled to see me, but I was hesitant to approach them about Puro Cielo's troubles. Ever since my "accident," as they liked to call it, they'd kept talk of camp business to themselves. "Finish college," they would say. "Keep up with your soccer training. Don't worry about Puro Cielo. The camp will be there when you're ready."

I could confront Daniel with what Pascal had told me. He would tell me to talk to my parents.

And Pascal? Nausea crept back into my stomach at the thought of facing him. I'd just have to take it one day at a time for now.

At the end of my jog, I stopped by Daniel's modest house, which sat at the top of the hill above the camp. The back door was open. Voices carried through the outer screen.

tracked

"They pointed a gun at one of the men and took the cash he offered... We already talked to the group about safety in numbers." Daniel's voice stopped me from barging right in. The pauses in his speech told me he was talking to someone on the phone. "I can't keep avoiding the board; I'm going to have to tell them eventually... I will. To top it off, William and Bennett's daughter showed up unannounced last night... They're still going to Africa... I don't know what Raven will do... Don't worry about things on my end... I'll handle it... Fine, bye."

The loud sound of Daniel banging something after he ended his conversation had me backing quickly away from the house, not wanting to get caught eavesdropping. My heart pumped hard in my chest, and I practically fell as I ran down the drive toward the camp. Who was going to Africa? My parents? Had to be.

Looked like they were keeping more secrets than I thought.

FOUR

Kyle

After a few restless hours of sleep, I sauntered up the hill to the dining pavilion Mr. MacMillan had pointed out the night before. A small group of about twenty milled about, drinking coffee and tea and enjoying casual conversation.

"You must be Kyle." A petite, round woman greeted me with a touch to the arm. I covered my mouth, trying to hide a yawn. "I'm Eva Forester, Daniel's wife." She pointed to a gray-haired man with a matching goatee standing by the coffee. While Daniel was American, Eva was not. She wasn't Costa Rican, either.

"Morning, Kyle." Daniel gave a nod in my direction before returning to his conversation with William MacMillan, the man who had picked me up at the airport.

"Daniel and I live at Puro Cielo year round," Eva said.

"It's nice to meet you." I shook Eva's hand while allowing my eyes to circle the room and take everyone in. It seemed like a nice enough group. There was Eva and Daniel Forester, the two who lived at Puro Cielo full-time, and William and Bennett MacMillan, who picked me up at the airport. The rest were volunteers, most likely. Probably there for a week or two, based on the description I got of the camp from its website and from Bennett and William on the ride from the airport.

"Welcome to paradise. I hope you found your cabin comfortable enough," Eva continued. "We were sure excited to get your phone call. We always need extra help in the summer."

"Thank you, ma'am. The cabin's fine. And I'm glad to be here." I wasn't sure how I was supposed to help the camp, but I would do what I could while checking out the local scene. A waft of smoky sausage reached my nose, and my stomach growled.

Bennett MacMillan squeezed around William and Daniel, who were deep in conversation, to approach me. "Would you like some coffee, Kyle?" She gestured toward the table of coffee and an assortment of teas.

"Good morning, Mrs. MacMillan. Yes, coffee is definitely in order."

"Please, call me Bennett."

I nodded.

"Where's Mac?" Daniel asked, stopping whatever conversation he and William had been having. If the scowl on William's face was any indication, their discussion had been an intense one. "That kid knows better than to be late for breakfast."

"Oh, Dan." Eva shook her head at her husband. "Give the poor child a break."

"You're right," Daniel said in a not-so-forgiving tone. "But Mac should be setting a better example for Kyle here, who didn't get in until well into the morning, yet managed to make it to breakfast on time." Daniel walked over to the stainless steel coffee carafe, poured another mug, and dumped a hearty dose of cream and sugar into it before giving it a quick stir.

tracked

"You need to meet Mac anyway," he said to me. "Take this and follow that path over there down to the river. Tell the lazy bum sitting down there to get up here for breakfast."

I took the offered mug and my own and weaved my way along the path down to the river. I didn't recall any talk of a "Mac" last night on the trip back from the airport with William and Bennett, so I had no idea what kind of guy I'd find or what he did at the camp.

I rounded a corner, and my breath caught when I faced the river with tall trees and vivid green underbrush along the bank. Blue sky and the glow of the sunlight snuck through sections of the forest canopy. River rapids that had annoyed me when I'd been attempting to sleep last night now sang a relaxing tune. But there was no sign of any people. Certainly no Mac. I shrugged and looked around again. I'd have to revisit this perfect spot of nature when I had the time. I turned to leave.

"Why did you come all the way down here if you had no intention of staying for the view?" a female voice called out.

I angled toward the voice and tripped on a large tree root, sending a splash of hot coffee to the ground inches from my left shoe. Muttering a curse word under my breath, I held the mugs out at arm's length and stepped to the side. Once I regained my footing, I saw a girl, around my age, wearing a black tank top and a flowery skirt. She sat on a rock holding a camera in front of her face, aimed high into the trees. A black braid trailed from underneath a plaid hat a quarter of the way down her back.

"That was a close one," she called out. "Nice recovery!"

"I'm sorry?" I stuttered, still staring at the slight curve of her biceps as she held the camera to her eye and snapped a few more pictures.

"Well, you walked all the way down here—double-fisting even." Lowering the camera, she gestured at the two cups of coffee. "Weren't you planning to enjoy your drinks and take in the view? You can sit here if you like. I spotted some toucans up in the trees." She scooted herself and her backpack over, making room for me on the rock.

"Maybe another time?" I asked. I looked for the toucans. I'd only seen the colorful birds on television. "I'm looking for a man by the name of Mac. Have you seen anyone else down here?"

"Nope, no men. But I sure would love a cup of coffee." She aimed her camera at the toucans, squinting into the viewfinder.

I stared down at the cup of coffee, wondering if it would be a bad first day if I gave away one of the camp's mugs. Shrugging, I walked toward the girl and handed her the coffee.

"Thanks. You sure you don't want to sit down?"

I glanced up toward the camp. "No, I better get back."

She shrugged. Her smile seemed to be code for some joke that was most likely at my expense. "Suit yourself. If I see a man named Mac, I'll let him know you were here. Who should I tell him was looking?"

"Oh. Kyle. Kyle Jones." I was close enough to see the vibrant sapphire color of her eyes, and I stared at her for several seconds before I turned and walked back up the path.

FIVE

Raven

I took a few more sips of coffee and scanned the trees for the scarlet macaws, heard but not seen yet this morning. I pushed myself up from the large rock I once used for morning yoga and meditation. Maybe I would find my way back to that routine, to finding solace in the quiet. I threw my backpack over my shoulder and inhaled the thick air, then let it out slowly. I couldn't believe I was back, so close to the place where my life was forced onto a path of escaped memories and hidden truths.

I shook the bad thoughts from my head and scurried up the hill in the opposite direction of this Kyle character, excited to have a little fun with the new brown-haired boy with amber eyes—eyes that were full of mystery.

I snuck up behind Dad, who was engaged in an animated conversation with Daniel. Careful not to spill my coffee, I slid my arms around him in a hug. "Hey, Dad!"

"Well, well, well. Look what the cat dragged in." Dad turned to face me and returned a warm embrace of his own. He towered over me even though I stood at a generous five-foot-eight. "I see you made it to La Fortuna in one piece. Your mom and I couldn't believe it when Daniel told us you flew in last night."

He kissed the top of my head. "Did you meet Kyle? We sent him to find you."

"I did." Raven raised an eyebrow. "Who is he?"

Kyle came around the opposite corner before my father could answer. He was dressed in khaki pants and a navy polo shirt, untucked. *Preppy.* I turned my back to him and eyed my father. I wondered when my parents planned to tell me they were heading off to Africa.

"Okay, Kyle, I see you found Mac," Daniel said, clasping his hands together. "Let's eat."

"I didn't actually..." Kyle began as I turned around and flashed a great big grin at him.

I held out a hand. "Raven MacMillan. Nice to meet you. Only Daniel calls me Mac."

Kyle stared, but managed to shake my outstretched hand. His grip was firm, and he held on a little longer than I found comfortable. I looked from our hands to his face. He appeared more amused than flustered by my childish prank. It wasn't the reaction I'd expected.

~~~~~

The weight of the camp's troubles, among other things, sat on my shoulders. I yearned to ask my parents about a visiting humanitarian being robbed at gunpoint. And about Africa. But breakfast was more about Kyle, it would seem.

Mom and I sat at a table with Daniel and Kyle. Over eggs, bacon, and sweet mango, I learned that Kyle was from Kentucky. Had just graduated from some boarding school I had never heard of. Swam for his school's swim team and was awarded All-American status last year. He was on track to finish college in only two years and had already been accepted

tracked

into some pre-med program at the University of Kentucky. He had thick brown hair that reached all the way down to his dark eyebrows, the warmest amber-colored eyes I had ever seen, and an infectious laugh that had people from other tables looking up from their conversations and smiling.

"Kyle, what kind of medicine do you plan on studying?" Mom asked.

I let out an exasperated breath. "Mom, you're grilling the poor guy." It had been question after question for fifteen straight minutes. And all I could think about was how I was supposed to discuss camp business with this new guy hanging around. I wished he would take his dimpled smile and go back to Kentucky. I didn't have time for this.

"I am not. I'm just interested in the newest member of our summer team."

Why? You won't even be here.

"It's okay," Kyle said. His eyes met mine.

Heat spread across my cheeks, and I looked down at my fruit plate. I risked another fleeting glance at Kyle and found him smiling at me while he continued to answer Mom's barrage of questions.

"I have a long way to go before I narrow my field of study, but I'm leaning toward something in the area of neurology. I'm still trying to figure things out a little."

Aren't we all?

Daniel turned to me. "Mac, what about you?"

"What about me?" I stuffed a huge bite of papaya in my mouth.

"Last we talked, you had just led your soccer team to the conference championship game, and as I remember, you'd knocked your head something good. How'd that game end up?"

I grimaced at the memory. I'd suffered a concussion during the Pac-12 conference championship game in the fall. "We lost."

"Oh, sorry." Daniel frowned.

"You said you attended Stanford, right?" Kyle asked. "I watched that game on ESPN. That was you? You hit the ground hard when that UCLA player tripped you. That was a vicious slide-tackle."

I looked from Kyle to Daniel to Mom before returning to playing with my food. "Yeah, it wasn't pleasant."

"Well, at least she got a yellow card for that." Kyle paused and looked around the table at everyone. "Did I say something wrong?"

Mom reached over and grasped Kyle's forearm. "No, dear. Raven suffered a severe concussion a while back, and this one... well, it wasn't good either."

"Mom." I shook my head at her in warning.

She shrugged and mouthed, "Sorry."

I was sorry, too. I just wasn't prepared to discuss my head injuries with a complete stranger. Especially one who had just admitted to being curious about neurology. The last thing I needed was this stranger getting inside my head.

Daniel tossed his napkin on his plate and scooted his chair away from the table, patting his belly. "Mac, I was hoping you'd show Kyle around town this afternoon."

I sat up. I couldn't stop the gaping expression I threw at Daniel.

tracked

"That is, since you've blessed us with your presence this summer," he joked, ignoring the resistance that was plastered all over my face. "Show him where to find the internet cafés, the grocery store, and anything else you think he ought to know. I'm going to keep him busy until after lunch. You two can go then."

I forced a smile, then bit my lip so hard I was sure I'd left indentations. "I was planning to visit a few people today. Maybe—"

Mom spoke up, stopping me before I could finish my objection. "Perfect. Kyle can tag along and meet your friends." She said "your friends" like I was eleven years old going for an afternoon play date.

"But first I need help unloading some supplies from the truck," Daniel said. "Kyle, do you mind?"

"Of course not."

"And Raven, I have an errand I need you to run this morning."

"Oh yeah?" I sat up in my chair.

"I need you to run to the hot springs and negotiate a new rate for our guests."

I sank back down. The hot springs meant one thing: I'd have to deal with Pascal earlier than I'd planned.

~~~~~

I filled the sink with scalding water and suds. By volunteering to do the dishes, I had delayed the dreaded chore Daniel had assigned to me. I had tried to tag along with a visiting team of volunteers to an elementary school where they were conducting a medical clinic, but I was informed that the project was already well in hand.

Quiet footsteps sounded behind me. I didn't have to turn to know it was Mom coming to check up on me.

"Hey, Mom."

"Hey, sweetie." She wrapped her arms around me, giving me a gentle hug. "What made you change your mind?"

"About coming here? Lots of things, really." I rinsed a dish and stacked it in a crate for drying.

"Did you see Dr. Anderson before you left?"

"I saw him last week."

"And?"

I turned. Water and suds dripped from my hands. "Mom, the appointment went fine. Why so many questions?" The visit with my shrink had gone well. For the most part. It was the conference call with my soccer coach after the appointment with the neurologist that had gone awry.

"I'm sorry. I know your father and I agreed to stop asking questions after *every* doctor's appointment."

"And I agreed to keep you guys informed if anything went wrong where my health is concerned." I went back to washing and rinsing. I wouldn't lie outright to my mom, but avoidance and misleading information were in a neck-and-neck race.

After a heavy sigh, Mom took a wet dish from me, dried it, and put it away. "Kyle seems like a nice young man."

"I guess. I've only had one conversation with him." I pushed hair off my face with my forearm. "Why was he hired anyway? Did you need extra help this summer?"

"He volunteered, I think, but yes, we can always use an extra hand around the camp."

I turned my head to hide my rolling eyes. "How do you know he'll provide good help? He hardly looks like he's seen a

tracked

day of hard work in his life. He was wearing a Ralph Lauren polo shirt for crying out loud."

"Raven MacMillan! What's gotten into you?"

"I was just asking." I shrugged. Maybe I was being harsh, but I didn't need the distraction. And he was definitely a distraction. "Why didn't you call and say you needed *me* to come?"

"Is that what this is about? You don't feel wanted?"

"No. Okay, maybe." I submerged ten more grimy plates into the soapy water.

"And we did ask you. Many times. You said no. Remember?"

I remembered. "It just seems you and Dad are keeping things from me."

"What? We never keep things from you. What would make you think that?" Mom set the towel on the counter. "Sweetie, we've just tried to give you the space you seemed to want. You're not a child anymore. We didn't want to push."

I narrowed my eyes. "I know, Mom. I'm sorry. You and Dad have been great."

"You're welcome at this camp anytime. You know that. This is your home, too, and I'm thrilled you're here. Are you going to stay for the whole summer?"

"I don't know. I haven't really thought that far."

Mom paused. "I'll be right back."

"Okay, that was sudden," I mumbled to the stack of dishes staring at me. "Perfect. Don't worry, Mom. I can do all this by myself."

"Need some help?" Kyle asked behind me.

I spun around. The plate I held slipped from my soapy fingers. I reached for it with both hands, but it crashed to the ground and shattered. "That's just great." I bent and picked up the pieces, stacking them from large to small. "Where did you come from?"

"The pantry." Kyle thumbed over his shoulder to the room just off the kitchen. "I was organizing the supplies we unloaded." He bent down to help.

"Do you make it a habit to eavesdrop, Kyle?" I tossed the pieces of earthenware into the large trashcan.

"Only if I think I'll learn something interesting." He grinned.

I stared daggers at Kyle for several seconds. I was about to turn down his offer of help, but he picked up the towel left by my mom and began drying.

We washed and dried in silence while I replayed in my mind what I thought had been a private conversation. When Mom came back in with Daniel and Dad, I faced them, not even bothering to dry my hands. "What's going on?"

My parents traded looks with each other.

"You guys look so serious. Is this an intervention? I haven't been here long enough to get into that kind of trouble."

"Not yet," Daniel smirked.

I evil-eyed him, then smiled, knowing he was right. The summer had barely begun. I still had plenty of time to stir up some mischief.

"Raven, your father and I have good news." Mom twisted her hands together, and I raised an eyebrow at her fidgetiness. "We've been asked to travel to Africa as part of a medical mission. As you know, it's something your father and I have always wanted to do."

tracked

"What? When?" I feigned surprise. So, they were really going to leave Puro Cielo, even though the camp was in trouble.

"It's for the summer. We leave Saturday."

I looked at everyone's face, including Kyle's. I was the last to know. I pressed my hand against the heat that spread across my neck. The warmth from the dishwater only exacerbated the growing anger. "What does that mean for me? Am I going to Africa with you?" Africa didn't excite me like it did my parents, but how did my parents plan to protect Puro Cielo from so far away?

"No, sweetie, we want you to stay here with Daniel and Eva until you go back to school."

I winced on the inside. I hadn't had the opportunity to inform my parents that I'd lost my scholarship to play soccer thanks to the late-season concussion. And my small academic scholarships were now also history, thanks to my less-than-adequate grades. Without the scholarships, there was no way my family could afford Stanford University. Not to mention, Dr. Anderson thought my declining ability to concentrate might also be attributed to repeated head injuries. He was recommending that I take a year off.

"What if I want to go with you?" I asked.

"I'm sorry, but not this time, kiddo." Dad moved across the room to put his arm around me. "You know we hate to leave you behind, but Daniel and Eva really need your help here."

Could it be that my parents didn't know the camp was in trouble? But how could that be? My parents had been working on a trip to Africa for several years—maybe Daniel was keeping the trouble from them so they could go.

I glanced at Kyle, who at least had the decency to appear uncomfortable, shifting back and forth on his feet. Then I turned my gaze back to my parents. "Why am I the last person to know?"

"We found out right before we left California. We had to talk to Daniel and Eva before we could even think about going. We didn't want to bother you with it until we knew for sure we would go. We're just glad you're here so we can tell you in person." Mom wiped her palms on her pants. "And..."

A silent exchange passed between Mom and Dad.

"And what?"

"We received an offer on the house."

"So basically I'm homeless." Which wasn't true. Puro Cielo was my home just as much as any house in California was.

"We didn't think it would sell this quickly." Mom touched a gentle hand to my arm.

"And you're here now," Dad added. "You've always preferred Costa Rica to California." There was hope in his voice.

My parents were purposely avoiding talking about last summer. "How exactly am I supposed to get back to college with you guys gone?" Now I was just making them feel bad. I was pretty certain there was no school to return to.

And what about the nightmares I was having? And the headaches? Would they even care about what Dr. Anderson had said about my multiple head injuries? I had planned to tell them about the doctor visit as soon as we were alone. And the lost scholarship. But now? I couldn't ruin their aspirations with my problems. I was an adult now. It was time to start acting like one and handle my own problems.

tracked

"Eva and I are fully prepared to get you back to Stanford in the fall," Daniel said.

"And we might be back by then." Dad reached out and lightly punched my shoulder. "We still don't know the length of the mission."

I pressed my fingers into my forehead and rubbed. I wanted to scream, *How am I supposed to be happy about this? When you're deserting Puro Cielo at such a messed-up time?* I wasn't even sure how messed up.

Instead, I gave my mom a hug. "It's okay. I'm happy for you guys. I'm just shocked, I guess. I'll be fine. Really."

Dad joined us in the family hug while Daniel motioned for Kyle to follow him outside. Kyle turned back just as I looked up. Our eyes met, but I immediately redirected my stare to the trashcan by the door.

I pulled away from both parents. "So, can we can talk more about this later? I've got an errand to run for Daniel."

I didn't give my parents time to respond before I made an abrupt exit. I had to escape the kitchen before my head exploded. I waved to Daniel and Kyle and pretended not to hear their questions as I took off toward town.

SIX

Kyle

In between the odd jobs Daniel assigned me around the camp, I took a break under the camp pavilion to check my phone. I had a voice message from Jonas: "Kyle, someone emailed me a video. It showed a couple of young children approaching a table in a Costa Rican restaurant. A woman turns, lifts her purse off the back of the chair, and hands it over to one of the children. She appears to be in some sort of trance as the children take her purse and then just walk out. Minutes later, the same woman seems to snap out of it and is stunned to find that her purse is missing. This is the second of this type of video I've received, the first being the one I sent you before you left for Costa Rica. Someone obviously wants us to see these videos."

I closed my eyes, squeezing the bridge of my nose with my fingers. Jonas was right. That video, along with the first video we watched, was evidence that someone in Costa Rica was using some sort of mind control for petty theft. But why? And how exactly? Was this related to the stolen trackers?

I sent a quick text to Jonas: *Got your video. Will keep a lookout for little thieves. Thought you said the daughter of owners wasn't coming this year. Was her name Raven MacMillan?*

Jonas immediately replied back: *Sounds right. Sources told me she wasn't returning.*

Well, your sources were wrong.

Why do I sense hostility in your voice? Is this girl a problem?

No. Of course, it depended on what Jonas defined as a "problem."

SEVEN

Raven

I'd been friends with Pascal Centeno for as long as I could remember, and yet I was terrified to face him after our heated phone conversation two nights ago. That and the fact that I hadn't laid eyes on him in a year had me wanting to avoid him for a while longer.

A cab dropped me off in front of Navos Hot Springs, one of several resort locations at Costa Rica's Arenal Volcano hot springs. After asking to speak with someone about the camp's rates for their volunteers, I entered the resort to wait by one of the springs.

Lush green foliage and flowers in shades of fuchsia and coral decorated the paths that led visitors to the many different springs of varying sizes and temperatures.

I skirted one of the pools. The sound of a waterfall drowned out the clinking of dishes and glasses as resort workers prepared for the lunch crowd to arrive. After removing a sandal, I dipped my foot into a small pool—one of the hotter ones—and wished I had the time to sink my entire body into water that had to be near 110 degrees Fahrenheit.

"*Hola*, Amagita."

I spun around, backed up, and nearly fell into the pool as I faced the one person I had hoped to avoid—at least until I'd had the chance to adjust to being back in La Fortuna. Pascal reached out and wrapped his fingers around my arm just above my elbow to save me from a very embarrassing fall.

"Pascal. *Hola.*" Once I had regained my footing, I gently pulled my arm from his grasp and rubbed the tingling spot where he had squeezed.

He shoved his hands in his pockets. An uncomfortable silence passed as his hazel eyes looked me over from head to toe. I averted my own eyes, desperately looking in every direction except at Pascal. A group of teenagers, giggling and whispering, passed behind him.

"What made you come?" he asked.

"Daniel sent me here to talk about the rate for our camp guests."

"Ah. Good ol' Daniel, huh? Always looking for a better deal." He chuckled. "But you know what I meant. I believe your words were, 'I have no intention of stepping foot on Costa Rican soil this summer.' What changed your mind?"

I looked down, slipping back into my sandals. When he inched closer, I looked up and met his gaze. He was just over six feet tall, and the top of my head reached just past his chin—a perfect height for him to probe my eyes for everything I wanted to keep guarded.

"I guess I changed my mind? You knew I couldn't ignore what you told me about the camp. Do you know anything more than what you told me on the phone?"

Pascal shook his head. "I just know that Daniel is worried, which says a lot. He doesn't worry."

tracked

I nodded. He was right. Daniel's gift was an ability to take things in stride. He had to, in order to run a nonprofit in a foreign country.

"It's been a long time," Pascal said after more silence.

"I know, but—" My voice barely reached above a whisper.

"You left so quickly last year. You had just gotten here and..." His voice trailed off. Surely he didn't want to talk about last summer. Not now.

"How about I buy you lunch?" he asked, holding out his hand.

I stared at it and then looked up. "Why?"

He dropped his hand back to his side. "It's just lunch, Amagita."

He had named me Amagita when I was fourteen and he was eighteen. He'd told me it meant "Spanish princess." I was convinced he'd made up the word, seeing as none of my Spanish teachers could ever tell me the word existed in any Spanish dialect they'd ever heard.

"Does this coolness toward me have anything to do with me not calling you after our date?" Pascal smiled.

"There was never a date." I scrunched up my brows. This was going to be harder than I'd thought—being back in La Fortuna and being near Pascal.

"I seem to remember feeding you dinner and ending the evening with a kiss. I don't know what Americans call it, but we Ticos call that a date."

"The dinner was a package of crackers and some water to rehydrate after overheating in the hot spring, and the kiss... well... that was a moment of weakness. I was simply grateful."

Pascal frowned. "You're angry with me. Why?"

"No, I'm not angry." My voice escalated. "It's just—" I stopped myself. I was starting to feel claustrophobic, even though I was standing out in the open. I was exposed with no escape.

"It's just what, Amagita?"

"It's been a while since we talked." Since we *really* talked.

When I hadn't joined my parents in Costa Rica for the December holidays, Pascal had tried to contact me, but I'd ignored every one of his emails. It had been too little, too late. I was finally finding the strength to live with my new normal, and I didn't need Pascal ruining that.

"Let's fix that." Pascal grabbed my hand and led me away from the pools, toward a restaurant at the front entrance to the springs. "I'll buy you lunch."

"Pascal!" I stopped and pulled my fingers from his grasp. "I'm not here for lunch. And you can't just go bossing people around."

He turned and took a step toward me. He brushed the back of his hand down my cheek. "I haven't seen or heard from you in almost a year." He sighed. "Please have lunch with me. We can talk about the camp's group rate while we eat."

"Why would you negotiate with me? Isn't that tedious work beneath your new fancy title?"

Pascal smiled. "So—you *have* been keeping tabs on me." He picked up my hand again and gave it a gentle tug. "Come on, Amagita. This negotiation fits perfectly within the perks of my new title."

Finally I gave in and followed him. "Don't call me that." I smiled, unable to hide the tiny crack in my armor.

tracked

During lunch, Pascal filled me in on his promotion to manager of the hot springs—and on the increased crime around La Fortuna.

"So you're saying that in addition to the weird kidnappings, petty theft is back on the rise?"

"Sí. Remember the bands of thieves in San Jose a couple of years ago that were mostly small kids?"

"Yeah."

"There have been reports of small children like that running around at night taking things from people at restaurants."

"In La Fortuna?" That surprised me, because this type of petty theft was more popular in the larger cities.

"Sí. I'm just saying: pay attention. Some weird stuff's been going on."

"And the board of Puro Cielo isn't happy about it."

"I'm pretty sure the camp's bookings are down this summer. When the U.S. Department of State issues high crime alerts for travelers, people tend to look elsewhere for summer travel. And with the camp's board already threatening to close the camp..."

"Daniel and my parents have to be quite nervous."

After lunch, Pascal walked me to the front entrance. "Let me drive you back," he offered.

"No," I answered quickly. Too quickly. "I'm sorry. You have work to do, and a taxi is fine."

"We still haven't discussed what we need to talk about."

Though Pascal had been open with me about the crime affecting Puro Cielo, he and I had both avoided the topic of what had happened last summer. However, the darkness was ever-present, hanging like an enormous storm cloud between us. "I'm just not ready, Pascal."

He nodded, then raised a hand and gestured toward what I thought would be a taxi, but a sleek, dark sedan pulled up beside us. A man dressed in a dark suit got out and circled the car. Pascal waved him off, but before the driver returned to his spot behind the wheel, Pascal said, "Deliver her back to Puro Cielo, please, Oscar." Pascal opened the back door, then turned to me. He picked up my hand and gave it a soft kiss. "We'll talk again soon, Amagita."

I only nodded in reply, withdrawing my hand and climbing quickly inside the vehicle.

~~~~~

I arrived back at Puro Cielo after one o'clock to find Dad eating a late lunch with Daniel and Kyle.

I avoided the gaze of the three men and ducked inside the building by the pavilion. I passed the entrance to the kitchen, quiet and dark this time of day, and entered the camp office—a room big enough to house a simple pine desk, a straight-backed wicker chair, and a metal filing cabinet.

I sat in the chair, leaned over, and buried my face in my hands. My heart raced, and I struggled to get in a good breath as I pressed a palm against my heart.

Though I had intended to see Pascal eventually, to inquire about what he knew of Puro Cielo's troubles, I hadn't expected him to be so... well... kind and gentle. The anticipation of what we might have talked about—a long-ago night—sent my mind churning into overdrive.

I pushed my hands into my knees and looked at the ceiling. I breathed in and out. *Get a grip, Raven.* If I had any hope of

tracked

helping the camp, or the people of La Fortuna, I just might have to trust Pascal again.

I *had* trusted him, once upon a time, with my life and my heart. And both were practically crushed. Now, many months and thousands of dollars of therapy later, I was still barely half a person.

I waited until I had talked myself into enough courage to face whatever was to come—even if it was only for the next hour—then stood and walked back outside.

Back under the pavilion, I poured myself a glass of lemonade. The men were still there, and I caught the tail end of a conversation about repairs to window locks on several cabins. This was what I needed—normal, everyday details of running the camp: repairs and upkeep, interacting with the short-term teams, showing the new guy around.

"Hey, honey. Want a sandwich?" Dad asked.

"No, thanks. I grabbed something at the hot springs." I turned and took a sip of the syrupy sweet lemonade. "Where are Mom and Eva?"

"They took a picnic lunch to the team at the elementary school in town," Dad replied.

"Did everything go okay at the hot springs, Mac?" Daniel asked.

I pulled out a chair to sit with the three men. It took extra effort to answer Daniel's question while concentrating on keeping my breaths slow and in control from the lingering anxiety. "Yep. Fine. I got us a lower rate, good for bringing a group one evening a week. The deal is good through next May. Pascal was especially kind today. He even bought me lunch." I winked at Daniel. They didn't need to know that I'd agreed to another lunch with Pascal in order to get the reduced rate. Dad would have a tough enough time with the fact that I'd seen Pascal at all.

"He must still have a thing for you," Daniel said, fully aware of the reaction he was getting from my overprotective father, whose jaw was set in a hard line.

My shoulders tensed. I chanced a glance at Kyle. Having him there made everything different. I wouldn't typically care about being teased by Daniel. It bothered me that I cared now.

"How's that boyfriend of yours feel about you having lunch with other guys? Colin is it?" Daniel asked.

Dad shook his head and went back to eating his sandwich. Kyle picked up his iced tea and leaned against the back of the chair. I caught him staring at me. The corners of his lips lifted just enough to annoy me.

"Kyle, you ready for a trip to town?" I asked, ignoring Daniel's question. It was no one's business just how much my life had fallen apart this past year, including my inability to maintain a healthy relationship with any boyfriend.

EIGHT

Kyle

The fifteen-minute walk to town started with avoiding puddles along potholed roads. We passed dilapidated dwellings as well as homes that appeared brand new. Raven pointed out several landmarks along the way and taught me things about La Fortuna that I hadn't read on the internet, like the fact that there was only one small medic station in all of La Fortuna. All serious illnesses and injuries require a medevac to a larger city like San Jose.

The sun roasted the top of my head. I was starting to understand why Raven wore the polka dot hat that covered her head and shaded her face. The brim tilted, shielding her eyes from my view.

I'd spent the past six months or so thinking that I would never look at a pretty girl with any possibility of attraction again. But this Raven MacMillan was intriguing—even with the attitude. Quite possibly *because of* the attitude.

"I need to visit the internet café," she said. "I'll show you where everything is, and you can meet me there when you're done." She shifted her backpack to her other shoulder, reaching up with her hand to massage the back of her neck.

"You okay?" I asked, studying her profile.

"I'm fine. Neck's just a little tight."

"So, Stanford, huh?"

"Yeah." She nodded.

"What are you studying?"

"Sociology."

I raised my eyebrows. "When are you due back?"

"I don't know."

"What do you mean, you don't know?"

"What is this? Twenty questions?" Raven asked.

"No, it's just a conversation, MacMillan. Looks like we're going to be spending the summer together, so I thought we could get to know each other a little." I sighed. Her tough exterior was definitely going to be a challenge. "Did I miss something?"

"What do you mean?"

"Did I make you mad? Surely you're not still angry over what you think I overheard this morning."

"No, of course not. I'm just not that good at answering personal questions." She glanced up from under the brim of her hat. "I'm sorry. I've been thrown a little, finding out my parents are leaving me here alone for the summer."

"What about Daniel and Eva? They seem thrilled to have you here."

"Oh, they are. And I love them. It's just... well, it's... I have a lot going on."

"I'm a great listener. You can talk to me."

Raven glared.

Smiling, I held my hands up to show her I was completely unarmed. "Or not. It's your choice."

When we reached town, Raven pointed out the large Catholic church in the middle of town and explained how most ma-

tracked

jor Costa Rican cities had a church directly in the center with a park across from the church's front doors. We walked through La Fortuna's park.

Raven stopped and smelled the colorful and fragrant flowers. "Aren't they beautiful?"

I turned a complete circle, taking in the layout of the town. People strolled along the sidewalks, going in and out of stores. Women chatted and laughed, cupping their hands over their mouths. Sharing secrets, maybe. Men walked with purpose. Kids darted across streets, chasing each other. From online news articles I'd read, most of the crime in La Fortuna happened at night or on personal property away from town. The scene before me was not that of a crime-infested town.

Yet the kids playing in the streets reminded me of the video Jonas had spoken of.

Raven's face brightened as she cradled the petals of tropical flowers, lowered her face, and breathed in. Some of her attitude seemed to disappear, if only for a fleeting moment.

She pointed to the two grocery stores and a couple of internet cafés. "You can make phone calls using U.S. dollars at stores around the internet cafés. I'll meet you at that café over there." She pointed to a storefront on the corner diagonally across from where we stood. A hand-painted sign above the store read "Internet."

I listened to the directions she gave, but a pang of something I didn't quite recognize unsettled my stomach as she walked away.

~~~~~

An hour later, after I'd picked up a few personal items at the grocery store and had walked around to get my bearings, I found Raven typing away at the internet café. I sat down next to her and logged on to a computer of my own.

"Did you find everything?" she asked.

"Yep. Do you mind if I check my email?"

Raven shook her head. "Take your time. I'm going to go pay for my computer time. I'll meet you outside."

The only email of interest was from Jonas. He had sent me a link to an article: *Man Murdered Near Arenal Volcano Resort*.

The article explained that a man had been stabbed to death just over one year ago near the Navos Hot Springs, and that an unidentified American female had also been injured in the attack. The female was questioned after regaining consciousness, but reports claimed she remembered nothing due to a head injury.

"Why did you send me this, Jonas?" I mumbled to myself.

I glanced out the window to where Raven stood waiting for me. Why did I have this horrible feeling that Jonas's choosing of Puro Cielo as a place for me to stay was not coincidence?

Fifteen minutes later, I walked out of the café and squinted against the bright sunlight. Raven was leaning against a light post, one leg bent and propped against the pole, reading a paperback.

She looked up from the book. "You ready?"

"Sure. What's next?"

"How about a treat?" She closed the book and stowed it in her bag. "A sort of welcome-to-paradise milkshake." She paused, looking down at her feet and then back up at me. "And a forgiveness milkshake."

I tilted my head. "I don't understand."

tracked

"I'm sorry I was rude earlier. I had no right to take out my bad mood on you."

I studied her dark blue eyes before she looked away, the polka dot hat shielding them again. I reached out and tapped her arm, urging her to look at me. When she did, I felt this strong desire to know everything about her. Something told me that getting to know her was going to be a challenge. "I forgave you already."

Raven bought a mango milkshake for me and a papaya shake for herself at Centeno's, one of the restaurants in town. The cool, fruity drink provided some relief from the heat. "The mangoes here taste so different from the ones we get in the states. They're so sweet."

"I'm glad you like it." She pushed her tall glass toward me. "Here, try mine so you'll know which one you like best."

A lean, youthful-looking boy approached us. "*Hola*, Raven."

"Miguel!" Raven stood and hugged the very tall boy. "Oh, how I've missed you." She said something else in perfect Spanish. Well, it sounded perfect to me. I knew very little Spanish, though. It was hard not to be impressed by Raven MacMillan.

She introduced Miguel to me, but all I could offer was, "*Hola*." I made a mental note to learn more Spanish.

"Sit with us for a few minutes," Raven said.

"Oh, I can't. Boss would slit my throat." Miguel made a slicing motion across his neck.

Raven tilted her head. "Miguel. He would not. Your uncle loves you."

He looked over his shoulder, chuckling. "I do have to get back to work. Have you seen Pascal yet?"

"I saw him this morning. He bought me lunch out at the hot springs. Why?"

"How did he seem to you?"

"He was... well... Pascal. You know. He seemed the same, I guess." Raven searched Miguel's face. "What's wrong?"

"I can't talk now. Let's get together later. I'll come by the camp the next day I'm not working. Just stay away from Pascal, okay?"

"I wasn't planning to be around Pascal, but why do I need to stay away from him?"

"He's obsessed, Raven. He's determined to figure out what happened that night."

A man yelled from behind the counter. "Miguel! Get back to work!"

Miguel's gaze zeroed in on Raven. "He won't talk to me about it, but I'm afraid for you. He wants to make you remember."

The muscles in my back stiffened at the warning. Miguel turned on his heel and proceeded to take a neighboring table's order.

After Miguel left, Raven stared past me, bewildered.

"Do you have any idea what that was about?" I asked.

She shook her head. "Not really. I've known Miguel for ten years. He's younger than me, but he's been a great friend growing up. Pascal is his older brother and, well, Pascal and I haven't always gotten along. But we're friends. He wouldn't do anything to hurt me." Doubt seeped through her words.

"Do you want to see when Miguel gets off? We can wait around to talk to him." I was definitely curious to know more. The severity of Miguel's tone was enough to make me want to

tracked

meet this brother of his and confirm for myself that he was a "friend."

"No, he'll come find me when he can. I don't want to hang out too long and make trouble for him. His uncle is pretty strict with him."

We sucked down the rest of our milkshakes and stood to leave. Raven turned and waved to Miguel as she walked toward the door, not watching where she was going.

"Raven, watch out." I reached for her arm but was too late.

She plowed directly into a man entering the restaurant.

NINE

Raven

"Oh, I'm so sorry." I looked up and found a pair of dark, deep-set eyes staring back at me, paralyzing me. The musky scent of aftershave assaulted me. "Have we met?"

"No," the young man said, his lips twisted into a smirk. "Definitely not. I would have remembered meeting such a lovely lady." His Hispanic accent was thick, but it didn't sound Costa Rican. Columbian or Venezuelan, maybe.

He picked up my hand as if to shake it. Instead, he raised it to his lips. I jerked it away and tucked it behind me. I was used to the over-flirtatious men of Costa Rica, but there was something different about this man. He had entered my personal space uninvited, and the coolness of his skin sent a chill up my arm.

"Who might you be?" he asked, still smiling and still standing just inside the restaurant's entrance.

Before I could answer, another man entered the restaurant behind the first. "Raven?"

My mouth went dry at the sight of Pascal. No "hello," just my name and a nod of the head in my direction.

"You know her?" the stranger asked, as if I were no longer standing there. I shuddered at the sound of his smooth voice.

"Hi again, Pascal." I glanced over my shoulder at Kyle to make sure he was close. "We were just leaving."

"Yes, I know her," Pascal answered, not once removing his eyes from mine. "Felipe, this is Raven. Raven, Felipe."

Felipe cocked his head. "Raven, you say?" His thick brows furrowed, further darkening his mysterious eyes.

"Now it's your turn, Amagita." Pascal nodded his head at Kyle.

"What?" I asked, confused. "Oh, right. Sorry. This is Kyle."

Kyle stepped forward with an outstretched hand. "Nice to meet you." He glanced sideways at me, studying me as if I had sprouted a single horn from my forehead.

I risked another look at Felipe's face. *Could* we have met before? I searched my memories and tried to place him. I flinched at Kyle's touch to my elbow.

"You okay, Amagita? Your face is whiter than usual." Pascal often taunted me with jokes about my American paleness compared to the dark complexion of many Costa Ricans, but this time his facial expression remained serious. It was a comment that would anger most people, but I knew Pascal well enough to know he wasn't *necessarily* trying to insult me.

"Yeah, I'm fine." What was Pascal trying to do? Two nights ago, he'd urged me to return to La Fortuna and save Puro Cielo, and now he was throwing pathetic insults at me? Miguel had said he was obsessed, but Pascal hadn't even mentioned "that night" when we'd spoken at the hot springs. And who was this Felipe, and how did Pascal know him?

"We've gotta go. It was nice to meet you," I said to Felipe. I grabbed Kyle's hand and pushed past the two men, making eye

tracked

contact with each of them one last time before pulling harder on Kyle.

He matched my long stride, following quickly until we rounded a corner back toward Puro Cielo. Then I dropped his hand.

"Slow down," he said.

I sucked in a deep breath, then slowed until I was barely moving.

"Are you okay? What was that?"

"I'm fine. But those eyes," I said, more to myself than to him. "They were so familiar."

~~~~~

I glanced over my shoulder several times as I walked. Somewhere deep within my consciousness, I knew Kyle was beside me. Watching me. But I didn't care. I could just add him to the long list of people who had witnessed me losing bits and pieces of my sanity over the past year.

It wasn't just the way Felipe's touch had made me shiver in the ninety percent humidity. Or the way his voice had resonated with me. It was the way he'd looked at me—like he was seeing straight into my mind, reading every thought, every secret. Like there was nowhere I could hide.

I pictured his black hair, his dark skin, and his eyes shadowed by thick eyebrows. I could still smell the overwhelming scent of his aftershave.

"What did you mean, 'The eyes were familiar'?" Kyle asked after several minutes of silence.

"I don't know," I said. "He looked like someone I've met before. I couldn't place him." But it was more than that. I was *sure* I had met this Felipe before. I reached up and rubbed the spot over my heart. The effects of my earlier panic attack lingered. "I'm sure it was nothing. Let's move on before it gets too late."

I needed to visit a few people, let some old friends know I was back in Costa Rica. Miguel and Pascal's mom, Lucia, was the perfect place to start. Maybe *she* could add calm to this anything-but-peaceful start to my visit.

I led Kyle down a narrow dirt road with small houses on either side. I pointed out the many two-to-three-room homes that sometimes housed as many as six people or more.

"Where are we going?" Kyle asked.

I closed my eyes, took in a deep breath, and let it out slowly. "I guess the trip to town was strange, huh?"

I raised my head, looking at the small concrete house we now approached. A clothesline stretched from the side of the house to a neighboring carambola fruit tree, and linens and garments dangled from it, soaking up the hot sun. A toddler girl holding a banana stood in the open doorway. In front of her, rough, raw boards had been nailed across the lower part of the opening to form a makeshift baby gate.

"This is where Miguel lives," I said.

I stopped in front of the house and turned in a circle to examine the other houses in the village. I pointed to a house two doors down. "See that house?"

Kyle nodded.

"That was my first roofing job. And that house over there? I helped the owners paint the outside." I turned back to the house with the little girl, then inhaled deeply before lifting my heavy foot and starting toward the home of Lucia and Miguel, and sometimes Pascal.

I bent down to the child's level. "*Hola. Como te llamas?*"

tracked

"Sierra," she answered and ran away. "*Mami. Mami.*"

I stood and knocked on the door. "Lucia. Alejandra," I called. "*Upe?*" Surely Sierra wasn't wandering alone too far from her mother or great-aunt.

"*Upe?*" Kyle asked.

"There's a lot of slang in the Spanish spoken by Ticos. *Upe* is a way of asking if anyone's home."

"And a Tico is?"

"That's how Costa Ricans refer to themselves."

"Raven." Alejandra came to the door carrying a large basket of wet clothing and linens. "When you get in?" She spoke in slightly broken English.

"Just last night."

"Come in. Aunt Lucia in here. She going be thrilled to see you." Alejandra held my hand, and I swung my feet, one at a time, over the wooden boards. Kyle followed.

Sierra ran between Alejandra's legs. She held on to both thighs and buried her face in the back of her mother's knee. Alejandra, a lanky girl the same age as me, and first cousin to Pascal and Miguel, didn't appear old enough to have a shy two-year-old daughter clinging to her legs.

"Lucia, look who came visit," Alejandra said when they found Lucia sitting in a worn-out upholstered chair.

Lucia, a large woman with graying hair, reached out to take my hand and greeted me in Spanish. I bent down and hugged the woman who had taught me so much about my own spirituality over the years. I couldn't help but hope for a little of that wisdom this time around.

"Oh, child, let me have a look at you," she said.

I spun around and curtsied. The sounds of children laughing and playing traveled through the open front door. Alejandra and I used to play just like that on many afternoons when we were younger—in and around this house with Miguel and Pascal and anyone else who joined in. The children who lived in the small village of houses played outside from sunup to sundown most days they were out of school. It seemed that not much had changed over the years. Just the children. And me.

"Lucia, Alejandra," I said. "This is Kyle. He's working at Puro Cielo for the summer."

While Alejandra and Lucia talked with Kyle, I eyed the rest of the large room. My eyes landed on a picture of Nicholas Centeno. I sat down on the sofa and picked up the photograph of Nicholas standing with his two young sons, Pascal and Miguel, when they were just small boys. I didn't notice Kyle next to me until his hand touched my forearm.

I flinched, almost dropping the framed picture.

"You okay?" he asked.

"Yeah, why?" Only then did I notice that Lucia and Alejandra were staring at me. "I'm sorry. I was just... Did one of you say something?"

"It's okay," Lucia said. "I was just wondering how you were feeling and what the doctors were saying?"

I sucked in a deep breath. "What do you mean?" A cold sweat broke out across my neck. I had thought I was ready to face Nicholas's wife after so many months, but I was wrong. Very wrong. I traded glances with Kyle. When I'd agreed to show him around, I had hoped to avoid any conversation about my past. What had I been thinking, coming here?

tracked

"Daniel and Miguel tell me you still have no memories of that night," Lucia said.

"I don't." I looked down at my hands, which played with the snaps on my cargo pants pockets. *Nor do I plan to.* Why would I want to relive that? "I'm sorry."

"Oh, dear child, don't apologize to me. You did nothing wrong. How's your head?"

I shrugged and fought against the lump that formed in my throat. The grief and the heartbreak that I squeezed and crammed into small compartments somewhere deep inside my mind surfaced with a vengeance. I was unable to answer Lucia for fear of letting even an ounce of emotion escape.

"I've prayed every day for you since that night."

I shifted on the sofa and looked up, uncomfortable with the idea that Lucia had been wasting her daily prayers on me. "Thank you." As I faced a woman who radiated love and intense faith, I knew that Lucia deserved any comfort I could provide about the night I tried so hard to forget. "I'm okay. I wish coming back here was easier." Tears escaped down my cheeks. "I'm sorry. I don't know what happened that night." I buried my face in my hands.

"Alejandra, dear, why don't you and Kyle give Raven and me a minute? Get those wet clothes on the line."

I lifted my head. Kyle locked his eyes on mine for a brief moment. When I nodded that I was okay, he stood and followed Alejandra out the front door.

"Child, I don't know exactly what happened the night you were injured either, but—"

"The night your husband was killed," I said, looking at her. My voice broke. "I'm sorry. I don't know why I'm so emotional.

It's being here... Seeing Pascal and Miguel... And seeing *you* for the first time since..." I gasped in an uneven breath. "I feel so responsible."

"Raven, no one blames you for Nicholas's death."

"Pascal blames me."

"Pascal is dealing with losing his father in his own way. But he doesn't blame you for what happened."

I massaged my temples. A dull ache pulsed behind my eyes. An impending headache.

"Sometimes, dear," Lucia continued, "bad things happen. You'll remember when you are ready to handle the evilness of that night."

"That's the problem, Lucia. I don't want to remember. What I want is to know why I survived and Nicholas didn't." I surprised myself by saying it out loud.

"Oh, you poor child, you survived because—"

The sound of the door interrupted our conversation. Pascal's body filled a large portion of the doorway, blocking the sunlight.

"Oh, Pascal, look who came to visit." Lucia's excitement permeated her voice, hiding the seriousness of the conversation taking place moments before.

"I know, Ma. Nice surprise," Pascal said. He was much more subdued than his mother. He walked farther into the room and leaned over, kissing his mom on the top of her head.

I wiped my tear-stained face with my hands, trying to destroy all evidence of emotion. "I have to go." I stood. "It was great to see you, Lucia."

"Oh, okay, dear," Lucia said, standing from her chair. "I am happy you've decided to spend the summer here. We've missed

tracked

you. Promise me you'll come back when we have more time to visit."

"I promise. Bye, Pascal." After a gentle touch to Lucia's hand, I squeezed past Pascal without so much as a sideways glance in his direction.

But Pascal followed me out the door and grabbed my elbow before I could step off the porch.

I stopped and closed my eyes. Queasiness settled into the pit of my stomach as the warmth of his hand radiated against my skin. "Pascal, don't." My voice barely rose above a whisper. When I reopened my eyes, I focused on Kyle playing with the children in a yard across the dirt road.

"What was that back at the restaurant? Did you recognize Felipe?"

"No. Maybe. I don't know. He seemed familiar, that's all. Have I met him before?" I turned toward Pascal. His face was close. Too close. My breathing sped up when I saw the pain in his eyes.

"He's lived in La Fortuna less than a year. I don't know how you would have met him," he said, then paused before adding, "You've been crying. Why?"

I jerked my elbow away. "I'm fine. It's getting dark. I have to go."

"Ma was asking you about that night, wasn't she?"

"I have to go," I repeated. I hurried off the steps and jogged to the road where Kyle played soccer with a gaggle of neighborhood kids.

"You're going to have to face it at some point, Amagita," he called after me.

Maybe Pascal was right. But I wouldn't be facing *it* today.

TEN

Kyle

I wasn't absolutely sure why I had avoided Raven the last couple of days. As I leaned against a pillar at the back of the pavilion, I watched her and debated whether I should help her.

She carried a box from the camp's supply building, crossing in front of me. She stuck out a lower lip and blew loose strands of hair from her face. A crease was etched into the spot between her brows. As she pushed the box into the camp's van, I decided I would go to her rescue, and stop being less than a gentleman, if she appeared with another heavy load.

I chugged a bottle of water and wiped my dirty hands on equally filthy khaki pants. I had dried blood on my knuckles, the result of a superficial injury obtained while helping William with a stubborn outside water spigot. I had craved the escape that the day of heavy labor had provided. Not only had it helped to clear my mind of why I was in Costa Rica, but it had also helped me manage to avoid—for a short time anyway—mourning Dani or thinking about Raven.

The camp was mostly quiet. William, Daniel, and I were taking a much-needed break from our projects. The visiting team of volunteers was still in town at the local elementary school. Eva and Bennett sat at a picnic table, discussing a shopping list for the coming week.

And Raven was busy doing... something. I continued to watch her from my position in the shadows of the pavilion's far wall. She was still traveling back and forth between the supply building and the van, carrying smaller items now. Finally, after shoving a couple of fishing rods into the van, she slammed the back doors, then leaned against them, bending over slightly at the waist as if she needed to catch her breath. My heart had tightened at the sight of her tears during the visit with Lucia, much like the constriction I was feeling now. What the hell was I doing? I had no business letting my emotions get the better of me, especially with everything happening in my life. And so soon after losing Dani.

"Uh-oh." Daniel approached and glanced from me to Raven and back to me. "I've seen that look before."

Quickly averting my gaze from Raven, I tipped back my water bottle for another large gulp. "She seems to work hard." I ignored Daniel's teasing tone and nodded in Raven's direction.

"She works *very* hard. Always has."

I opened my mouth to ask Daniel about a night last summer when Raven was injured and a man was killed, but I stopped myself, deciding it would be better coming from Raven herself. I also wondered if that night was somehow something I wasn't supposed to be curious about.

What was really nagging me was that Jonas knew about the incident and had sent me a news article detailing the murder. Had I not overheard several conversations between Raven and others since I arrived, I might not have linked the article to Raven and this camp.

tracked

"You need anything else from me today?" I asked.

"We're done for today. Thanks for helping me with the rest of those window locks."

"No problem."

"The rest of us are going to dinner at Navos Hot Springs tonight. We'd love for you to join us. You'll love the springs."

I tipped my water bottle at him. "Thanks—can I let you know later?" He nodded, and I pushed away from the pillar and started to walk away.

"Kyle." Daniel stopped me, his voice lower than before.

He stared over my shoulder in the direction of Raven, then to the ladies at the picnic table, deep in their own conversation. He motioned me forward. "Look, I'm sure you've picked up on the fact that something happened the last time Raven was in Costa Rica."

I nodded.

Deep trenches formed across Daniel's forehead. "You seem like a nice guy, and your background check came in clean..."

I cocked my head. "You ran a background check on me?" I had underestimated the people of this modest camp. However, I knew he wouldn't have found much in my background. Jonas and Lexi had made sure of that.

"We run one on anyone who works for us." He crossed his arms. "Your background didn't give any information about your family. Which was strange. All checks come back with something about a person's family."

Sweat formed on my palms, and I resisted the urge to wipe them on my pants. "I don't have any family."

Daniel's eyes didn't move from mine, but he paused briefly, as if he was processing whether it was possible for someone to have zero family. "I'm sorry," he finally said. "I didn't mean to imply anything by that... Look, you seem like a nice guy. And I called your school. The president of your old boarding school verified everything in your background and gave us a glowing report about you."

I nodded. My long-time friend Lexi Matthews was now owner and president of Wellington Boarding School. She, of course, would have nothing but wonderful things to say about me.

Daniel continued to speak in a hushed voice. "I was hoping you would do me a favor and keep an eye out for Mac while she's here."

That was the last thing I had expected. Lexi had obviously been convincing.

I glanced in Raven's direction. "Is there a specific something I should be watching for? Or is this just out of general concern?"

"Let's just leave it at general concern for now." He also turned toward Raven. "That's one tough girl. She knows about as much as there is to know about La Fortuna and running this camp. She practically grew up here. She knows how to stay safe..."

When Daniel's voice trailed off, I drained my water bottle. If Raven knew how to stay safe, what went wrong last summer?

"Yeah, I'll watch out for her," I said. That strange tight feeling returned to my chest, and I didn't like it. I wasn't sure why I had just volunteered to watch out for Raven, seeing as I had no intention of sticking around very long. But if whatever had happened to Raven last summer had anything to do with my world of cloned humans and mad scientists, I'd stick to Raven like glue.

I left Daniel and followed Raven back toward the supply building. It was time to find out exactly what had happened here last year.

~~~~~

If I hadn't been watching for it, I would have missed Raven's cringe when I entered the storage building.

She lifted a box from a shelf then turned toward me. She was almost to the door where I was standing, blocking her way, when she stopped. Her blue eyes were determined and maybe a little frosty. "You want something? Or are you going to get out of my way?"

I sidestepped and gestured with my hand. "By all means."

She stared at me a moment longer before taking another step toward the door. She adjusted her grip on the box. It was obviously heavy.

"Let me help you with that." I tried to keep my tone light and airy.

When I reached for the box, she turned slightly. "I've got it, if you'll just hold the door," she snapped.

Was she mad at me? For two days I had said no more than an occasional "Good morning" or "Hello" when I saw her. The fact that she was acting irritated meant one of two things: either she didn't like me, which was my initial thought in the day or two after I'd first met her... or she was angry that I had ignored her. Which meant...

Hmmm. Interesting.

I reached out and grabbed her arm. Her head tilted down in the direction of my grip, then up, her eyes meeting mine. I smiled. "Let me take you to dinner."

Her entire body stiffened. "No." She tried to take another step, but I tightened my hold.

"Why not? You need to eat. I need to eat. Everyone else is going to the hot springs. We could go there for a big night of fun, or—"

Her entire demeanor suddenly changed at the mention of the hot springs. Her eyes lifted to mine. "Okay. What did you have in mind?"

Strange. Was it that she didn't want to go out with everyone else, or was it the location that had her agreeing so quickly? "Great. But I wouldn't have the first clue where to go."

She balanced the box against her knee and looked at her watch. "Up for a small adventure?" she asked.

"Always."

"Meet me at the pavilion in fifteen minutes. Come prepared for a small hike, and wear your swim trunks."

ELEVEN

Raven

I sat aboard a moped and watched Kyle walk up the small hill to the pavilion. With one foot on the ground and the other on the peg, I admired the shape of his well-defined muscles beneath his form-fitting T-shirt. He had mentioned that he was a competitive swimmer at boarding school; swimming had apparently done nice things for his upper body.

Dark clouds approached from the direction of Arenal Volcano and cast a shadow over parts of the camp. A light wind picked up and turned the leaves on the trees inside out.

"Make sure you don't have anything with you that you don't mind getting wet." I pointed at a huge storm cloud.

"Should we still go?"

"Of course. You're not scared of a little rain are you, Jones? In case you haven't noticed, it rains every day here. That's why they call it the rainy season. We wouldn't get anything done if we let rain stop us."

"It doesn't bother me. I was worried about you."

I scoffed at him. "Sure you were."

He climbed onto the moped behind me and reached his arms around my waist. The mountain-fresh smell of his shower gel tickled my nose, and my stomach tightened at his touch.

He leaned into my back. "Are you sure this thing will hold both of us?" His breath warmed my ear.

I laughed. "Relax, Jones."

Relax, Raven. It's a couple of arms. And hands. Touching your waist. Not a big deal unless you let it be.

~~~~~

A scarlet macaw squawked in a tree less than thirty feet from us. I ambled along the trail that led to the La Fortuna Waterfall, careful not to lose sight of the rare bird. Thankfully, man-made steps and a metal railing made the trek down a little easier in the steepest sections.

Kyle hiked a couple of steps in front of me. He was sturdy and confident with each stride and stopped every so often to glance behind him. Did he really think I couldn't handle the hike or what?

Distracted, I suddenly lost my footing when I stepped off the last wooden stair. My foot slipped on the wet foliage, and I fell forward with a yelp.

Kyle turned when he heard me call out—just in time to reach out a hand and grasp my forearm before I plowed into him. "Whoa." He caught me in his arms and saved both of us from tumbling the rest of the way down the side of the mountain.

Resting against his chest and looking up at his light brown eyes, I felt red heat cross my face.

His brows lifted. "You okay?"

"Yeah. Sorry." I placed a hand on his rock-hard chest. His thumping heart beneath my palm clouded my ability to think. "I was looking for a scarlet macaw. Can you hear them?" I winced on the inside. *A macaw? Really, Raven?*

tracked

"Is that a bird? You were looking for some birds when you almost slipped down this steep trail and took me with you?"

I nodded. *I'm an idiot.* "They're very rare," I said weakly.

His grin broadened. He looked toward the trees. "What makes them so special that you would risk our lives? Besides being so rare."

A few hikers approached. Kyle hugged me closer and pulled me to the side so they could pass. After finding my footing, I stepped back and straightened my clothes.

"Well," I said, "they often travel in pairs or in families. And I could hear two distinct sounds, but I only saw one. When I fell, I was trying to spot a second."

"Why do they travel in pairs?"

"They're monogamous birds. When they mate, they mate for life."

"Ah. Pretty cool birds." Kyle's eyes focused in on mine. I could feel the flush on my cheeks. I really was an idiot. Was I seriously talking about birds that mate?

"Should we keep going?" I said.

When we reached the final bend in the path to the waterfall, I grabbed Kyle's arm and stopped him. "Are you sure you're ready for this?"

"Isn't it just a waterfall? We have waterfalls in Kentucky."

"Just a waterfall? See for yourself." I backed away, and Kyle made the last turn to see the La Fortuna Waterfall for the first time.

"Oh, my," he said, his eyes huge.

"Isn't it wonderful?" The result of a lava flow from the dormant Chato Volcano, the La Fortuna Waterfall dropped seventy meters into a swimming hole of clear, blue-green water.

"It's impressive, that's for sure."

I giggled and ran past him. "Come on."

Halfway undressed by the time Kyle caught up to me, I shoved my clothes into my backpack, adjusted my swimsuit, and climbed up on a large rock. I looked down into the large pool of water, rippling from the force of the waterfall. Easing out to the edge of the rock, I bent my knees and leapt into the air, doing a perfect swan dive into the swimming hole.

My arms stretched in front of me, I soared through the water, allowing it to cleanse the worry that had plagued me since arriving at Puro Cielo.

I surfaced just in time to witness Kyle cannonballing in after me. When he came back up, he could barely catch his breath. "It's freezing!"

I smiled and swam closer to him. "Nice form on the entry, Mr. Swim Team." The tension that had sat on my shoulders since I'd decided to return to Puro Cielo lifted, if only a little. I opened my mouth to speak, but Kyle disappeared underwater. I turned all around, looking for him. Any second he would wrap his hand around my ankle and pull me under. I knew this game.

But he didn't. I turned another complete circle. Laughter from a couple of swimmers caught my attention as they dunked each other under the water. But no sign of Kyle. I sucked in a quick breath and looked under the water. Still nothing. I searched the sides.

"Boo!"

tracked

I gasped, and my heart sped up. I whipped around and socked him in the chest. "That wasn't funny. You were under a long time."

"Were you worried about me? That's so cute."

I started to swim away, but he grabbed my arm. "Hey, I'm sorry. I didn't mean to scare you."

"Well, you did."

"I told you I was a swimmer. I always won the award for being able to hold my breath the longest."

"Well, aren't you multi-talented?" The frigid temperature of the water crept back into my heart.

"Says the Olympic diver." Kyle's fingers moved down my arm to brush against my hand. "Seriously, I *am* sorry."

The sincerity of his words and the touch of his fingers heated the blood leading to my heart and pushed against the coldness from the water. "Don't do it again," I said.

It *was* amazing how long he'd stayed under. And if I hadn't been so jumpy from being back in the rainforest, I probably would have thought it was funny. Allowing a small giggle to escape, I placed both hands on his chest and pushed him backward. He grabbed my arm again, pulled me closer, and with a hand on top of my head, pushed me under. I grabbed his foot and pulled him down with me. Two could play this game. I came up laughing, then swam away.

I climbed back up onto the rocks and stuck my arms to the side to balance on the uneven ground.

"Where are you going?" he called after me.

"Getting out. It's freezing." I reached into my backpack for a towel and dabbed at my face.

A group of swimmers gathered their belongings and began the climb back up the mountain. The chatter of other hikers faded in the opposite direction as an eerie quiet fell over the forest. A twig cracking behind me sounded like the pop of a shotgun over the sound of the falls. No one was there, though. I glanced toward Kyle, who was swimming toward the thunderous waterfall, away from me.

I tucked the towel back inside my backpack and traded it for a T-shirt. As I slipped it over my head, a chill moved up my arms and down my spine, and I trembled. I felt the stare before I saw the man.

The Tico was dressed in faded black jeans and a dark gray button-down. Odd for a hike, and definitely strange for a visit to the waterfall. When I looked at him, he lowered his eyes, which were shaded by a New York Yankees hat, and continued past me and around the bend in the path, alone. He didn't look back.

Kyle climbed up the bank and sat on the rock beside me. I handed him a towel and proceeded to squeeze the excess moisture from my hair. At first I didn't remove my eyes from the spot where the Tico had disappeared, but then I shook the paranoia from my head. Surely I was imagining things.

The setting sun broke through the trees and cast a warm glow on us. Lying beside me, Kyle propped his head up by his elbow to face me, while I lay back on the rock using my backpack as a pillow.

"How long have you been coming to La Fortuna?" he asked.

"Since I was eight. So, thirteen years. My parents are college professors at Cal-Poly. Well, they were. I guess they're

tracked

done with that now. They've always taken summer months and sometimes a month in the winter for volunteer work."

"That had to be hard on you. Spending every summer here, I mean. It's beautiful, but it's not home."

"It's home to me, sort of." I couldn't help but think how I'd skipped coming last winter. The memory of last summer had been too fresh. And now, with the camp in trouble...

"So, you grew up in San Luis Obispo?"

"Yep. Been there since I was three."

"But you've worked with your parents to run Puro Cielo in the summers?"

"Yeah. My parents started out giving me small chores when I was younger. As I could handle more, they gave me more to do." I sat up and wrapped my arms around my knees, then angled my head to look at Kyle. "What made you come to Costa Rica?"

Deep trenches formed across Kyle's forehead. He looked away briefly. When he turned back to me, his brows continued to tilt inward, like he was contemplating what to tell me. "I lost someone close to me recently." He swallowed hard.

"I'm sorry."

His breathing picked up. I was about to tell him he didn't have to talk about it when he stared into my eyes and blurted, "She was murdered."

If someone had told me a couple of years ago that someone they knew was murdered, I probably would have freaked out and run full steam in the opposite direction. I'd always led such a sheltered life. Even while I lived in a foreign country, I was surrounded by people—Mom, Dad, Daniel, and even Pascal—who overprotected me. But while under the protection of others, something horrible had still happened in front of me—and *to* me.

I reached out my hand and placed it over Kyle's. "I'm sorry about your friend." A few beats passed. I removed my hand.

Kyle remained very still while he stared into the waterfall in front of us. "That's not really what you asked, is it?" He turned to me again. "I came here partly to escape the memories, I think."

"But you can't, can you?"

He shook his head. "There's no escaping the memories of someone you've loved and lost. There's only learning to live with what's no longer."

"What was the other part?"

He met my gaze. "The other part?"

"You said you came to Costa Rica partly to escape bad memories. I don't think I can help you with that. But maybe I can help you with the other part of why you came here."

At that, Kyle's lips twitched into a warm grin that almost pushed all the sadness from his eyes. Almost.

"I think I came to find someone. Maybe myself. Maybe someone else. A friend got me the job at the camp. His last words to me were direct orders to take in some sights—go ziplining and soak in the hot springs. To have some fun."

I bit my lip, trying to hide my grin. If it was fun he was looking for... "Well, I might not be able to help you forget your past, but I can sure help you experience Costa Rica."

He matched my smile. "This was a good start. Thank you for forcing me to come out with you this afternoon." He sat up. The seriousness of our talk from moments before evaporated like the mist of the waterfall behind him.

tracked

I laughed. "Forcing you? No one held a gun to your head, Jones."

He nudged me with his shoulder, and the back of his hand brushed against my knee. "Seriously, thank you for showing me this place." The heat from his fingers lingered long after he pulled his hand back. "Do you feel comfortable telling me what happened last summer?"

The question caught me off guard. I could feel my smile slip away from my lips. I sat up and looked straight ahead, searching the waterfall for an answer. Kyle had overheard part of the conversation between Lucia and me. I was sorry for that.

"I know you witnessed something awful. And I know you weren't expected to return. It might help to talk about it."

I took in a deep, pained breath. "I can't." I turned my head away and squeezed my eyes tight. Behind my lids I saw Nicholas—how I remembered him in my dreams. Dead. Eyes open and glassed over.

Kyle grazed my arm with the back of his hand. "It's okay. I'm sorry that I pried. It just seems that no one talks about it around camp, so if you ever do want to…"

I opened my eyes, and the dark images faded. "Thank you." I stared at the place his hand had just touched, then at his eyes. "I'm just not ready." I swallowed, forcing a smile. "But I am ready for dinner. Hungry?"

I looked for disappointment on Kyle's face, but instead I found warmth, understanding. Strange. What *did* he know about last summer? I would have thought someone planning to stay at Puro Cielo all summer would insist on knowing more about a murder that had touched our camp last year.

"Starving," he said. He stood and reached down with both hands, helping me to my feet. The calm expression on his face gave away nothing.

As we began our trek back up the trail, I glanced over my shoulder. There he was again: the man in the New York Yankees hat lurked in the shadows of some not-too-far-away trees, watching us.

We were definitely being followed.

TWELVE

Kyle

Raven's silence on the trip back to camp troubled me. I had pushed her too hard for information about last summer. She'd seemed fine when I dropped the subject, but then she'd visibly trembled during our hike back up the trail and had been quiet most of the ride back.

And that wasn't the only thing troubling me. If Raven hadn't been with me, I would have had a "conversation" with the hiker in the New York Yankees hat. He looked out of place, and he seemed to have Raven in his sight a little too much for my comfort level. I had to constantly remind myself that I was the medical experiment, not Raven. No one was after her, and no one knew I was in La Fortuna.

Still, something felt off.

We made it back to Puro Cielo at five thirty as darkness descended on the camp. Showered and dressed, I entered the kitchen thirty minutes later. Standing just inside the doorway, I watched Raven knead pizza dough, pressing the gooey substance onto a baking stone. She wore flip-flops and a sundress that flowed to just above her knees. A clip pulled her hair away from her face and held it in a twist on the back of her head, exposing the delicate line of her neck.

I approached her slowly. "You look nice." *Nice?* What a stupid compliment. She looked more than *nice*. This girl was equal parts hot and vulnerable, and both elements played with my intent to stay away from all complications this summer.

"Thank you." She blushed, and the weird feeling returned to my stomach—a feeling that set off alarms telling me I was getting too close.

I wasn't even emotionally available. But there was something about this black-haired, doe-eyed woman in front of me. She carried herself with confidence most of the time, but there was a certain amount of distrust deep within her azure eyes that had me eager to know everything there was to know about her.

But since I'd already failed in my earlier attempt to talk to her about her mysterious, traumatic event last year, I decided that my La Fortuna business was on hold for the night.

She darted back and forth from the pizza that was taking shape to the stove where she poked at a frying pan holding sizzling meat.

"Can I help?" The smell of Italian sausage made my mouth water.

"You can grab yourself something to drink. There are sodas and bottled waters in the fridge over there, and there's iced tea behind me." She lifted her head in the direction of the stainless steel refrigerator.

"What can I get you?"

"I'm fine, thanks. I've already got some tea."

"How have you gotten used to all the sounds around here at night?" I asked as I cracked open a Coke. "I thought the roar

tracked

of the river was the worst of it the first night, but then I woke to—"

"The frog?"

I turned, shaking a finger at her. "Yes! Exactly."

She raised a brow, and a smirk played with the corners of her lips. "Kermit is always outside my window when I'm here. It's the one sound I don't like. I sleep soundly by the river and I love the birds singing in the a.m., but the frog drives me nuts."

"You're in the cabin next to me, right?"

She nodded. "The one on the end with the hummingbird painted on the outside." Every cabin at Puro Cielo had some tropical bug or animal painted outside the door.

"Why don't I ever see you coming or going?"

"I'm up way before you, and I go to bed early and read most nights." She shrugged. "I'm a boring girl. I've spent so many summers here that I settle into a routine in no time." She turned around and put the pizza in the oven.

I grabbed our drinks. When she rose and turned back around, I stood only inches away. Her eyes widened in surprise. I handed her the glass of tea and tipped my Coke to it. "Here's to an excellent first week at Puro Cielo. Thank you for making it a pleasant one."

Oh, how I wished I could read what was behind those intense blue eyes. Why didn't I get the mind-reading gift that my fellow cloned friends, Jack and Jonas, possessed?

"I hardly made your first week enjoyable," she said. "I wasn't even that nice to you when you first arrived." She lifted herself up onto the center island. "I'm sorry for that."

"You already apologized. Remember? With the milkshake. And I forgave you. The trip to the waterfall today was incredible. And now you're making me dinner. I'd say you've more than made up for your initial cold shoulder."

"It wasn't that I didn't want you here. Besides, you'll be too busy to notice me starting Sunday. The next group arrives late Saturday night, and it's much larger. We'll also have more to do after my mom and dad leave. We're booked with a different group every week this summer."

I lifted myself to sit next to her. "It'll take more than fifty strangers around camp to keep me from noticing you, and although I don't know you well enough *yet*, you seem far from boring." What was I saying? I mentally berated myself.

Her cheeks reddened further. I admired the soft lines around her meek smile and how her hands thumbed the sides of her glass. She looked down at her tea and jiggled the ice, avoiding my gaze.

"Can I get you some more tea?" I asked.

She shook her head. The smile that was there moments ago faded. Her eyes fluttered toward me for a fleeting moment. She set her glass behind her and wiped her palms on her skirt. "You were right." She inhaled. Her hands twisted in her lap. "Something happened here last year that *was* awful."

I stayed very still and quiet so as not to spook her back into silence.

"Miguel's and Pascal's father was murdered. Stabbed. I saw it happen, I think." She bit her lower lip. Sadness swirled in her eyes, further defining the vulnerability that lived there most of the time.

"You *think* you saw it?" I wanted to scoop both of her hands into mine, to hold them tightly. I wanted to help her talk about this traumatic event. I could see that she needed to. How could I convince her that she could trust me?

She lifted her fidgety hands and wrapped her arms around her stomach in a hug. "I don't remember any of it. I remember being at the hot springs one night with one of Puro Cielo's largest groups ever, and the next thing I remember, I was lying in the hospital."

"What did the police say?"

"They found enough evidence to verify that someone else was there, and that whoever it was killed Nicholas. They assumed I had just stumbled onto a bad scene. Wrong place, wrong time."

"So they never found who killed him?"

Raven shook her head. The corners of her lips tugged into a frown.

"Is that how you got the scar?" I reached out and followed the groove of the scar on her temple with gentle fingers.

She nodded, her eyes glued to mine. Swallowing hard, I pulled my hand back.

She lifted her hand and touched the same spot, as if she needed to remember the smooth feel of the newer skin, the indention on her face left as a souvenir of a night she'd tucked far away inside her head. "The doctors say I either blocked the memories because of the shock, or the concussion caused me to forget."

"Is it difficult being back?"

Her hand slipped around to the back of her neck, where she absentmindedly rubbed a spot at the base of her skull. "It's hard seeing the people whose lives were changed forever when Nicholas died. Miguel and I have talked about it. Through email, mostly. And Lucia... well, she's the most loving and forgiving woman alive, but..." Raven's voice trailed off.

"But?"

"Pascal." She paused. "He took his father's death hard. I'm not sure he'll ever forgive me for not remembering."

I studied the scar that decorated the skin dangerously close to her eye. If I'd known her back then, Lexi or Jack would have healed her. I would have tried to heal her. I had gotten better at healing the last couple of months, thanks to Lexi's help. "Thank you for sharing your story with me."

She nodded, swallowing hard. She met my gaze again, the features of her face gentle. She was starting to trust me.

A pain stabbed my heart. I wanted to put my arm around her and pull her close. I wanted to hug her fear and anguish away the same way I'd hugged Dani during the nights after Sandra Whitmeyer inserted a tracker into the back of her neck. But this wasn't Dani. And just like I hadn't been able to comfort Dani, or even save her, I couldn't help Raven now.

Although the barriers around Raven's heart had seemed to soften a little, those walls were still there. And even if I were to bring those walls down, is that what I really wanted?

THIRTEEN

Raven

I tossed and turned for several hours. I counted animal sounds outside my window, read for a while, even tried meditating myself to sleep. Nothing worked against the paralyzing fear that the monsters were waiting for me in slumber.

The hour grew later and later. Finally, my eyes became too heavy.

I ran through the trees. Footsteps thumped behind me, growing louder and louder. I opened my mouth to scream but produced no sound. Perspiration ran down the sides of my head. I dodged low-hanging branches, and thick underbrush stung my ankles as I sprinted away. The rumbling of the volcano thundered in the distance.

A loud banging grew over the sound of the booming footsteps and the volcano grumbles, and I sat straight up in bed.

I covered my heart with both palms and sucked in a deep breath. A dream. Just a dream. The banging, however, was real—someone was at my door.

I illuminated my phone. Two a.m. I approached the cabin window, my mini-Maglight gripped tightly in my hand. As if a tiny flashlight would stop whoever was banging on my door from murdering me. I glanced out at an angle, then let out a huge breath of relief. *Pascal.* What was he doing here?

I grabbed a hooded sweatshirt off the bedpost.

With another rise and fall of my chest, I cracked open the door enough to see his face. "Have you lost your mind?"

"Please, can I come in?"

"No, you may not. Are you drunk?"

His face hardened. "Amagita, I am not drunk. If I can't come in, will you please come out?"

I looked up at the dark ceiling and took another exasperated breath before giving in. "Fine." I huffed. "Let me get some shoes."

I walked to my suitcase and searched under a pile of clothes for a pair of flip-flops. I returned and swung the door open to face Pascal, who bit his lower lip and stuffed his hands in his front pockets.

He followed me across a stretch of grass to an old concrete picnic table overlooking the river. I prayed no one would hear us at this hour. I would have no answers for Daniel or my father if they caught us out past the camp's curfew.

I sat on one of the benches and placed my elbows on the table in front of me. Instead of sitting across the table, Pascal sat right next to me, the length of his body touching mine.

I stared at the connection, willing him to scoot over.

When he didn't move, I shifted just slightly to break the contact. "Why are you here?" I asked when I couldn't take the silence any longer.

"Do you remember the night that you, Alejandra, Miguel, and I stayed up all night? We played down by the river. Flashlight tag, I think?"

tracked

"Yeah. And Alejandra fell out of that tree. She scraped up her legs and arms pretty bad." I smiled at the memory of her laughing it off. "I also remember getting caught and grounded for the rest of the summer." That was about the time a curfew was implemented at Puro Cielo.

"I need to know what you remember about that night. The night my dad died."

The silence rang loud in my ears. I hadn't needed his clarification; I knew which night he had switched to without warning. I took in a deep breath and held it there a few seconds before letting it out slowly. "I don't remember anything."

"Nothing at all? Do you remember being at the hot springs?"

"Yes. And I remember waking up in the hospital. But nothing in between."

Why was he asking me these questions? Why the sudden interest, when for months after the murder, I'd heard nothing from him?

I hadn't wanted to face Pascal. Facing Miguel was no problem. Seeing Lucia was difficult, but survivable. Pascal made me want to crawl into a hole in the ground. To burrow deep within a rabbit's warren. Hiding was easier than confronting Pascal's inquisitive and sad eyes. Would he ever forgive me for not coping with the details of that night? For not being more courageous?

"Miguel said you lost your college scholarship because of your head injuries."

"He shouldn't have told you that." I looked away from Pascal toward the sound of the river—hoping to lose myself there. Miguel was the only person I'd told about my scholarship.

"Why wouldn't you want me to know that? We all lost something that night, you know."

"Don't you think I know that?" I swung my head back to look at him, and my voice climbed just above a whisper. "What do you want from me?" Rage bubbled up in my chest and threatened to spill over.

"I don't want you to avoid me all summer. I don't want you to see me as the enemy. I want you to remember."

"What?" I asked as calmly as I could manage. "What are you talking about? What if I don't want to remember?"

"You need to deal with this, Amagita. *We* need to deal with it."

"Why can't you leave this alone?"

"Why are you shutting these memories out? Even worse, why are you pushing everyone away who wants to help you?"

"Help? Is that what you're doing? Trying to help *me*? From where I'm sitting, it looks like you're trying to help *yourself*."

"Don't you think I deserve to know what happened to my father?"

"Of course you do," I whispered.

"I ran into Miguel last night. He confessed that he said some things to you about me. He said he told you to stay away from me."

"That's true; he did. And why did he ask me to do that? Did something happen between the two of you?" Miguel had never come to the camp like he'd promised.

"No. Not really. He thinks you're better off not remembering, and he thinks I shouldn't interfere." Pascal shook his head and looked out toward the river. "Dammit, Raven, I just want to

tracked

know who killed my father. I want to know if that person..." His voice trailed off.

"If that person... what?"

"Nothing."

"If that person what, Pascal?" I grabbed Pascal's shoulder and forced him to look at me. "You think whoever killed your father is still here, don't you?" My entire body began a slow shake. I climbed from the bench and stumbled backward. "You asked me to come here, and you think..."

He was on his feet and in front of me so fast. "No. Raven, no. I wouldn't have put you in danger. Whoever killed my father would be stupid to have stayed here."

I searched Pascal's eyes for any sign that he believed what he was saying. He struggled to maintain eye contact, blinking and refocusing on me each time his gaze drifted away. He wanted to believe that the killer was long gone, to convince me of the same, but it didn't take a mind reader to see that Pascal was scared.

"I want you to leave," I said.

"Raven... I..." He tried to pull me closer.

"Right *now*, Pascal." My arms and hands began to tremble slightly. I lifted my arms up and away from his tight grasp before he could feel the quake in my limbs or sense my fear.

"Hey, Raven. Nice night for a moonlit chat?" Kyle announced himself with calm sarcasm.

I jerked my head in his direction. Just perfect. Now I'd have to explain myself to the new guy. Just when I was starting to like having him around.

Pascal backed up a couple of steps.

"Great. Just great," I said. "I guess introductions are in order. Kyle, Pascal. Pascal, Kyle. Oh wait. That's right. You already met." I didn't mean to take out my frustration on Kyle, but, well... I didn't need him, or any other man, here this summer. I didn't need the distraction. I could handle whatever crisis the camp was having. Without him. Without Pascal. Without my parents. Alone.

The two guys in front of me stared at each other without saying a word. It was a contest to see who was going to leave first.

I looked from Kyle to Pascal. A frustrated growl vibrated in my throat. "I'm going to bed. Pascal, it's been real. Kyle, thanks for galloping in on your white horse." I stomped off toward my cabin. Once I was inside, I slammed my cabin door and kicked off my flip-flops.

This time when my head hit the pillow, I slipped quickly back into my nightmares. I ran faster from the footsteps, as fast as I could, until I hit a wall. The wall was a man. A man with dark eyes set deeply in the shadows of his brows—eyes that looked so familiar.

FOURTEEN

Kyle

I followed her through the forest as she ran, careful to stay out of sight. If she saw me in this dream, she'd definitely be confused.

Slipping into a person's dreams or subconscious was a gift I'd received when scientists tampered with the DNA they'd cloned me from.

I was pretty sure Raven would be convinced she'd just incorporated her own thoughts into her dreams, but I didn't want to risk her freaking out and pushing me further away.

Her dream ended every time she came face to face with the man—the man with dark brown eyes but no other distinguishing features. As soon as she encountered him, she'd wake up—then drift right back into the same dream. Over and over again this happened, until she finally fell into a deeper, non-REM, stage of sleep.

I didn't sleep much after that. I was thinking about what she'd shared with me about the murder, and I was concerned about the early morning visit from Pascal. Raven had claimed that Pascal was her friend—but what kind of friend woke a girl in the middle of the night to talk about a year-old murder that had frightened her enough to cause suppressed memories?

The look on her face when she'd stormed off was not one of anger, as I would have expected, but a mixture of confusion and anguish. This was a girl who had closed herself off to dealing with what had happened. She had bottled up way too many negative emotions. But her guilt over not being able to help Pascal and his family was tearing her apart.

One thing was certain: I was way too involved. And it was becoming more and more difficult to walk away from this girl. This girl who struggled in her dreams less than twenty feet away from me, yet wanted little to do with me.

How could I tell her that I could meet up with her and actually help her *inside* those nightmares?

~~~~~

Early the next morning, Raven's mom, Bennett, was on a mission to find some sort of sweet coffee drink for her daughter. I decided to tag along to the grocery store to get a better feel for the town.

I surveyed the store's selection of junk food, something I was now craving after having eaten nothing but fresh fruit, some version of black beans, and fried plantains with the past dozen or so meals. And after getting less than two hours of sleep the night before, I needed comfort food.

Loud voices, including Bennett's, interrupted my analysis of some sort of sugar-covered jellied fruit snacks. When I heard Bennett cry out, I dropped the package and took off toward the front of the store. At the end of the aisle, I leaned carefully around the corner.

The store clerk was crouched down behind the counter. In a security mirror above her, I could see two men forcing Bennett out of the store.

tracked

My pulse beat loudly in my head. As soon as they were outside, I ran to the door and peered through the glass. Bennett struggled as they pulled her along toward a dark sedan.

I quickly looked around for a weapon—or anything I could use as one. I spotted an aisle end cap with a display of machetes. I darted over, grabbed a stupid-huge knife, and flew out of the store. A man in a dark suit had the back door of the sedan open and was preparing to push Bennett into the vehicle.

"You're going to want to stop right there," I said. I slowly removed the outer sheath housing the blade.

The two men turned to face me, both of them smirking. One still had a hand gripped tightly around Bennett's upper arm. I held the uncovered machete in front of me, prepared for whatever fight I had to have in order to keep Bennett from being shoved into that car. Bennett's wide eyes bounced from the men to me. She grimaced in pain from the hold on her arm.

One of the men stepped toward me. "Look what we have here. An American meddling in our business." Pushing his suit jacket back just slightly, he revealed a revolver tucked in a holster at his waist.

I studied his light brown eyes and dark hair. He looked incredibly similar to the friend who had sent me to La Fortuna. This man was Jonas—an older version of Jonas, anyway. Jonas had been right. His DNA donor clone, Dr. Jeremy Porter, was here in Costa Rica.

The man's gun didn't scare me, but this proof that Jonas was right about his donor being here did.

Dr. Porter cocked his head, eyeing me closely as I made the realization. I had no idea what I was dealing with. Was he running another lab? Was he as evil as Sandra Whitmeyer? Was he one of the original geneticists who had created me, Jonas, Jack, Lexi, and the others?

And did he recognize me? I looked from him to Bennett's terror-filled eyes. I had to get her out of here.

I stood straighter. "That's right. I'm also an American who will use this little knife to make short order of both of you if you don't release the lady right now."

Dr. Porter laughed.

A white SUV with the word "policia" on the side pulled up to a street corner half a block away. It was my lucky day.

I nodded in the SUV's direction. "Or we could ask the lovely policewoman for help in resolving our differences."

Dr. Porter scowled. "Let her go, Paulo."

"Let her go? Really, boss?"

After a stern look from Dr. Porter, Paulo released Bennett with one last push. She stumbled forward, but quickly turned to face them.

Jonas's DNA donor clone smiled, then saluted Bennett. "We will meet again, Madame."

I pulled Raven's mom backward and positioned myself between her and the two men.

Dr. Porter's eyes locked on to mine. "Watch your back, pretty boy." He leaned in to my face and, in a whisper that only I could hear, said, "Give Jonas my best."

He and Paulo then climbed into the car and left.

Only when their car had turned the corner did Bennett let out a huge breath behind me. Her hand covered her heart.

"You okay? Did they hurt you?" I asked, sliding the machete back into its protective sleeve.

tracked

She looked up at me. Strength poured from her eyes and from the words that came next. "Not a word about this to Raven."

FIFTEEN

Raven

I journaled in the dining pavilion after breakfast the next morning. The visiting volunteer team milled about, preparing for their departure and taking some last-minute pictures by the river. Only when an old school bus crept down the long drive—chartered to deliver the team to the San Jose Airport—did I realize I was alone in the pavilion.

As a matter of fact, I hadn't laid eyes on Kyle since the middle of the night. Not even for breakfast.

I stood and did a three-sixty, looking for any sign of my parents, Kyle, or Daniel and Eva. I placed the cap on my pen and stuffed it and my journal into my bag, still studying the perimeter. Daniel, at the very least, should be helping the team preparing to leave.

I entered the kitchen, where the smell of breakfast casserole lingered. Voices carried toward the door. I stepped lightly in the direction of the storage room behind the kitchen, where apparently a staff meeting was being held. Without me.

I inched up toward the door.

"The important thing is you're okay." Daniel's voice.

My breath caught. Who was he speaking to? *Who* was okay?

"I think Raven should go home," Dad said. "Can we send her with this group to San Jose? She can get a ticket when she gets there."

Go home? I'm not going home.

"She just got here," Daniel said. "I'm not disagreeing with you, but you know how she is. We can't force her to jump on a plane after she just got the nerve to return here for the first time since... I'm just saying, it had to take a lot of courage for her to get on a plane and come here. Besides, where will she go for the summer? You sold your house, remember?"

"They didn't hurt me," Mom said.

Hurt her? Who? What happened?

"It was just a random crime," Mom continued. "I think Raven will be fine. She'll just need to take extra precautions. Everyone will. I don't think anyone should be wandering alone."

My eyes darted back and forth between a couple of stains on the wall, unable to focus as other people argued about what I should do. I was tempted to barge in on their little meeting, but thought better of it.

"Excuse me if I'm speaking out of line," Kyle said. "But I think you'd be better off telling her the truth."

You tell 'em, Kyle. I think I might like having you around after all.

"Kyle, I know you mean well," Dad said. "But you don't know the extent of what happened to her. No one does."

"Let's not overreact," Daniel said. "For now, we'll stick with the original plan. We'll make sure everyone travels in small groups. At the first sign that it's unsafe for Raven to be here, I'll put her on a plane myself. We all know crime happens everywhere. La Fortuna is just as safe as any California town."

tracked

I stood with my back straight against the wall, squeezing my eyes shut.

"Kyle, I'm sorry to be such a downer on your birthday," Mom said, her tone more casual, and my eyes popped open.

Kyle's birthday? I gave my head a quick shake. *Focus, Raven.*

Sensing the end of the conversation, I ducked inside the small office.

"Well, I've got to see this group off." Daniel stepped out of the storage room. He walked past the office and out the door, with Dad following close behind.

The banter between Mom and Kyle continued. They stopped just outside the office where I was hiding.

"You're not a downer. I'm just sorry about what happened to you," Kyle said.

"I'm thankful you were there. And I'm glad you'll be here this summer, with William and me leaving."

I massaged the bridge of my nose. Who would hurt my mom?

"Kyle," Mom continued. "Please don't say anything to Raven."

"Why not? I think that's a big mistake."

"Please, Kyle. I will tell her. When the time is right."

SIXTEEN

Kyle

I wiped the sweat from my brow. I wasn't used to this heat and humidity, so unlike the Kentucky weather most of the year. I scuffed my feet along the dirt path that led down to the river, feeling tired from digging holes for the new gate at the entrance to Puro Cielo. I had to find a private spot where I could call Jonas.

He needed to know that the DNA donor from whom he had been created was, in fact, in Costa Rica—and kidnapping innocent Americans. And, although Dr. Porter didn't outright admit to knowing *exactly* who I was, he clearly recognized me, and he knew I was tied to Jonas in some way.

Was it a coincidence that someone from the camp where I had agreed to work was a target of an express kidnapping? That's what William and Daniel were calling it. I was sure there was more to it.

Armed with my phone, I skirted around a tree and stopped short; Raven had beaten me to the quiet spot where I had planned to call Jonas.

However, I had to admit that it wasn't such a terrible thing to find Raven sitting on a large rock, her slender legs stretched out in front of her, a book open on her lap.

I watched her for a moment. Her face tilted up toward the sun that peeked through the trees. She wasn't even reading the book.

I thought back to the scene that morning—Bennett nearly stuffed into a car. I wanted to march over and tell Raven the truth: that she might be in danger here; that she should go home. But I had assured Bennett I would let her talk to Raven. She'd have to do it soon, though, since she and William were leaving for Africa first thing in the morning.

After a deep breath, I put my phone in my pocket and climbed onto the rock to sit beside Raven. "Hey." I nudged her shoulder with mine.

Barely looking sideways and in a bored tone, she said, "Hey, yourself." She closed her book and held it in her lap while her fingers traced the letters of the title. In addition to sounding curt, she refused to make eye contact.

"Have you had a good morning?" I caught a trace of her fruity scent, and something in my stomach played with the lunch I'd just eaten.

"I guess. I finally unpacked."

"Is that a big step for you?" I glanced sideways at her, hoping to catch the slightest twitch of her lips at my sarcasm.

"Nope." No hint of a smile surfaced. "Unpacking just wasn't first on my list of priorities when I arrived. Or second. Or third. But since I hit the waterfall last night..." She shrugged. "I figured unpacking had to be next." Finally, a hint of a smile kissed her lips at the joke attempt.

At least she was talking to me, but she was definitely in a mood. How was I going to get her out of this mood without offering up the truth? I liked being around her, but dishonesty

tracked

wasn't my thing. I'd watched two of my friends hide things from each other off and on for the past year, and the lies had nearly cost them not only their relationship but their lives. Then again, I wasn't lying to Raven. Not technically. I was just withholding information. For her own good, maybe. *That's probably how Lexi and Jack justified their secrets, too.*

Also, Raven and I were *not* in a relationship. The question was: would it stay that way?

Did I *want* it to stay that way?

Raven raised her head and looked out over the river. I counted the freckles on her nose while pondering what subjects weren't off limits. Just when I was about to ask her about Pascal's late-night visit, she tossed her book aside and straightened her back, her eyes angled up into the trees. I followed her line of vision.

She laid a firm hand on my forearm. "Don't move."

"What's wrong?" I looked from her to the trees and back. The look on her face made the muscles in my back tense.

She took my hand and pointed it toward the trees. Her movements were slow and deliberate, as if a bomb might go off if she shifted too abruptly. "Shhh. Look!"

There in front of us, several monkeys swung from branch to branch, not all that far from where we sat. My shoulders and back relaxed in a sigh. Raven dug through her bag, then held her Nikon up to her eye and snapped away.

"What are those?" I asked. I sat up, taking in the sight of monkeys in the wild.

"Uh... monkeys." She left the word "dumbass" off the end of her statement, but it was definitely implied.

"I know they're monkeys, Miss Smarty Pants." I tilted my chin into my shoulder and raised my eyebrows. "What kind of monkeys?"

She lowered her camera but continued to watch the monkeys swing through the limbs. "White-headed capuchins."

"How close will they get to us?"

"Close enough to throw poop at us if they don't want us here."

"Really?"

She nodded, smirking.

Did she want the monkeys to throw feces at me? She had been pretty mad in the middle of the night, and not just at Pascal.

A grin tugged at the corner of my lips. She was pretty cute when she was angry.

The monkeys disappeared through the trees, and Raven replaced her camera in her bag. When she turned back around, our eyes met. "Something on your mind, Jones?"

I paused. "You want to tell me about Pascal?"

"I told you about Pascal. He's Miguel's older brother." Her smile faded, and her less-than-rosy mood returned. "You'll see him when you go to the hot springs, most likely. I'm sure you two will get along just swimmingly."

"Why do you do that?"

"Do what?"

"Use sarcasm as a defensive weapon." When she just stared at me, I continued. "What was that middle-of-the-night visit all about?"

"That was nothing. Pascal has a way with the dramatics. That's all."

tracked

"Well, I think Daniel should know that Pascal showed up uninvited at your cabin at two in the morning." Maybe then Daniel would explain to Raven the importance of the curfew and making smarter decisions. Especially now that it was clear something strange was going on in this little town in the middle of the rainforest.

"You can't tell him. Why would you do that? It's none of your business." Raven closed her eyes tight and massaged the points on either side of the bridge of her nose.

"Give me one good reason not to."

She hesitated for a few seconds, then opened her eyes. "You'll cause him and my parents unnecessary worry. Pascal would never hurt me."

"How do you know that? Do you *really* know him?"

"Yes, I know him very well. As well as anyone can know Pascal."

I cocked my head. What the hell did she mean by that? I decided to let that one go, for now, reminding myself that Raven and I were not in a relationship. "You were yelling at him pretty good when I came on the scene."

"Well, we had a lot of catching up to do."

"Again with the sarcasm?"

"Sorry." Though I could tell she wasn't. "But this truly is none of your business."

For some reason, her words stung. For a reason I couldn't form fully, I wanted it to be my business. I wanted *her* to be my business. And I could think of a dozen reasons to tell Daniel about Pascal—and another dozen reasons not to get involved with Raven or the drama of this camp.

"Please don't say anything to my parents or Daniel. My parents don't need anything more to worry about before they take off for Africa. They'll fret about me enough as it is."

More than you know. I replayed the earlier conversation about the kidnapping in my head. I was losing track of how many secrets I was keeping from each of the people at this camp. Dishonesty was never an admirable quality in a friend. But were Raven and I becoming friends? And was it betrayal to keep a secret that wasn't my tale to tell?

"All right. I'll leave it alone for now."

She stood and lifted her shirt over her head, revealing a very small white bikini, and thus ending our conversation.

"What are you doing?" I tried to avert my eyes from this beautiful girl—no, woman—in front of me. White. Purity.

My thoughts were anything but pure.

"Going for a swim. Come on." She climbed down from the rock, tiptoed along the path closer to the water, and dove into a deep portion of the river.

I wanted to go in after her, but I was entirely too conflicted by what this mind-boggling creature was doing to me. For one thing, she was making me question my own judgment about how to watch out for her like Daniel had requested. Second, she was making me feel things I wasn't ready for—things I didn't know I'd ever be capable of feeling again this soon after saying goodbye to Dani.

From my perch on the rock, I watched her swim. Raven was at home in Puro Cielo. She interacted well with humanitarians she hardly knew. The Tico children flocked to her like she was sent directly from heaven. And she didn't shy away from hard work. But from everything I had witnessed in the short time I'd

tracked

been in La Fortuna, I knew something suspicious was going on in the area. And some of it hit a little too close to Puro Cielo—which reminded me way too much of the trouble I had witnessed at home in the past year after discovering that my friends and I were cloned humans.

SEVENTEEN

Raven

I spread icing on the cake I had prepared for Kyle's birthday. Chocolate cake with raspberry filling was my specialty, even though it was my least favorite to eat. Guests of the camp always loved it, so I took a chance that Kyle would as well. Why I cared if he liked it, I had no idea. He certainly didn't deserve anything special from me after he'd agreed to keep secrets from me.

I licked a smudge of icing from my finger, tasting the rich chocolate. Baking was usually a therapeutic pastime for me, but now it did little to take my mind off what had happened to my mother. Or whether the incident was truly random. It occurred away from camp—that was good. And Daniel wasn't overly concerned, based on the conversation I'd overheard. I had been too scared to confront him with what I knew for fear that he would suddenly realize I was better off on a plane back to California.

I placed the cake on a glass platter. After strategically decorating the edge with raspberry garnishes, I covered the birthday dessert with a glass dome. Stepping back from my masterpiece, I admired the final product, then grabbed the knife to place it in the sink.

"Good afternoon, Raven."

I whipped around at the sound of a man's voice, the knife still gripped in my hand, to find Pascal's friend, Felipe, standing in the Puro Cielo kitchen. A crisp button-down and equally pressed slacks hung against a trim but muscular body. His hauntingly familiar eyes sent a chill along my arms and had the hairs on the back of my neck standing at attention.

"Hello." My tone sounded harsh, unwelcoming, even to my own ears.

"Pretty cake." He grinned as his eyes shifted to the knife I was white-knuckling. "Is Daniel around? I've got some supplies he ordered."

"Supplies?"

"Yeah, we got him a pretty good deal through the resort for some bulk food supplies."

"Resort?" *Stop*, I ordered myself. I sounded like an idiot with each one-word question.

"The Navos Resort and Spa, the sister location to the Navos Hot Springs...?" he said with a drawn-out enunciation and a lifted eyebrow. "You've heard of it, no?"

"Of course I've heard of it. I just didn't know you worked there."

"I own it," he said. "Well, my father owns it, which is close to the same thing." His words were steeped in smugness. It made my heart constrict to know that this guy and his father had taken over Navos after Nicholas was killed.

I placed the knife in the sink and wiped my hands on a dishtowel. "I'll get Daniel." I started to head out, but Felipe blocked the doorway, an intimidating sneer plastered across his face. My fingers curled into fists as I looked him up and down, and a sweat broke out across my neck.

tracked

He leaned in, his face close to my cheek. "I appreciate your help." His breath was hot on my ear and made me want to knee him in order to get him out of my way.

I breathed through my mouth in order to escape the musky assault of his cologne, then dipped under his arm and squeezed past him, all the while trying to calm my fast-pumping heart.

I could feel his eyes like a firm hand to the middle of my back as I walked away in search of Daniel. It was as if he was following me closely and could direct my movement with a simple guiding touch. Who did he think he was?

I did a three-sixty in the middle of the driveway, having no idea where anyone was. The sound of clanking echoed off the pavilion walls. I turned and headed up the hill toward Daniel's house.

Daniel was banging on some pipe in the ground. Kyle wiped his forehead with his sleeve. Both were covered in dirt.

"Felipe's here," I yelled over the clanking of metal on metal.

"What's he want?" Daniel looked up, out of breath.

"Something about some supplies."

"Oh, yeah. Great." He tossed aside the wrench he'd been using for the pipe-beating and climbed out of the hole he was in. "We could use the break," he said to Kyle.

I followed Daniel back down the hill to the kitchen. Felipe was leaning against the kitchen island, playing with his cell phone. I rolled my eyes as I breezed past him.

"I see you met Raven," Daniel said.

"I *have* had the pleasure already." Felipe nodded in my direction, his tone pleasant, not arrogant like before.

I pretended to clean up my mess from an afternoon of baking, wiping down counters that were already clean, even though I had already done most of the work. All an act to appear busy while studying Mr. Creepy.

Daniel, Kyle, and Felipe unloaded food and supplies from the resort truck and carted them into the storeroom next to the kitchen. Kyle glanced my way each time they entered the kitchen. And every time, I looked away, folding the same three dishtowels over and over.

With the truck emptied, Daniel shook Felipe's hand. "Care to stay for dinner?"

Felipe looked at me and grinned. I quickly grabbed a stack of dishcloths and knelt down to put them away.

"Oh, no, sir. Father is expecting me back at the hot springs tonight."

I breathed a sigh of relief before standing back up. When I did, Kyle was staring at me with a raised brow.

Daniel and Kyle walked Felipe back to his truck, and I escaped to my cabin for a quiet moment before dinner.

Kyle caught up to me as I dug in my backpack's side pocket for keys.

"What's wrong with you?" he asked, matching my steps.

"Nothing. Why?"

"A local business helps the camp, and you turn your nose up at it?"

"Who are you to judge me? Besides, he gives me the creeps. I've never known Daniel to order shipments of food or supplies through another business. Don't you find that odd?"

"Why would I?"

I crinkled my nose. "I guess you wouldn't."

tracked

I puffed out a large breath before tossing my backpack on the bench outside my cabin. I mumbled my frustration and leaned over, digging through every pocket. "Where are my keys? I know I put them in this pocket."

"Problem?"

"I know I put... here they are." I rose and dangled my key chain in front of his face. A crease formed across Kyle's forehead and his lips tightened into a straight line. I smiled. "You're cute when you look like that."

His face softened. "Like what?"

"Oh, I don't know. Like you're a little irritated with me, but not really."

He really was cute. Actually, no. Handsome was more like it. I studied the blond highlights in his otherwise brown hair and imagined running my fingers through them.

The way he looked at me unnerved me slightly—like he had known me forever, or like he knew some deep dark secret about me. He hadn't given me too hard of a time about Pascal's late-night visit. So, there was that. And he had stood up for me when the others had wanted to over-protect. Now he chastised me about Felipe, which I deserved, I guessed.

I shrugged as he continued to stare at me like he was trying to figure something out. It was all very interesting.

I turned and unlocked my cabin door. "I would love to continue this conversation"—or whatever it was—"but I can't right now. I have things to do. I'll see you at dinner."

And with that, I closed the door in his surprised face.

~~~~~

Daniel was spreading butter on thick Italian loaves when I entered the kitchen. Eva measured noodles and threw them in the boiling water.

"Hola, Raven." Eva greeted me with a hug and a warm smile. She held me out by my shoulders. "You okay, honey?"

"I'm good. Just a little tired today. I'm fighting a small headache."

Eva frowned and enveloped me in her motherly embrace. She turned and handed me a large bowl of salad. "Be a dear and put that over on the serving counter. Then go sit and relax. Dinner's almost ready."

I did as I was told, joining the others who were gathering in the pavilion. It was just the six of us for dinner that night. I breathed a sigh of relief, thankful I didn't have to sit across the table from Felipe, then felt immediately remorseful for thinking bad thoughts about someone I hardly knew.

Once we had all sat for dinner, Daniel didn't take long to launch into business talk, something we couldn't really do when camp guests were present. "The newspapers have reported some tourist kidnappings for very small ransoms." Daniel's eyes circled the table, pausing at Dad, then landing on Mom. "Families or friends have come forward and paid the money, and the tourists have gone on their merry way in a matter of hours. And on many occasions the kidnappers have simply driven the tourists to an ATM, forced them to take out three hundred dollars or so, and then released them on the spot."

"Yeah, so they can run to the nearest airport," I said as I twirled spaghetti noodles with my fork. This was exactly what Pascal had warned me about. If this kind of crime escalated,

tracked

American-run camps such as this one ran the risk of having to close, and I would be evicted from another home.

"Probably. The point is, no one has been willing to give the authorities enough information to help catch these criminals."

The term "express kidnapping" wasn't new to me, yet I'd never seen a reason to fear the possibility. Express kidnappers usually targeted wealthy tourists, not volunteers inside humanitarian organizations like this one. *Until now*, I thought as I glanced toward Mom. Had my mom been practically kidnapped that morning? And if so, was it truly random?

I gave my head a little shake when Daniel continued.

"No one is to walk around in town alone for now. Any questions?" he asked.

"Isn't that a little unreasonable?" I asked. "How are we supposed to run errands for the camp? Are you saying I can't even run to the store for milk without a chaperone?"

"Raven," my dad said, "you are not to leave camp alone. Day or night. Anywhere," he ordered. "If you feel the need to go to town, Eva, Daniel, or Kyle will go with you."

"I think this is a bit ridiculous, but fine. Whatever." I stuffed a large bite of garlic bread in my mouth.

"Your mom and I are leaving tomorrow," Dad reminded me. "Promise me you'll make smart choices."

"I will make smart choices," I recited, making air-quotes around "smart choices." I leaned back in my chair in a huff and drank the last of my iced tea. I looked across the table and found Kyle staring at me with a smirk.

He lifted a brow, chuckling.

"What are you laughing at?" I practically spat.

"Raven..." Mom choked on her tea.

"Yes?" I asked, never taking my eyes off of Kyle. He returned the stare, causing me to squirm in my seat.

"And another thing, little missie." Daniel pointed a fork at me. "What was that about earlier? With Felipe?"

"What are you talking about?" Dad asked.

"Your sweet daughter here—"

"There's something freaky about him. Makes my skin crawl." I pointed my garlic bread at Daniel as I spoke. "Who is he anyway?"

Mom shook her head in that I-can't-control-my-daughter sort of way.

"Well, he helps his father run the Navos Hot Springs and the resort," Daniel said. "They've done a lot to help the camp and many people of this town, including Pascal and his family. I'm not sure we would have survived the slow part of winter without their help."

"Yeah, but where did they come from?"

"They're from Venezuela, and they're very nice," Eva said somewhat defensively.

Eva's sweet accent disarmed my attack. Eva thought everyone was nice. I'd just save my questions for Miguel. He'd tell me anything I wanted to know.

Either that, or I'd have to confront Pascal about his employer and his son.

EIGHTEEN

Kyle

After sitting around the dinner table for more than two hours, I was starting to understand the family dynamic between the MacMillans and Daniel and his wife. And while they all doted on Raven, they also poked fun at her from time to time. Especially Daniel.

"Remember the summer Raven and Alejandra decided it would be a good idea to teach some visiting children a bunch of Spanish cuss words?" Daniel tossed back the rest of his drink.

Raven laughed and waved a hand in dismissal. "Oh, they were harmless words."

"What words were they?" William tried, but failed, to cast his daughter a stern look.

"They were all just parts or functions of the body. No big deal." Raven shrugged, trying hard to suppress a smile. "You know. Words like ass, shit, and piss."

William laughed while Bennett erupted with, "Raven Mac-Millan!"

"Try telling the evangelical Christian missionary parents that the words their children were yelling and calling each other were simply 'parts of the body.'" Daniel shook his head at the memory.

"I meant no harm by it. I was fifteen and bored."

The group grew silent for a moment, but then they all erupted in laughter. It was interesting to see Raven let go like she did. She grew silent, though, when the others continued their banter. She looked down and played with the condensation on her glass, her smile completely gone. When her eyes drifted to mine, she blushed as if realizing for the first time that I was sitting across from her.

She shifted uncomfortably in her seat, but then sat up suddenly. "Oh my gosh, I almost forgot."

Everyone turned to her.

"I'll be right back." She rose from her chair and sashayed toward the kitchen with the grace of a ballerina.

I crossed my arms, studying the looks on the faces of the others. They looked just as puzzled as I felt.

Daniel pushed away from the table. "I need to stretch my legs." He reached down and grabbed his wife's hand and pulled her to him.

William stood and moved to sit beside me. When he looked at Bennett, she nodded, then stood, gathered some dishes, and headed for the kitchen.

"Something wrong, William?" I asked. He had the look I suspected fathers get when they're about to warn a boy away from their daughter.

"No. At least, I hope not." He leaned his elbows into his knees and looked up at me. "I know the attempted kidnapping left us all a little on edge this morning."

To say the least. "But...?" I prodded.

"No buts. Bennett and I have a favor to ask of you. She and I have discussed it, and we're not planning to send Raven

tracked

home. I don't think she would go even if we tried. Crime happens everywhere. And we'll worry about Raven no matter where she is. But this is her home. And if Bennett and I can't be with her, Daniel and Eva are the next best thing."

"What's the favor?" I knew the crime against Bennett hadn't been random, but I had no proof that I was willing to share just yet. I certainly couldn't tell these people that I'd recognized a man because I knew his genetic clone.

William ran a hand through his hair. "Please keep an eye out for Raven. She *will* try to leave the camp alone. She's grown up here, and until last summer, she's never witnessed crime in La Fortuna firsthand. She'll act strong. She's been told over and over that she was simply in the wrong place at the wrong time."

"You don't think that's true?"

"No, I do." He didn't sound convincing. "But she's our baby. I just... I would feel better knowing that people are looking out for her. Making sure she doesn't leave the camp alone. Stuff like that."

I nodded in understanding. William wanted someone closer to Raven's own age looking after her so it didn't look like Daniel and Eva were hovering. "Of course."

I would try. But from everything I'd seen, Raven *was* a strong, independent woman. This would be a challenge.

William patted my knee and stood. He took a step away, but stopped and turned back. "Oh, and if there's something going on between the two of you, treat her with the respect she deserves." He gave me a half smile, then joined the other adults talking at the entrance of the pavilion.

While I could hear the concern in his voice, I was convinced that William and his wife were one hundred percent wrong in not sending Raven home. However, I could stick close to Raven and help keep her safe. And at the same time, I needed to learn everything I could about this city and what Jonas's DNA donor was doing here.

Minutes later, Raven returned carrying a chocolate cake with lit candles on top.

My mouth fell open. I squinted, studying her face. *How did she know? I didn't tell her it was my birthday.*

The others began singing "Happy Birthday." I couldn't remember the last time anyone had made a big deal about my birthday.

I blew out the candles. Eva and Daniel sliced and served the cake. Scooping up two pieces, I walked toward Raven, who had moved away from the others and had propped her feet up in a chair across from her.

She smiled up at me. "Happy birthday."

"How did you know?"

"I make it my business to know certain things, Mr. Jones." She winked.

"I don't know what to say." I placed the cake on the table and set another slice in front of Raven. "I suppose I could start with 'thank you.'" I made a slight bow before taking the seat beside her.

"Kyle." She leaned closer to me. "I'm sorry I snapped at you earlier today. And I'm sorry for the less-than-nice things I said to you. I'm afraid you continue to catch me in not the best of moods."

tracked

"You don't need to apologize. And you're forgiven." I took the first bite of cake. Moist, chocolaty, melt-in-your-mouth goodness. "Did you make this? It's delicious."

She beamed. "I'm very glad you like it."

Out of instinct—or stupidity—I let my knee brush against hers as I enjoyed the cake. And I didn't move my leg away when she shifted uncomfortably, also without breaking contact. What the hell was I doing? I could *not* get closer to Raven. Not in *that* way. This could only end badly. Yet there I was, leaning forward, probing her eyes and desiring to learn more about her. I found myself wanting to help her, protect her, watch over her like her father had asked.

"Why were you so reluctant about coming back here after what happened last summer?" I asked. Did she think she was still in some sort of danger?

If her nightmares were any indication, I already knew the answer to that question. I also needed to know if last summer's murder had anything to do with what was happening in La Fortuna now.

She tipped back a bottle of water, her eyes glued to mine, then set the drink on the table in slow, calculated movements.

I glanced in the direction of the others, who were still deep in conversation on the far side of the pavilion, then met her gaze again. I took another bite of cake. I was good at silence. But so was she, apparently. She took another drink and then screwed the cap back on the empty bottle.

She leaned forward again. The gold flecks in the blue of her eyes sparkled with mystery. "I was scared."

"And now you're not?"

"Dozens of hours and thousands of dollars of therapy have taught me that I should turn my fear into something more productive than hiding."

Hiding, huh? I lifted a brow. "So, why did you return to Puro Cielo? You could have done something productive in California."

She shrugged. "I'm here to make sure Puro Cielo has a future."

I raised a brow. The dazzle in her eye told me she was being coy, that her vagueness was intentional. "Is that so?"

"Yeah." She looked toward the others, still a safe distance away. "The camp's board of directors thinks La Fortuna is plagued with crime. Bookings are down. The camp is losing money. I came to prove that it's just a temporary problem. That the crime is no more than what any other impoverished city suffers. If I can show the board I'm not afraid to be here after everything that's happened, then they'll have to rethink their position. I can't let them close this camp."

I stuffed another bite in my mouth, then sat back in my chair, a little shocked by her knowledge of the camp's troubles. I didn't think her parents, nor Daniel, had any idea that she knew all that. But she was also leaving something out. The way her eyes drifted down and away from me told me almost as much as mind-reading would. "Are your parents aware that you know all this?"

"I had planned to tell them, but I don't see the need now that they're leaving for Africa."

I had severely underestimated the strength of the woman in front of me.

tracked

"Raven, I need to tell you something." She needed to know about her mother's incident, including the fact that the crime was not necessarily random.

But before I could start, the rest of the group, armed with desserts, pulled up chairs to sit with us. I closed my eyes briefly. I couldn't get enough time alone with Raven. We were always interrupted.

"Always nice to have a birthday at the camp." Daniel stood behind Raven and placed a hand on her shoulder. "Great excuse to get this one baking again."

Eva reached over and touched Raven's knee. "How's your head, sweetie?"

I narrowed my eyes at Raven.

"It's feeling mostly better, thanks." She darted her eyes from Eva to me, but just as quickly looked away while reaching a hand to massage the back of her neck.

"Did you have a headache, honey?" William asked.

"Just a small one. I'm fine," she said in a "stop fussing" sort of way.

"Raven," Bennett said, "Daniel and Eva are taking us to the airport first thing in the morning."

Raven nodded. "All right."

"They have all the information about how to get in touch with us while we're in Africa. We hope to be able to use email, but we just don't know yet." Bennett proceeded to go through her long list of necessary bits of information to tell her daughter.

"Mom, I know. We've been through this. And Daniel and Eva are here if I need anything." Raven reached across the table and grabbed both of her parents' hands. "I promise everything will be fine. Don't worry. You're going to be gone less time than I'm away at school for a semester."

They smiled back. I suspected that Raven's parents *had* to worry about her, because she apparently never worried about herself. She was too laid back for her own good.

Eva placed her arm around Bennett. "Everything will be fine."

Raven stretched and yawned, then stood and gathered everyone's empty plates.

"Oh, no you don't. The one who bakes doesn't clean up." Daniel took the dishes from Raven. "Come on, wife. You and me. We'll clean this stuff up while these old folks get to bed."

"Who are you calling old?" William laughed.

Everyone wished me happy birthday again. After we said goodbye to Bennett and William, we began the treks to our beds—Bennett and William up the hill to their small house, and Raven and me toward the cabins.

Raven paused in front of my cabin. "I believe this is your stop, Mr. Jones." She paused for the briefest of moments, then continued walking slowly toward her own cabin.

With a pit bull gnawing at my conscience, I ran a hand through my hair before following her. Here was my chance to finish our conversation, and to come clean—to tell her about her mother's near-kidnapping and to let her know that both Daniel and her father had asked me to watch after her.

"The least I can do is walk you to your door after you made me that incredible birthday cake," I said. I walked behind her, only inches separating us.

tracked

At her cabin door, she turned and faced me. The moon reflected off her black hair. The urge to reach out and run my fingers through it was overwhelming.

"I can't believe you figured out it was my birthday," I said.

"You can't hide those kinds of things around this group. And private conversations are difficult to have around camp."

I cocked my head. There was something hidden in her words, in the sly expression on her face.

She rose on her tiptoes while placing a gentle hand on my arm, lifted her head, and kissed me lightly on the cheek. It was unexpected, and the light scent of her fruity shampoo caused my head to spin slightly.

"What was that for?" My gaze drifted to her rosy lips. Warmth lingered from their touch on my cheek, and I imagined the sweet taste of them on my own lips.

"Happy birthday, Kyle." Her voice came out in a whisper. Her body lingered close to mine, heat radiating between us.

Unable to stop myself, I slid my hand around the back of her neck and allowed myself to study the depths of her eyes. There were so many stories hidden there, but mostly I was witnessing the strength of a woman who tried to mask fear with manufactured joy. I was lost, pushing away the nagging feeling that said I had no business getting this close to her.

I tilted my head to one side, then the other, before lowering my lips to cover hers. Raven trembled as I made contact. Her lips were soft and warm and tasted of the raspberry filling from the cake. Her hands gripped my shirt at the waist, and my stomach tightened at the touch. My heart sped up, and I couldn't help but press my lips harder against hers.

I snaked one arm around her back and brought her even closer as her hands moved to my back and pressed firmly.

When we finally paused for air, her face remained inches from mine. We both breathed heavily. "Thank you for the cake." I leaned my forehead against hers as I pushed hard against the guilt that was trying to seep into my psyche.

Her quick breath feathered my cheeks.

"You're welcome," she whispered. She pulled away, then turned and unlocked the door.

I rubbed my fingers back and forth across my lips. I certainly hadn't planned on kissing her, but what had surprised me more was the way she had reacted. Still, something nagged at the corner of my mind. Like a fleeting thought. Before Raven could enter her cabin, I spun her around slowly, placing my hands on her shoulders. "You never said how you knew it was my birthday."

She smiled, stood tall on the tips of her toes, and touched her lips to mine one last time. "You worry too much."

The only conversation I'd had about my birthday had occurred when the group was discussing Bennett's near-kidnapping. Raven hadn't even been there. Or was she? "You didn't answer the question."

"I never heard one." She slipped through the door with little more than a glance over her shoulder, then closed it behind her.

There was only one explanation: she'd overheard the conversation. Which meant she knew about the attempted kidnapping, knew that she'd almost been sent home. I stared at the door, wanting more than anything to spend more time with her. But for now, I'd savor the taste of her kiss.

tracked

~~~~~

One peaceful night of sleep later, I rolled out of bed with the chickens. Not cheerfully, of course. Not at first. I never willingly arose at five a.m. But Daniel had given me a special birthday present. A tip. An inside track. According to Daniel, Raven jogged every morning. And when Daniel expressed his nervousness about her going alone, I volunteered to join her.

That was before I discovered that she jogged so early.

I sauntered up the hill to the pavilion with a University of Kentucky cap on my head, rubbing my eyes with the heels of my palms. When I opened them again, Raven stood a few yards away, smiling and holding a bottle of water.

"You look as if you haven't seen the five o'clock hour in a long time, Jones. Maybe not ever." A smirk reached all the way to her eyes.

"Not excitedly, anyway." I was never thrilled for all the early morning swim practices at Wellington Boarding School.

"What's the special occasion?"

"I thought we would spend the day together."

She straightened, letting her hand fall to her side. "You did? Any particular reason why?" Her voice held a slight sound of alarm.

"Nope." I pulled my ankle up behind me to stretch my quad and rolled my neck around, warming up my muscles. Apparently Raven would need a few seconds to settle into the idea.

"Sheesh, you give someone one little peck, and everything changes." She rolled her eyes, then proceeded to do a little stretching of her own.

"There's that sarcasm again, MacMillan." And it had been a far cry from a "little peck."

With the sky now lit, we headed for the road and jogged toward Arenal Volcano.

"You can see the top of the volcano this morning." I pointed ahead of us. White clouds framed the large mountain in front of us, but the flat top remained visible against a baby blue sky. I studied the very top of the mountain, imagining what lava spewing from its mouth would look like.

"See what you miss out on when you sleep your life away?" Raven asked. "Typically, clouds cover the top by eight or nine o'clock this time of year, but now and then you can see it later in the day."

"It's active, right? Does it ever erupt?"

"Technically, the experts say that it's in a resting phase. Until recently, it erupted many times every day. Now, not so much."

I swiped at the sweat running down my forehead and took measured breaths. "So, when are you due back to Stanford for soccer training?"

Raven didn't answer. It was a personal question, after all—not her specialty. When I looked her way, she was frowning, her eyes distant.

"Something I said?"

"No." She paused, refusing to look at me. "I lost my scholarship. There is no more Stanford."

"What? Why?" I almost stopped and forced her to have this conversation, but something told me she would be more likely to continue if I didn't stop and draw attention to the enormity of what she'd just shared.

She hesitated again. "I saw my doctor the week before coming here. He advised me that my last concussion left me at

tracked

high risk for severe brain injury if I were to suffer another. I already get a lot of headaches because of a couple of bad knocks to the head. It's too risky for me to play college soccer any longer. At least that's what the doc tells me." She shrugged, but the crease between her eyes told me she was fighting to hold back her emotions. "So, no soccer; no scholarship. Besides, my grades have plummeted. Which is also thanks to two concussions. So, even the small amounts of money I got from academic scholarships are off the table. My doctor recommended I join my parents in Costa Rica and give my brain time to heal."

"Your parents don't know any of this, do they?"

"Besides my doctor, a couple of friends, and Stanford, you're the only other person I've told."

"What are you going to do?"

"Not sure yet. I'm hoping to work here until I figure that out. I was thinking that taking a semester or two off would do me some good."

"Don't you think you should've told your parents before they left? Or at least tell Daniel and Eva?"

"I'll tell them eventually. This is my problem to solve, though."

Like mother, like daughter, I mused. I was pretty sure Bennett had never planned to tell Raven about the attempted kidnapping. This family was hell-bent on not worrying each other.

I dodged a pothole in the street. I considered asking Raven for more details, but decided she'd already had a tough enough time sharing what she did.

"I won't say anything," I said. For now, anyway. I would, however, be examining the inside of Raven's head in the near future. Maybe it was time to bring Lexi to Costa Rica.

NINETEEN

Raven

Kyle and I reached the pavilion just after six a.m. We'd made it through the run with very little talk about last night, but it was stupid of me to tell him about my lost scholarship. I was just about to escape him to take a quick shower when Dad arrived in a huff.

"Raven MacMillan." *Great. What did I do?*

I turned toward Dad. "William MacMillan." My tone mirrored his anger, teasing at first, but then I grew more concerned. I let my arms fall. "What's wrong, Dad? I thought you'd already be gone."

"Why didn't you tell me that Pascal showed up here in the middle of the night?" His face turned an alarming shade of firehouse red.

I looked around. Daniel, Eva, Mom, and Kyle all looked on. The size of Kyle's eyes doubled at the harshness of Dad's voice. *Please, God, let the ground swallow me into another time. If only I could time travel.*

"Because I handled it." I crossed my arms. "Why are you so angry?"

"You should have told your mother and me when it happened."

"Really? So you could do what, exactly? Send me on the first plane out of here?" I did my best to keep my voice down, wishing he would do the same. How could he embarrass me like this? "Seriously, Dad. You're totally overreacting."

"Raven, don't you speak to me like that. I'm still your father. I realize you're an adult, but..." He paused. "Pascal had no business showing up here in the middle of the night. You two aren't kids anymore."

"Meaning what?"

"Meaning... Meaning he has no business coming to your cabin and pulling you out of bed at all hours. What would people think?"

"I don't know. What *would* people think? That's what you're worried about? Or are you worried I'm not making smart decisions?" I lifted my hands and made air quotes around "smart decisions."

"That boy is no good for you."

The temperature of my blood rose. A cold sweat broke out across my forehead. "For argument's sake, why is he no good for me?"

"He's too old for you, for one." Dad's gaze drifted from my face to the faces of those behind me. His expression softened, and he lowered his voice, but he didn't stop berating me. "He lacks morals, he's a loose cannon, and he's..."

"Yeah, Dad?" I looked long and hard into Dad's eyes. "He's a bad influence? Different from me? Never going anywhere? Which is it this time?" My voice shook. I'd had these discussions with Dad before, mostly concerning Pascal's "bad influence" over me. They never ended well. And it never mattered

tracked

when I insisted that Pascal and I didn't feel that way about each other.

Dad breathed heavily. I had rendered him speechless.

"William," Mom whispered behind me. "We need to go."

Blinking back tears, I turned and wrapped my arms around my mother. "Have a safe trip. Let us know that you've arrived safely."

Without another word or glance, I stormed off to my cabin, not even looking back when Dad called my name.

~~~~~

"How could he?" I undressed and threw my clothes at the dresser. "Aren't we here to encourage people? Help them in any way we can?" Besides, Pascal was a good guy.

I slammed the door to the bathroom. When I saw my splotchy face in the mirror, I turned away in frustration and swallowed hard against the lump in my throat. Dad had embarrassed me in front of everyone. In front of Kyle.

Just when I thought I had found someone I might open up to, Dad had swooped in and humiliated me.

My father had never given Pascal a chance. Despite the age difference, Pascal and I had a history. We, along with Miguel and Alejandra, had spent our childhoods building a lifetime of memories. I would not let Dad strip me of those.

I turned on the shower and stepped under the cool spray of water, letting it extinguish the fire of anger that spread over me.

When I was showered and dressed, I stretched a beaded necklace around my neck. A silver lotus charm hung at my throat. I chose a white canvas hat and tossed it on the bed beside my backpack. While rubbing my fingers along the shape of the flower—a symbol of the meditation that often grounded me, and a reminder of the period in my life when I had questioned everything—I stared at the spot where my hat had landed: on top of the journal that I used to record my sleep patterns, headaches, and other things my doctor suggested. I hadn't written in it since arriving in Costa Rica.

A knock sounded at the door, interrupting my thoughts.

I opened the door so abruptly that Kyle jumped back.

Puffing the hair out of my eyes, I rested a hand on the doorknob, blocking him from entering. I guessed I'd have to face him sooner or later. "What do you want?" I said, turning away and leaving the door open.

"I didn't tell him about Pascal's visit," he said.

"What do you want, Kyle?" I repeated.

"I told you. I aim to spend the day with you."

"Sorry, but no thanks. I'm not great company right now." The edge in my voice irritated even me.

"Sure, I don't mind if I have a seat." Kyle breezed past me and sat on the opposite bottom bunk from where my stuff lay scattered.

As he passed, I inhaled his clean, citrus smell—a smell that reminded me of California oranges. I shook it off. He had distracted me last night with the kiss, but I wouldn't let that happen today. My life was obviously way too complicated to impose on someone like Kyle, who was kind and... well, other interesting things I didn't want to think about. Besides, I had encouraged the kiss with the innocent peck, hadn't I? How could I have been so stupid to have invited him into my life when I wasn't ready? I wasn't being fair to him.

"You're awfully confident, aren't you?" I said.

tracked

He lay across the bed, placing his hands behind his head. "So, what do you want to do today?"

"Some would say arrogant." I braided my hair loosely around to the side.

"I was thinking after a bite to eat, we could read by the river and relax. Maybe later we could walk to town and visit the internet café. What do you think?"

"You're not listening to me." I sighed. He wasn't going away, and maybe I didn't really want him to. "Look, Kyle, that's sweet of you, but you don't need to babysit me today. I was planning to hang around the camp."

"Babysit you?" He cocked his head.

"I assumed Daniel and Dad asked you to keep an eye on me while Daniel and Eva were in San Jose."

Kyle stood and walked around the bunk to stand in front of me. He slid his finger under my chin and lifted it so he could see my eyes. The dark amber of his irises and the comfort behind them paralyzed me. "I want to spend the day with you because I want to spend the day with you."

I remained still, my mind washed blank by his touch. "What did you have in mind again?"

"Well..." He released my chin, walked over to the door, and grabbed something from outside. "Since you skipped out on breakfast, I thought a picnic for starters." He held up a backpack, which he opened to reveal containers of food and bottles of water.

I *was* hungry.

He wiggled the backpack, smiling. "How 'bout it?"

What would a little brunch hurt? "Bless that Eva." I grabbed the white hat and smashed it onto my head. And bless Kyle for persistence. I didn't deserve his kindness. I grabbed my backpack and followed him out the door.

~~~~~

We hiked over to the watering hole, close to the rock where I enjoyed quiet time most mornings and where I had swum the day before. I followed Kyle closely, admiring his broad shoulders and the size of his biceps as he carried the bag full of food. I couldn't stop myself from imagining the strength of his arms around me. But why? Did I even have the right to crave his affection while I carried an entire cargo hold of baggage?

I knew the argument with my father would blow over, but why did it have to happen at all? Especially just before he was to leave for Africa.

"Watch this branch," Kyle said over his shoulder; he held up a low branch, allowing me to pass under it.

I added thoughtfulness to his list of attractive traits.

At the picnic site, I spread a blanket for us to sit on. Thanks to Eva, we enjoyed a wonderful breakfast of fresh fruit, pastries, and large bottles of water.

Kyle finished off his mango while giving me a sideways glance. "I promise I didn't tell your father about Pascal."

"It doesn't matter." I threw our empty containers into the backpack and grabbed another bottle of water.

"It does to me." He placed a hand on my forearm, stopping me from raising the bottle to my mouth again. "I told you I wouldn't say anything, and I didn't. It's important to me that you trust me."

I looked down at his hand and then up at his eyes. My skin tingled beneath the warmth of his touch. "I believe you." But if

tracked

Kyle didn't tell my father that Pascal had showed up uninvited, who did? I gave my head a little shake. It didn't matter, really.

Kyle stood and ran a hand through his hair before tossing me a grin. "Want to go for a swim?"

"I don't have my swimsuit on." When he frowned, I turned and reached inside my backpack, pulled out a wad of fabric, and waved it in the air. "But I have it with me!"

My problems could wait. There was fun to be had.

Kyle eyed the fabric and raised a brow. "And what good does that do us?"

I let my lips lift just a little, definitely ready for a little bit of mischief. I pulled out a tropical-colored sarong from the bottom of my backpack and wrapped it around my body. Then I made a swirly motion with my hand. "Turn around."

I slipped my clothes off under the large piece of fabric, then eased into the swimsuit. When I was sure the suit was adjusted to cover all the important parts, I removed the sarong and stuffed my clothes inside the backpack.

"Ta-da." I struck a pose with one arm stretched above my head and one down by my waist.

Kyle gave me his best impression of a golf clap. "Impressive." He took a deep breath in, then let it out slowly. "And frightening. Your father would have me skinned if he knew I'd seen that."

I giggled. "What? I was discreet. We're in the middle of the jungle. Sometimes you just have to improvise."

"Oh. Is that what you call that? Improvisation?"

I passed him, heading for the edge of the riverbed. The sun filtered through the tall trees surrounding the watering hole—a pool of crystal-clear water that promised to be refreshing.

"You look scared to death," I said over the sound of the rapids. "What on earth are you thinking about?"

He walked closer to me. "I'm thinking how cold the water looks. Maybe this wasn't my brightest idea."

"You big baby. It isn't that cold."

He grabbed my hand and led me over to a flat spot next to the water. We dangled our feet while he rubbed my hand with his thumb. I thought about the kiss we had shared. His lips had been soft and gentle at first, but when he'd pressed harder, unmistakable desire had erupted behind the kiss. I'd had a few serious boyfriends in the past, but this felt different. *He* was different. There was a certain sadness about Kyle. It lurked there behind his chocolate eyes. He masked it well with an easygoing air, but it was there nonetheless. And I craved to be closer to him.

"Your turn," he said. "What are you thinking about?"

"I'm not thinking about anything." Nothing I could share at that moment.

"Liar."

I leaned away from Kyle but still held on to his hand. "Did you just call me a liar?"

"Yes, I did. You can't be sitting there thinking about nothing. It's impossible. So, be honest."

I bit my bottom lip, watching a dragonfly hover above the water. "Well, let's see. Honest, huh? I was thinking how my chest felt tight. That this must be what the beginning of a heart attack feels like." I didn't dare look up at Kyle.

"Really? I can't imagine you anxious about anything."

I raised our locked hands. "This makes me nervous." I lifted my eyes and met his gaze. The warmth there threatened to

tracked

swallow me whole. I simply didn't know what to do with whatever was happening between us. "How 'bout we swim?"

I shoved off the rock and slipped into the river. A dip in the cold water was exactly what we both needed. Kyle swam beside me while I floated on my back with my eyes closed.

"I can feel your eyes on me," I said. "Something else on your mind?"

He took a few seconds before answering. "I'm not the type of guy who steps on another guy's toes when it comes to a girl."

I moved to treading water in front of him. "What are you talking about? Pascal? There's nothing going on between Pascal and me." Not really. Maybe some unfinished business. But nothing romantic.

"Really? Because..." He threw his head back. "Man, I seem so insecure." He made eye contact with me again. "Your father and Daniel have mentioned Pascal in conversations several times the last few days. Daniel seems to think Pascal is responsible for luring you back here this summer."

I frowned. My blood boiled just thinking about Daniel and my father discussing my personal life in front of others. But then again, my father had reached new depths of embarrassing me today. "Oh, is that all?" I leaned into the water again, floating on my back and breaking contact from those eyes that threatened to break through all the barriers I had constructed.

"Is that *all*? You kissed me last night."

"Uh, no... No, I didn't. *You* kissed *me*." I bit my lip, attempting to hide all signs of teasing, knowing he was staring at me.

"You're toying with me. I'm putting myself out there, and you're taunting me."

"Why did you kiss me last night if you were worried about a boyfriend?"

"I wasn't thinking about some guy I've only met briefly."

"Do you regret kissing me?" I couldn't stop the smile from playing at the corners of my lips now.

"For the record, you kissed me first, and no, I haven't regretted it for even a second. I'm looking forward to doing it again. But I might not have kissed you if I knew you had a boyfriend."

I opened one eye to look at him. "That's interesting."

"Why is that interesting?"

"It's admirable." I rolled over and swam around him. "So, if I tell you that I do, in fact, have a boyfriend, you'll just back off and not try anything further with me?"

He ran his fingers through his wet hair and angled his head toward the canopy of trees. "It would be difficult, but yeah. Making a play for another guy's girl isn't how I roll."

I dipped my mouth and nose below the water, leaving only my eyes above the surface, directed at Kyle's. I raised my mouth above the water again. "What about you? Any girlfriends back home?"

The expression on his face twitched slightly. It was that look again. He was burying something deep down. And that *something* dulled the sparkle in his eyes. "No. I wouldn't have kissed you if I had a girlfriend."

"So, I must not have any morals. Since, according to you, I have a boyfriend, and I allowed you to kiss me anyway."

"You're putting words in my mouth, Miss MacMillan. And you still haven't answered the question."

tracked

"Pascal and I have never dated. And until the night before I arrived here, I hadn't spoken to him in over a year."

"Why haven't the two of you talked?"

"Does it matter?"

"Hmm." He narrowed his eyes, contemplating that. "I'm not sure."

I dipped my head under the water one last time before climbing out. As I twisted and wrung the water from my braid, I glanced back at Kyle, who was still floating on his back. "A little competition's not always a bad thing, you know?" I joked.

Kyle lifted his head, squinting at me.

"Keeps things interesting." I shrugged, and he flashed me a full-on grin.

TWENTY

Kyle

"Look, Kyle," Lexi said. "I would come to Costa Rica if I could, but I can't right now. Jack thinks we might have a lead on Addison."

Addison was the youngest of the clones that we'd met at Wellington; she was thought to have been completely brainwashed or programmed by Sandra Whitmeyer, the doctor behind the entire cloning operation. Addison had double-crossed all of us, but especially Jack and Lexi.

Addison also disappeared shortly after Lexi handed Dr. Whitmeyer over to the Secret Service. She literally *disappeared*. That was the unnatural talent that had been awarded to her through the cloning process. She could force people to see things that weren't there—or to see nothing at all.

I possessed the ability to get inside people's dreams and to control the actions of someone while he or she was unconscious or asleep. I'd controlled Lexi many times. With her permission, most of the time. And I'd been inside Dani's dreams.

Lexi could control people's actions with her mind and mindspeak with other clones. But her true gift was the power of healing. She could heal many ailments, and what I needed right now was for her to take a look at Raven's brain.

"Can you set aside your obsession with Addison for a few days?" I asked.

"I'm not obsessed," she countered.

"You know she's going to show up eventually, with the most fabricated lie she's ever told. Addison will be found when Addison wants to be found."

"Listen, Kyle. You know how to examine this girl's head. What did you say her name was? Some sort of bird, right?"

"Raven." I didn't even bother to hide the irritation in my voice. It was unlike Lexi to be this distracted. And after everything we'd been through, I had expected her to help me.

"Raven. Right. Anyway, we practiced this. You know how to examine someone for internal injuries and other medical issues. You know what a concussion looks like and what normal brain activity looks like. Once you have a look inside her head, let me know what you find. Maybe Jack and I can make time to come down in a couple of weeks."

"I'm terrified of what I'm going to find when I examine her brain."

"Kyle Jones! Have you fallen for this girl?"

An uncomfortable silence settled over the phone line. My first love, Dani, had been Lexi's best friend—like a sister to her. But she had been much more to me. When she died, I swore I would never love anyone else.

"You have," Lexi said. "You've fallen for her. I can tell by your silence and by the way you're irritated with me. First, for not agreeing to hop on the next flight out of Lexington, and second, for forgetting her name."

I could almost hear a smile in her voice, yet I still felt an enormous guilt. I was not over Dani, and this felt an awful lot like I was cheating on her.

"It's okay to like someone, Kyle." Lexi's voice lowered to almost a whisper.

I tipped the phone away from my mouth for a couple of beats. After a heavy sigh, I brought it close again. "Lex, I don't know what it is about this girl. I loved Dani. I thought she and I... I don't know what I thought."

"You thought she was the one."

"I did." I slammed a hand through my hair.

"But Kyle..." Lexi's voice was soft, soothing. "Dani of all people would want you to be happy."

"I know." I rubbed a hand up and down, over my face, then stopped to drill my thumb and forefinger into my eyes, attempting to rub away the tension mounting behind them. Dani would want me to find happiness. I knew this with my brain. It was my heart that was tripping me up. "And this girl... I don't know... Can I really let someone get close to our world again?"

Lexi had never told Dani about her special mind abilities. In fact, we all kept Dani in the dark until the day Sandra placed a mind-controlling tracker at the base of Dani's skull—and then used that tracker to kill her. I couldn't save Dani, and I would regret not saving her every day for the rest of my life.

"Dani's death was not your fault, Kyle. It was none of our faults."

"Really? Is that why you went off all crazy in search of Sandra last year? You're telling me you haven't once thought about Dani's death being your fault?"

Lexi's silence gave me my answer.

"I'm sorry."

"It's fine."

It wasn't fine. I was an idiot. "Please come when you can."

"I have to go for now, but call me back as soon as you've had a chance to examine her more closely. We'll go from there."

"All right. I will." I dropped my hand to my side and stared out from the pavilion toward the hypnotizing sound of the river below. "Lexi?"

"Yeah?"

"I love you. It was no one's fault."

"I love you too!"

"I'll be in touch."

I hung up and continued to stare out toward the river. The camp hummed, a soothing orchestra of nature's noises. With no visitors around, this place was a quiet sanctuary.

Lexi was right. There was no need for her to come down here unless I got inside Raven's head and actually found something Lexi could heal.

The clearing of a throat behind me startled me. I turned and found Raven standing at the opening to the pavilion in a short, pale blue sundress with spaghetti straps. I stepped slowly toward her. "You look... amazing." My voice was strained from emotions left over from the conversation with Lexi.

"Thank you." She looked away for a moment, pressing her lips into a thin line. "Lexi?" She met my gaze, and I saw an emotion I didn't recognize.

How much of my conversation had she heard? "Oh, the phone call?" When she only stared blankly at me, I continued,

tracked

"Yes, one of my longest and dearest friends from boarding school."

I stepped closer to her. I lifted my hand to push a lock of black hair out of her face, but she retreated a step, out of my reach. A small breeze actually picked up her hair and blew it off her shoulders, revealing a hint of a sapphire-colored bra strap peeking out from under her sundress.

"What's wrong?"

"Look, Kyle. I can play a mean game of flirting, but if you have a girlfriend at home, just tell me. We can be friends. We'll have a great summer, but..."

"But...?" I prompted. I couldn't suppress a smirk. She'd obviously only heard the tail end of my conversation with Lexi. And what was this? Jealousy?

Suddenly she turned around. "Forget I even said any of that. Of course this was just innocent flirting. Nothing more. What else could it be? We'll both be going our separate ways at the end of the summer. You back to Kentucky. Me back to... well... wherever I'll be going." She took a few steps, then turned back to me. "Let's just go to town. Forget that entire conversation." She gave her head a shake. She was completely rattled. It was interesting to watch.

I leaned my hip against one of the pillars and crossed my arms. "Is that what that was? A conversation? Because all I heard was you freaking out."

She cocked a brow. "Freaking out? Are you insulting me?"

"That wasn't my intention. Come here."

I raised a hand and wiggled a finger, motioning her to come closer. And by some miracle, she did walk a few hesitant steps toward me, but not close enough for me to touch her.

"That was Lexi on the phone, my long-time friend from boarding school. We've swum together since we were eleven. She's practically married to another of my friends, Jack."

Raven took another step closer. "Oh?" A rosy glow lit her cheeks on fire.

I reached out a hand, grabbed her forearm, which was crossed tightly with her other against her chest, and pulled her the rest of the way to me. "I told you I lost someone close to me."

She nodded.

"Her name was Dani. She and Lexi were best friends." Hell, they were more than best friends. When you attend a boarding school and live your life away from your blood relatives, your classmates become your family. We were *all* family.

I watched as realization flitted across her face and compassion entered her eyes. "I am so sorry, Kyle. I had no right to freak out like that. You and I aren't..."

"We aren't what?"

"I don't know." She looked down at her feet, then met my gaze again. "You seem to be having fun with my severe discomfort, though."

I tilted my head from side to side. "Maybe a little." She tried to pull away, but I held tight, smiling. "I have no idea what we're doing here, or if I'm even capable of whatever this is. But I know I like you." *More than like.* "And I know I want to spend time with you. Can we just start there?"

She nodded hesitantly, and I knew that would have to be enough for now.

TWENTY-ONE

Raven

My parents called just before boarding their plane, the first of several flights that would take them to eastern Africa. I apologized to Dad for our misunderstanding, and he seemed genuinely upset that we'd fought, but then he tried to talk me into returning to California for the summer. I refused, saying that I was nineteen years old, and besides, Daniel and Eva were here to watch over me.

Not that I needed anyone to watch over me.

Needless to say, Dad and I pretended to be okay, though our voices were strained when we hung up.

Daniel and Eva had driven my parents to the airport in San Jose and planned to spend the night. The next group of volunteers would arrive late tomorrow night, so Kyle and I had the camp to ourselves for the next thirty-six hours or so.

In the afternoon, we walked to the internet café in town. Kyle pecked away on a nearby computer while I scrolled through several articles about express kidnappings, each story adding to the anxiety in my chest. I also did a search for Felipe and his father.

A search page of sites and articles popped up on the screen, including the website for the Navos Hot Springs Resort and Spa—the business Felipe's father took over when he came to

La Fortuna—and related La Fortuna websites and articles. Three articles down, a link about an express kidnapping caught my eye. I opened it.

Some local businessmen had been hailed as heroes after leading police to perpetrators in an express kidnapping. The teen was in Costa Rica with a group of high schoolers from Colorado to learn more about saving the rainforest. The kidnapping had occurred outside a restaurant in downtown La Fortuna; the kidnappers took the victim to a nearby ATM and forced him to withdraw five hundred American dollars. A local businessman stumbled upon the kidnapping in progress and called the police. No one was injured. The victims claimed no weapons were used.

Strange. I enlarged the picture beside the article and translated the caption: *Local businessman, Leonardo Rojas—witness to recent kidnapping.*

"Five hundred dollars?" I asked in a low voice to myself. I wrinkled my brow. "That's all?" My thoughts turned to my mother. She must have been so frightened.

"Hey," Kyle said, two seats down. "Why do you look so serious?"

"Was my mom okay yesterday?" I asked, avoiding his gaze. "Was she hurt at all?"

He sighed. "I knew you must have overheard that whole conversation. That explains the birthday cake." He pushed away from his computer and wheeled his chair over to me. "She wasn't hurt. She was only shaken up a little. She was more worried about what the police would say if she reported it. I guess the government wouldn't want an American-owned company who supported a lot of tourism in the area reporting that Costa Rica is full of crime."

Especially if the company was already in trouble with their governing board. I turned to face him and swallowed hard. "Why would someone try to take her?" I quickly blinked tears away, but not before Kyle saw them.

"Hey, come here." He pulled my head into his shoulder. "It's okay. She was okay. She's strong, just like her daughter."

I looked up from his shoulder, our faces close. "Sorry." I brushed at the dampness I'd left on his T-shirt.

He wiped my cheek with his thumb, his touch gentle. "I think the shirt will survive."

I laughed. He cupped my cheek, then slowly retracted his hand, retreat apparent in his eyes. But he remained close, our knees touching. The nerves in my stomach twisted and bent like acrobats. Something in his eyes told me that his life was complicated. He'd said very little about himself other than the fact that he'd lost someone special, and so far, I hadn't wanted to pry, no more than I'd wanted him to invade my past.

I turned back to my computer. "Look, I'll meet you outside," I said, closing the browser windows. "I have to make a phone call."

He wrapped his fingers around my hand, stopping me from pulling away. "Why can't you call from in here?"

I cocked my head. "Seriously?" I pointed to the window right behind him. "You'll be able to see me right outside the window. I'll be fine." I grabbed my bag, paid for the computer time, and dashed out the door. I needed room to breathe.

And a distraction.

I called my advisor at Stanford. I had sent her an email in the hope that she might advise me on financial aid available to me next year. I knew my parents would be devastated if I had to drop out of school; this was my last-ditch effort. On the other hand, I was starting to like the idea of taking some time off—with the head injuries and all. As devastating as it would be to my parents, maybe a break was exactly what I needed.

My adviser's voicemail picked up just as three Ticos climbed out of a black sedan about ten yards away. I turned and stared through the window at Kyle's back, still seated at the computer.

I turned back; the Ticos had gathered around a man in a sports coat and jeans. The man shook his head at them, clearly trying to get away.

I bowed my head, hiding my face from the Ticos' view, and ducked into the darkened entrance to an alleyway. My heart beat faster, and sweat pooled in the lines of my palms. Surely I was just on edge because of the articles I had just read, and because of what had happened to my mother. I had hung up on my adviser's voicemail greeting, but I kept the phone to my ear, pretending to have a conversation.

The Ticos harassed the man a few seconds more, then suddenly pushed him toward the sedan parked at the curb. They almost had the man in the car when my instincts kicked in. "Hey!" I yelled, stepping out of the darkness.

The Ticos turned toward me.

"Let him go. What are you doing?"

Onlookers and passersby sped up. Everyone distanced themselves from whatever was happening. Except me. I seemed hell-bent on jumping right into the middle of the fracas.

tracked

One of the Ticos, the biggest one, shoved the innocent man, and he took off running. A second Tico chased after him. The big Tico and his friend stepped toward me. Any second, the sweat forming on my palms would begin to drip like a running faucet. I backed away slowly, then turned to run—but one of them had grabbed hold of my backpack.

I whipped around, swinging. The man ducked as my fist came within inches of his head. He raised his hands in defense.

"Hey! Whoa! I not hurt you, chica." His long dark hair hung straight, framing his pale face; it reminded me of a horse's mane. His body looked like that of a professional wrestler. "I just talk to you," he said. "You just the chica I's looking for."

Horse Mane was joined by another man—a younger Costa Rican. The youthful Tico's eyes were unblinking as they darted from his buddy to me. Horse Mane placed his arm around me, holding my shoulders firmly and pushing me away from the internet café. I was no longer in sight of Kyle. I didn't even know if he was still at his computer.

I tried to jerk away, but Horse Mane tightened his grip. He reeked of body odor.

Scream, Raven, scream. Don't let him put you in a car, my inner voice told me. I stiffened my legs into the sidewalk, resisting the forward movement.

Horse Mane pulled a syringe from his pocket. He struggled as I squirmed, but he managed to flick the plastic lid off of the needle.

I opened my mouth to yell, but as I did, Horse Mane adjusted his grip on the syringe and stuck me in the arm. As the needle penetrated my skin, Horse Mane loosened his hold—but not before emptying the substance into my arm.

I flinched at the pain of the needle, but managed to wriggle from his hold enough to stomp on his foot and elbow him in the stomach. The syringe and needle went flying. I let out an angry growl as I turned and kicked him where I knew I would do damage. He doubled over, stumbled backward into a large plastic garbage can, and fell to the ground. I quickly turned—

And smacked right into a wall of a man. Felipe.

Kyle was at his side.

"Hey, slow down. Where's the fire?" Felipe steadied me, gripping my arms and holding me up. "What happened here?"

I looked from Felipe to Kyle, whose brows were furrowed, shadowing his dark eyes. He seemed to stand taller than I remembered, and he looked like he was ready for a fight.

"Felipe?" I tilted my head, studying his deep-set eyes, which were filled with an expression I couldn't decipher. Concern? No. Irritation? Possibly.

"What's going on here, Raven?" he asked again. "What did you do to this poor soul on the ground?" The corners of his lips curved upward as he peeked around me at the large man leaning against the garbage can.

Horse Mane wiped blood from his lip, then stood and dusted himself off. He pulled a knife from a sheath hidden beneath his shirt.

Kyle grabbed me and positioned me behind him. My hands shook at my side, so I tucked them into my armpits. What was happening? Was this some failed attempt to kidnap me for petty cash?

tracked

My vision blurred and I swayed slightly. I had no idea what had been inside that syringe, but I was sure Horse Mane had meant to drug me in order to kidnap me.

The other Tico—the kid—had so far done nothing more than stand by and watch events unfold. Now he looked back and forth between Horse Mane, Kyle, and Felipe before turning and bolting.

Kyle lunged at Horse Mane. But Horse Mane was quick. He swiped at Kyle, and I was sure the knife made contact with Kyle's chest.

I screamed, drawing attention. Pedestrians slowed. A crowd of onlookers gathered several yards away. I saw the owner of the internet café standing at his store window, a phone at his ear.

Horse Mane came at Kyle again. This time when he tried to take a swipe, Kyle ducked, then nailed him in the jaw. Horse Mane's eyes rolled back, and he collapsed to the ground, out cold.

TWENTY-TWO

Kyle

"Kyle, get Raven out of here. I'll deal with this thug," Felipe said, grabbing my arm and pulling me away from the asshole sprawled out on the ground.

I jerked my arm away from Felipe. I wanted him to think I was upset, irrational—just an overprotective boyfriend of sorts. Which wasn't too far from the truth.

My chest rose and fell in heavy breaths. I looked toward Raven. Her eyes darted from me to Felipe to the piece of shit on the ground. She didn't look hurt, but something was off about her.

I wanted to get inside the thug's head and force him to talk to me—find out what he had hoped to accomplish and see what he wanted with Raven. But I couldn't; for obvious reasons, I'd have to keep my supernatural abilities hidden for now.

"Should we call the police?" I asked Felipe. I didn't want to get involved in police business in this country, but a crime *had* just occurred—the second in less than forty-eight hours—and this time it was Raven who had almost been shoved inside a car for who-knows-what reason. I was almost positive this wasn't random. Just like the attempt to kidnap Bennett hadn't been random. Raven had to be thinking the same thing.

"I'll take care of it," Felipe said. "Just get Raven out of here."

I was about to tell Felipe where to shove his command when Raven darted forward and reached down by the soiled curb to pick something up. Then she walked a couple of steps and picked something else up. Her back was to me, but I could tell she was fiddling with something. When she turned, she hid whatever it was in her palm.

I reached out and grabbed her by the elbow. She looked up at me with bloodshot eyes. Her head bobbed backward slightly. I looked more closely at her eyes and saw that they were dilated, and she seemed to be having a hard time focusing. I didn't think she had hit her head, but something was wrong.

"Felipe's right," I said. "Let's get out of here." My fingers skimmed down her arm and wrapped around her wrist. Her pulse was beating wildly, out of control. Her eyes were crazed. "What's wrong with you?"

Her eyes rolled back into her head, and I barely had enough time to slide an arm around her and catch her as she passed out.

What the hell?

I glanced over my shoulder. Felipe was patting the face of the oversized jerk who I'd laid out moments before. I only had seconds to decide what to do next. I didn't trust Felipe, and I needed to get Raven out of there.

I made my decision. I slid into Raven's brain and mind-spoke softly.

Raven, can you hear me? I need you to open your eyes.

Her eyes began a quick flutter, then opened wide. She reached a palm to my cheek. "Kyle? What happened?"

"Is she all right?" Felipe asked from behind me.

Can you stand?

tracked

She nodded, hearing my mindspoken words loud and clear. I guided her to her feet. She had no idea she was unconscious right now, but I had to get us away from people as quickly as possible. My power to control people's actions while they were unconscious was limited to how long they were out and how long I could hang on to their dormant minds.

And when Raven did eventually snap out of her unconsciousness and back to full awareness, I would be temporarily blinded—the lovely side effect of my supernatural power.

Look at Felipe and tell him you're fine.

Raven narrowed her eyes at me, confusion dotting the lines that formed when she scrunched up her brows. She knew something wasn't right.

Do it. Now!

"Okay. Fine. Keep your pants on." Raven turned slowly toward Felipe and said, "I'm fine." She assessed the situation before her. There was recollection in her bewildered look.

The sound of a police siren had us all turning our heads. I tugged on Raven. "We have to go."

"Yes, go," Felipe ordered. "I'll take care of the police."

I didn't quite understand why he was telling us to run from the police. It seemed wrong, but I didn't have the time to think about it.

I wrapped my fingers around Raven's hand and pulled her forward, away from the busy sidewalk.

I want you to walk quickly. Act normal, like we're just a couple out on a date having a good time. I looked over my shoulder as we walked. *Laugh.*

Raven's head jerked back and she let out a sweet laugh. Then she angled into me, placing her opposite hand gently on my bicep as we continued to walk.

What the hell had we gotten ourselves into?

I glanced back once more before we rounded a corner. I waited until we were more than two blocks away and on the broken-up country road that led back to Puro Cielo, then I squeezed her hand and urged her to slow down. No Ticos were following us, and I didn't hear any police sirens either. I grabbed Raven and pulled her to me in a tight embrace.

"Are you okay?" I removed her hat, which had miraculously remained on her head during the entire ordeal. I stroked her hair and hugged her close.

When I was sure I was cutting off her circulation, I pushed her back to look at her face, tucking long, loose wisps behind her ear. "Talk to me. Are you okay? Did they hurt you?"

She looked up at me with the strangest of expressions.

I pulled her back into my chest, but she remained silent.

Please talk to me. I let my words slip inside her head and tried to soothe her racing mind.

"I feel so weird," she said into my shirt, muffling her voice. She turned her head farther to the side. "And I heard you. Earlier. I heard you inside my mind, but you weren't talking. Your lips weren't moving. I don't understand."

How was I going to explain this to her? How would I explain that I was a cloned human with the supernatural ability to get inside her dreams and speak directly to her subconscious? I couldn't imagine anything that would make a woman run from a man faster.

Let's get back to camp. We have a lot to talk about.

tracked

We needed to be somewhere safe before I lost control of her mind—and lost my sight.

Hand in hand, I led her along the mostly gravel and dirt road back to Puro Cielo. Several cars passed, but thankfully none of them slowed or seemed to take the slightest interest in us. At the camp, I secured the new gate that Daniel and I had installed and turned on the alarm that would alert us to visitors.

When we reached the pavilion, I pulled Raven into a hug, knowing it might be the last time she would ever let me touch her at all. *When she discovers the medical experiment I am...* She and Daniel would probably kick me to the curb. Or worse, tell someone about me.

After a minute or so, Raven pulled away, took a few steps back, and held out her closed fist, palm up, in front of me. Then she slowly uncurled her fingers, revealing a metal and glass syringe lying flat against her palm. This must be what she'd picked up off the curb.

I looked from the syringe to her eyes and back to the syringe. Tiny droplets of a strange neon blue liquid glowed from within the tube. I raised my fingers and let them hover over the syringe, scared that whatever was inside was now flowing through Raven's bloodstream.

"Did that man touch you with that?" I asked. A panic hummed along my skin and pooled in my neck, forming an enormous knot of tension.

Raven nodded. Her expression was still largely void of emotion. Where she should have been frightened, she appeared only mildly mystified instead. And slightly drunk. All the result of whatever was in that syringe.

I grabbed the syringe, broke off the needle, and slid the tube into my back pocket.

Stepping closer to her, I brushed my fingers along her temple. Lexi had taught me how to examine a person's bloodstream and internal organs when we thought Jack was dying last year. She'd also taught me how to slip inside someone's head to assess brain damage—and to detect when something foreign was affecting a person's mind.

But while Lexi could force a foreign substance out of someone's body, I had never done so. Had never even tried. I still had so much to learn.

Up until now, I had been scared to see the type of head trauma Raven had suffered, because I didn't know if I could help her. And it pained me to know that she was losing so much—her scholarship, the ability to play soccer—due to her injuries. But now I had no choice but to slip inside her bloodstream. And as the syringe with the remnants of a mysterious substance burned in my back pocket, I was terrified at what I might find.

I narrowed my mind and slipped beneath Raven's skin. I immediately recognized the same neon blue substance mixing with the blood running through her circulatory system. I traced it upward, toward her brain; a high concentration of it seemed to be pooling at the base of her skull. The substance had obviously been designed to knock her out so she could be stuffed into that car and taken away. I continued to search, now directing my attention toward her brain. And as I homed in on the area where the neon blue substance seemed to be the greatest, I received a surprise I wasn't expecting.

tracked

I immediately pulled out of her head and stared into her eyes. "Who are you?" I asked.

Raven cocked her head. A smile touched her lips. "Silly, you know who I am. I'm Raven." The sound of her voice reminded me that she was completely high on the blue drug running through her veins.

I slipped back inside her brain and stared once more at my worst nightmare.

A tracker at the base of Raven's skull.

~~~~~

I led Raven to her cabin. The camp was quiet, and I managed to secure all the buildings while hanging on to Raven's mind. Darkness wrapped around the base of the trees lining the riverbank, and for the first time since being in Costa Rica I was scared of everything I might discover here.

I pulled Raven's key from her backpack and helped her inside.

I need you to lie down. When I slip out of your mind, you're going to sleep off whatever substance that guy slipped you. Okay?

"Where are you going?" Vulnerability shone in her eyes.

I glanced around her cabin. It was nearly identical to mine. "I'll sleep in the bunk beside you."

With Daniel and Eva still in San Jose waiting to pick up the next group visiting the camp, I couldn't bear to leave her alone. I wouldn't. Especially now that I knew that Raven, and this camp, were tied to whatever was happening here in La Fortuna with the trackers.

Raven nodded, turned, and walked to a small dresser. She pulled some clothing out, and before I realized what was happening, she was undressing.

I turned quickly, but not before seeing the smooth skin of her back in the dim glow of twilight coming through the small cabin window.

She's going to hate me when she wakes up. She'll think this was all a bad dream at first, but then too much of it will ring true, and she'll discover that I'm not at all who I've pretended to be.

I glanced behind me. She had changed into a thin, short cotton nightgown and was sliding under a sheet on one of the lower bunks.

God help me, she was gorgeous. I kneeled beside her bed and stared into her eyes, still bloodshot and slightly glassy from the drug. My heart constricted. How the hell had someone else in my life managed to get a tracker placed in her skull? And did she know it was there? I couldn't ask her while she was unconscious. But I had so many questions.

"You're not leaving, right?" she said. "Promise me you're staying with me."

"I'll stay as long as you want me to." *Now go to sleep.* I leaned in and kissed her forehead.

She slipped a hand around the back of my neck, preventing me from pulling away. The look in her eyes grew intense—hungry even. I leaned in and nuzzled her neck. Desire pooled in my gut and caused me to hesitate before I finally pulled back. I wanted to be close to the girl staring up at me, but not like this. *You need to sleep. I'll be here when you wake up.*

She closed her eyes and slipped into a pattern of deeper breathing almost immediately.

After kicking off my shoes, I lay on top of the sheet and stared straight at Raven until I couldn't hang on to her mind

tracked

any longer. As soon as I felt her slipping away, the blindness set in, and all I could see was black.

The cicadas' shrill cries rang in my head, drowning out the voices that were telling me I needed to run from Costa Rica—that I should let Jonas come here and take care of whatever was happening in La Fortuna. Obviously, his clone donor was tied to it in some way; so he should be the one to take ownership of this mess.

Whatever was going on here in La Fortuna had Dr. Sandra Whitmeyer and Dr. John DeWeese written all over it. And I couldn't forget the International Intelligence Agency. They were the agency ultimately responsible for creating the tracker: a small device that, when inserted into the brain of a human, gave scientists full control over their mind.

I rolled to my back and closed my eyes. At least with my eyes closed I could pretend that I wasn't lying there defenseless. I knew that if someone were to come after Raven during the night, I would be helpless without the ability to see.

I clenched my hands into fists and beat them against the mattress at my sides.

I thought about Dani—the love of my life. She had been so innocent. According to Lexi, until Sandra inserted a tracker at the base of Dani's skull, Dani had had no idea that Lexi, Jack, or I had been created as human clones of famous geneticist doctors and scientists.

The day Sandra Whitmeyer inserted a tracker into Dani's neck was the day everything changed. That was when her innocence was stripped from her.

And now the girl beside me had been implanted with a nearly identical device. I couldn't watch another girl die like

Dani had. I just couldn't. What did these people want with Raven? Who knew about it? How long had this device been in there? And how had it escaped the doctors who had treated her for her concussions?

These questions and so many more ran through my brain until I couldn't hold on any longer. After listening to the sounds of the camp for close to an hour, I gave in to sleep.

TWENTY-THREE

Raven

I paced outside my cabin for thirty minutes, wringing my hands, stopping to stare at the door, but not entering to wake Kyle.

Images of the night before filled my head. At first I thought the images were from my dreams. Or nightmares. But the longer I thought about the man who'd stuck me with some sort of needle, the faster my heart thumped inside my chest.

I thought about calling Pascal.

No, that wouldn't do. I needed to *see* him. Even though we'd been at odds the past year, I trusted him. He'd be able to help me.

So as not to risk waking Kyle, I left him a note on the kitchen island: *Be back soon. Went to the hot springs.*

~~~~~

"Raven."

I whipped around and faced Pascal. Despite the ninety degree weather and hundred percent humidity, he wore black slacks and a black polo with the Navos Resort & Spa logo.

"Hi," I said, barely able to meet his probing eyes. "Can we talk?"

"We can talk in my office."

He led me around the various pools that made up the hot springs. Workers were setting up chairs and getting the place ready to open.

"I was surprised to hear from you this morning." He touched a hand to the small of my back, manually directing me toward the resort offices.

"Why's that?" I peeked up at him. It didn't take long for the heat of his palm to permeate the thin fabric of my peasant-style shirt. For some reason, I was nervous around him. Or maybe I was just jumpy from the night before.

"Aren't you getting ready for a new team to arrive at the camp? Didn't Daniel and Eva take your parents to the airport yesterday? They haven't yet returned with the next group, right?"

"All of that's correct, but that doesn't answer my question." Why would he be surprised to get a phone call from me? And how did he know that Daniel and Eva had gone to the airport? They didn't always transport the groups themselves.

"It just seems you've been avoiding me since you returned."

I couldn't completely deny that.

We entered an office decorated with sleek modern furniture. The black furniture rested on dark hardwoods. White walls were decorated with artistic photographs from around the hot springs—various tropical plants, colorful cocktails from the bar, a pretty woman meditating beneath a waterfall in a bikini. The last photo sent my eyes rolling toward the ceiling. It was tasteful, but... seriously?

"Nice office. Yours?" I asked.

He nodded. "Can I get you something to drink? A water? Soda?"

tracked

I sat in one of his guest chairs. "Water would be great." I wiped my palms on my cargo capris. "So, how did you know Daniel and Eva were in San Jose?"

He handed me the bottle of water from a small fridge, already sweating with condensation, then he leaned a hip against the desk and crossed his arms. "I saw your father a few days ago. He mentioned it."

My father wasn't a fan of Pascal's, so this came as a slight shock. "When?"

"When what?"

"When did you see my father?"

"I don't know. Friday."

"Friday," I repeated while I stared at a scuff on the floor and scrolled through the events of the past few days. I stood and walked around the chair. "When Friday?" Dad had been fine at dinner when we celebrated Kyle's birthday, but he was more than pissed early the next morning before he left for the airport.

Pascal shifted, lowering his hands to cup the edge of the desk. "Why don't you tell me what you're doing here, Amagita? You wanted to see me, but I have work to do, so what's this about?"

"You're changing the subject. And you're being vague. You came to the camp late Friday night, didn't you?"

Pascal's lips twitched slightly, but he remained silent.

"You're the one who told him that you dragged me out of bed in the middle of the night."

"Why would I do that?"

I crossed my arms and tried to stand taller. "That's a good question." I searched my mind for possible reasons. "Why did you?"

"Raven..." He stepped around the chairs and approached me slowly. "Your father and Daniel needed to see how easy it was to gain access to your cabin. And I wanted to know who this new person that the camp hired was. Kyle, is it?"

My back stiffened, and I hoped Pascal didn't notice. I had thought I wanted to talk to Pascal about Kyle, but now I wasn't so sure. Something had happened last night after I was attacked, but I wasn't completely sure what, and now that I was standing in Pascal's office, I wasn't sure Pascal would believe me if I told him.

"Why is Puro Cielo any of your business?" I asked, going on the defensive.

"Don't be like that." He reached out a hand and ran it down my arm, leaving a trail of goose bumps in his wake. "*You* are my business."

At that declaration, I stepped back and out of his reach. "What does that mean? What I choose to do or not do has nothing to do with you." My eyes studied his. He was nervous about something. "This isn't about Kyle. You knew that telling my father about your middle-of-the-night visit would anger him. You upset him on purpose." I narrowed my eyes. "You knew he would threaten to send me home if you put the idea in his head that I was unsafe here. What happened last summer is in the past, Pascal. It's not going to happen again."

"Oh, because you can take care of yourself?"

"Yes." My breathing picked up just thinking about last summer. And with what had happened last night... once again I

tracked

hadn't done a very good job protecting myself. My fingers massaged the spot where the needle had punctured my skin.

Pascal looked past me toward the door. "You shouldn't have come to Costa Rica."

A hysterical laugh reverberated through my throat and past my lips before I could stop it. "You're the one who talked me into coming." And now not only was I having nightmares about the murder I'd witnessed last summer, but my mom and I were nearly kidnapped.

"I know, but I was wrong. And now I think you should return to the States."

"You were wrong," I deadpanned. "Unbelievable." I threw my hands up in frustration. Pascal had always been controlling. From what games we played as children to which rules we broke and who took the fall when we got caught—which happened to be him most of the time even though we were all responsible. Instead of turning and storming out of his office like I wanted to right then, I walked past him and stared through the window behind his desk, out over the pool with the built-in bar. It was the pool most likely to draw the biggest crowd at night, so it only made sense for the administrative staff to have visual access to the activity there.

"What have you learned about this Kyle person?" Pascal asked behind me.

That he was drop dead gorgeous. That he loved a girl named Lexi. That he'd loved a girl named Dani more, but she'd died. That he was a great kisser. That he could speak inside my head with his mind. I cringed at the last thought and wrapped my arms tightly around myself.

"Not much, why?" I said. "What have you learned?"

"Absolutely nothing. His background checks out. The boarding school he attended claims he was a top student, captain of the swim team, and not a single blemish on his conduct."

"You did a background check on him?"

"Yes. As did Daniel."

"Well, then, what's the problem?"

"No one's that perfect."

A group of women spread towels on chairs by the pool. I imagined they'd be drinking fruity drinks from pineapples within the hour. People came to the springs to let off steam, relax in the hot pools, and have fun in the cooler ones. I wondered if these women were on a girls' trip. Or were their husbands off ziplining or golfing?

And did they run the risk of being kidnapped for petty cash when they went to dinner later?

I changed the subject. "Tell me more about the express kidnappings." When Pascal remained silent behind me, I added, "Don't worry about hiding the recent attempt on my mom. I know all about it."

"I didn't realize it when I phoned you last week, but all the recent kidnappings have been aimed at people from your camp."

I turned. "The camp? Why would someone target people from the camp? Doesn't that seem strange to you?"

"It does, unless—" Pascal stopped abruptly. He squeezed the bridge of his nose.

"Unless what?"

"There's not a lot of crime in La Fortuna. These kidnappings started up a couple of months ago. No one is ever hurt.

tracked

And the kidnappers never take very much money from the victims. But the criminals do manage to scare them enough that they almost always leave immediately. So, I'm thinking... what if the real target is Puro Cielo? Maybe the kidnappers are trying to scare Daniel or your parents."

Or maybe they were hoping I would hear about them and would refuse to return to Costa Rica.

Pascal's phone buzzed at his hip. He read a text and typed a response as I pondered the express kidnappings further. I should have told him what had happened to me last night, but something stopped me.

His expression changed as he read a second text. His brows furrowed and his entire body went rigid by the fourth text. His head jerked up at me. "When were you going to tell me that someone attacked you last night?"

My spine stiffened. "Who are you texting?"

He sent a couple more texts, then shoved his phone back into the clip at his hip. "That doesn't matter." He took several steps closer to me. When I took a step back, he stopped and ran a hand through his hair. "Tell me what happened."

"I'm fine." I wasn't. "Some guy tried to grab me outside the internet café. But I'm fine," I repeated.

"You're fine. You're always 'fine,' aren't you?" He started to reach for me again, but then retracted his hand and stretched his fingers wide at his side. "Did they hurt you?"

Should I tell Pascal that the guy drugged me? What would he do? "Felipe was there. Is that who texted you?"

Pascal's jaw tightened further; his eyes shot daggers over my shoulder. "Why were you with Felipe?" He wouldn't even look at me as he spoke. I could tell he was scanning the area of the hot springs outside his office window.

So, it wasn't Felipe who had texted him. "I wasn't *with* him. He showed up shortly after I kneed my attacker in the—"

He held up a hand to stop me. "I get the picture. Where was this Kyle person? I thought he was supposed to be with you at all times?"

"And how would you know that? My dad told you?"

"And Daniel." Pascal ignored his instincts this time and placed his hands on my arms just below my shoulders. With effort, I didn't flinch. He held me in place while he pierced me with his intense gaze. "You have to go home."

I studied the features of Pascal's face: the thick lines across his forehead, the hardened jaw, the dark eyebrows—shadows over warm, hazel eyes. Eyes that screamed very contradicting messages. On one hand, he seemed angry, maybe even at me. On the other hand, he appeared vulnerable, worried, and possibly even scared.

"Why are you ordering me to go home? I thought you *wanted* me here." Pascal *had* wanted me to return to Costa Rica. Miguel had said that Pascal asked me here to remember what had happened the night his father was killed.

"I did. I do." He loosened his grip on my arms. "I thought I did, but not if you're in danger."

"Why would I be in danger? They didn't succeed last night, did they? What are the odds of someone trying to kidnap me *again*? Especially now that we're on high alert." But he didn't have to say what I knew to be true: if the kidnappings weren't random...

tracked

I stared up at him. "I don't have a home to go to. Puro Cielo is my home now."

Pascal pulled me to him, and I leaned my forehead against his chest.

"I don't want to be scared anymore," I said. "I've spent the last year in therapy, and I'm exhausted."

I sensed his hand hovering over my back. He finally let it land up near my neck and massaged the muscles there.

"We'll figure something out," he said.

There was a knock at the door. Pascal pushed me back just slightly. "How well do you trust this Kyle person?"

"His name is just Kyle, Pascal. Say it with me."

"I don't really care. How well do you trust him?"

It had been all too easy to trust this stranger that had showed up at the camp the morning after me. He was an outsider with none of the dark history that La Fortuna held for me. And he was easy to talk to—not to mention easy on the eyes. I feared that maybe I had *wanted* to trust him so badly that I'd let my guard down.

And though he'd saved me last night, something strange had occurred that had left me fleeing from him this morning.

But if I told Pascal that I didn't trust Kyle, Pascal would be sure to harass my parents and Daniel until he personally strapped me into a seat on a flight out of Costa Rica.

"I trust him," I said in a small voice. At least I planned on finding out if I could trust him. He had a lot of explaining to do.

Another knock sounded.

"Do you promise you'll tell me the minute anything else happens? If you feel unsafe at all, I want to know about it."

Control freak. I nodded.

He crossed the room and opened his office door to reveal a very panicked-looking Kyle on the other side. When his eyes found mine, his face softened just slightly, but he said nothing.

I looked from Kyle to Pascal. "*Kyle* texted you?" How would Kyle have Pascal's phone number?

"Daniel gave Kyle and me each other's contact information in case we needed it while he and Eva were in San Jose," Pascal answered as if reading my mind.

"Have you told Daniel about last night?" I asked Pascal.

He shook his head. "Not yet. I'll let you tell him—as soon as he returns." There was a hidden threat behind his words.

Pascal redirected his gaze from me to Kyle. "And if I find out that you're anyone other than some random American here to help out my friends at Puro Cielo, I will—"

"We get it." I crossed to Kyle and stood between him and Pascal. Kyle had yet to utter a single word. His hands were fisted at his sides. I faced Pascal. "You've proven you have the ability to insert yourself into my life uninvited, but—"

"That wasn't my intention. I'm just worried about you. The camp is not secure."

I held up a hand to stop him. We were working on the security of the camp. Kyle had already helped Daniel install a new, more secure gate, and new windows with better locks had been placed on all the cabins. "I'm willing to give you the benefit of the doubt that you have my best interests at heart, but if you try to manipulate me again by going to Daniel or my father instead of me, I will cut you out of my life."

"Amagita, you don't—"

tracked

"Mean it? I absolutely do. Promise me you won't go behind my back and hide things from me again."

Pascal nodded.

"And I promise to tell you if I remember anything about your father."

And with that I turned and exited Pascal's office.

TWENTY-FOUR

Kyle

When I woke that morning, my blindness was gone, but it had been replaced with a killer headache. Controlling Raven long enough to get her home without letting Felipe see that she'd been drugged had exhausted me to the core.

I had thought that if I slept in the same cabin with Raven I would hear her if she woke up earlier than me. I was wrong. When I finally scrubbed the cobwebs from my brain, I discovered she was already gone.

I searched the camp for her: her favorite spot to meditate, the pavilion, the picnic table by the river. She was missing, and I knew that the best-case scenario was that she had run from the monster I was. The worst case was that someone had come to Puro Cielo and finished the kidnapping they had attempted last night.

It wasn't until after an hour of searching that I finally found the note she'd left me on the kitchen island: *Be back soon. Went to the hot springs.*

I wadded it in my fist and called a cab.

I received a text from Pascal just as I arrived at Navos Hot Springs: *Lose something? Raven is here at the hot springs.*

Relief at knowing she was safe far outweighed the anger I felt over her recklessness at leaving the camp alone—and the jealousy that gripped my ego when she ran straight to a guy she'd known most of her life. At the same time, I couldn't delude myself into thinking that Raven was anything more than someone that needed my help. I knew that any hopes of something more happening between us had been squashed the moment I found the tracker at the base of her skull.

Raven was simply part of the puzzle Jonas sent me here to solve.

Standing outside Navos Hot Springs' corporate offices with Raven, my heart constricted. I knew that someone was targeting her, and I had to assume that she had no idea. But I couldn't protect her alone. And I couldn't watch yet another person I cared about go through what Dani had suffered.

While I debated with myself, Raven began walking toward one of the pools. She still hadn't said anything to me. I had no choice but to follow her. I needed to know what she remembered from last night. Was she feeling any effects from whatever the goon had injected into her?

I had tried calling Jonas again on my way here, but he didn't answer. Neither had Lexi. I had left messages for them both, telling them they needed to get here fast.

When Raven continued around one of the more private pools, I reached out a hand and touched her arm. "Raven," I said in a low voice. She spun around so quickly that I jerked back.

She opened her mouth to say something, but closed it again. She swallowed. Her breathing was heavy. The silence between us wrapped around my neck like a noose.

tracked

Finally I couldn't take it any longer. "How are you feeling?"

She quirked a brow. "How am I feeling? That's what you want to know?"

I tilted my head side to side. "For starters."

"Well, let's see. I'm confused, and I feel violated."

I nodded. I glanced around the pool. We were alone in the back of the hot springs beside a pool with a waterfall. Steam rose from the pool, indicating it was one of the warmer ones.

Raven wrung her hands at her sides.

"We don't have to talk here," I said. "We can go back to the front of the hot springs, somewhere a little more public."

"Why? Are you planning to hurt me?"

"What? No. Of course not." I sucked in a deep breath. "You just look nervous. I don't want you to feel nervous around me." More than anything, I didn't want that. She was going to need me.

"I want to trust you."

I cocked my head. "You have no reason to trust me."

"Yet here I am. Alone with you. And I'm going to trust you to tell me the truth."

"Then why did you run this morning? I was going to tell you everything the minute we woke up."

"I was scared. And confused. I've known Pascal since I was a kid. I thought he might have answers." She laughed. "Why I thought he could help me with this, I have no idea."

"Did you tell him anything?"

"I should have." She looked down at her feet. She wore flip-flops, and her toenails were painted blue to match her eyes. "But no, I didn't."

"Why not?"

She looked up through a veil of dark eyelashes. "Because I've chosen to trust you. That, and anything I told him would make me sound crazy."

I didn't know what to say next. How was I going to explain my world to her?

"I heard you last night," she said quietly. "Inside my head. Please tell me that I didn't imagine that."

"You didn't imagine it."

She pulled in a huge, labored breath, then let it out slowly almost in a sob as she hugged herself. I reached out a hand, attempting to steady her.

"Why do I get the feeling you're relieved at this news?" I asked. "You should be terrified of me right now."

Raven gave a slight nod, as if coming to a decision. "I've been hiding something for months now—from my doctor, from my soccer coach, from my professors, and from my parents." Raven glanced over my shoulder and looked right and left as if confirming no one was around. "I... I thought I was going crazy. So, yeah, hearing that you might have an explanation for my ability to hear voices inside my head *is* good news."

Was I hearing her right? She'd been hearing voices inside her head? I stared at her. And she at me. "What kind of voices? When?" Who could be inside her head? The only people I knew who could get inside people's heads were my fellow cloned friends—plus the clones I'd met who had been under the evil Dr. Sandra Whitmeyer's thumb.

"I don't know. Voices. When I was at school. Mostly in my dreams."

"In your dreams..." I repeated.

tracked

She backed up a step and her eyes widened. "You don't believe me. You think I'm crazy. Which is exactly why I didn't tell anyone!" She turned and started to walk quickly away.

I caught up to her and grabbed her arm. She turned those beautiful azure eyes on me, big and round. If she hadn't been afraid of me before, she was now. "You misunderstood. I *do* believe you. I'm just trying to process what this means. I expected you to be terrified of me this morning."

The muscles of her slender arm relaxed beneath my grasp. "I've got some serious questions about last night. But since last summer, I've spent countless hours on a psychiatrist's couch while they analyzed whether I suffered from post-traumatic stress disorder or some other form of mental breakdown. I've come to accept some strange things since that night... because the alternative would be to let a doctor commit me."

"What kinds of strange things?" I asked. I was taken aback. I had been expecting a difficult conversation with her, where I would have to explain a world of supernatural powers that most people would never believe without a lot of evidence. What I hadn't expected was for her to be relieved to hear that I was, in fact, inside her head.

"I don't know." She was nervous again. "Things like seeing people I've only met once inside my dreams and it seeming real." Her cheeks reddened. Was she talking about me? Did she know that I was inside her dream a couple of nights ago?

"What else?"

"At times, I've sensed an outside force telling me to do things. And I would do them. But then I would wonder later why I'd chosen a certain thing."

"Can you be a little more specific?"

"Well, I heard voices in my head when I was completing my class schedule this past semester. I was scheduled to take a lighter load, but at the last minute a voice inside my head told me to change my schedule around and add another science class. And when I went to schedule my flight to come here over Christmas last December, a voice in my head told me I shouldn't travel to Costa Rica."

"And you just listened."

"I didn't really want to come here in December. The voice only helped me make up my mind."

I thought about Lexi and her ability to manipulate people's actions. And Jonas—he could talk a girl into removing her clothes just to see her naked.

"Say something," Raven finally said.

I gave my head a shake. "I'm sorry. It's just—"

"You can explain these things to me, right? This has to just be symptoms of multiple hits to my head. I'm not crazy, am I?"

Despite the things she was telling me, nothing explained the fact that she had a tracker at the base of her skull. "No, you're not crazy."

"I know I'm not telepathic. I don't hear people's thoughts. But you were speaking directly to me. How is that possible?"

A group of women appeared and slipped into the pool behind us. They each had a drink in either a carved-out coconut or a pineapple. I sighed in irritation. "We need to go somewhere else. There's more you should know, but I can't tell you here."

"Okay. Where?"

tracked

"No one's at the camp." Daniel wasn't due back with another group until later that night. "Let's go back there. I'm going to need to make a couple of phone calls on the way."

"Okay."

I wanted to grab Raven's hand, hold her in my arms, tell her everything was going to be okay, but I couldn't. Because I simply didn't know if that was true. She thought she was just experiencing some sort of weird variation of a telepathic power. How was I going to tell her that she'd basically been given a death sentence when someone inserted a tracker in her head?

TWENTY-FIVE

Raven

Kyle appeared at the doorway to the kitchen just as I removed two large pans of coffee cake from the oven. At his questioning look, I shrugged my shoulders. "When I'm stressed, I bake." Besides, this would save Eva from having to scrounge up something in the morning.

He walked into the room, remaining silent.

"Did you make your phone calls?" I had given him the space he'd needed. He'd been very distant and quiet since I'd revealed that I'd heard voices in my head.

"Yes. I have some friends coming to Costa Rica. Could they stay here? They'll pretend to be visitors like me. But if that'll be a problem, they can stay at a hotel in town."

"That won't be a problem. There are plenty of cabins."

"I'd like them to stay in *our* cabins. I think you—we—could use the extra security."

"No, you think *I* need the extra security." I crossed the kitchen, grabbed a couple of glasses, and turned them upright. I then proceeded to pull a pitcher of iced tea from the refrigerator. My hand shook as I tipped the heavy pitcher.

He reached around me and placed a steady hand over mine. "Let me." He poured the tea, then handed a glass to me.

The tea soothed my dry throat. Kyle stood close. His eyes drifted downward from my eyes to my lips. I licked them free of the remnants of sweet tea.

His eyes closed briefly before he backed up, taking with him the fire that had threatened to consume me.

"What's changed between us?" I asked, my voice cracking as I said the words. "Why are you not talking to me? You can't stand to be close to me for longer than seconds at a time. Yesterday you were promising to kiss me again, and now you can't even be near me."

"Is that what you think? That I don't want to be close to you?"

"What am I supposed to think? I tell you I hear voices, and now you can barely look me in the eye." I squeezed my eyes tight. "Why don't you tell me why you're really in Costa Rica. You said there was more I needed to know."

When I opened my eyes again, Kyle's forehead was scrunched up like he was in pain. He took my tea from me and set it on the counter, then led me to a couple of barstools. "Sit."

I did as he requested. "You're scaring me."

He sat opposite me, close enough that our knees intersected, and scooped up both of my hands in his. "What I'm about to tell you is not something many people know." He swallowed hard. "I am a member of a very unique group of individuals."

"What kind of group? You mean like some sort of secret society?"

"Not quite. I'm a human clone."

TWENTY-SIX

Kyle

Raven pulled her hands from mine and leaned away. "Come again?"

My heart constricted into a tight ball of rubber bands at the absence of her touch. I wasn't sure if I wanted her to kick me out of the camp after she heard everything or embrace me for who I was. "I'm the result of a human cloning experiment that a group of doctors decided to conduct almost twenty years ago."

"Okay..." she said slowly. "But you look absolutely normal."

I chuckled. She wasn't freaking out. That was good. "Looks can be deceiving, but yes, from the perspective that most people assume that cloned animals will be born with extreme deformities, yes, I'm normal."

"So you're a human clone. Go on."

Not quite the reaction I was expecting, but neither was her reaction to hearing my voice inside her head. She *was* from California. Maybe people from California were more accepting of the strange and different.

"I'm one of seven cloned humans that survived the original experiment—although there are many younger ones, too, from later experiments. We still have no idea how big the operation is. We're starting to suspect that there are various labs around the United States. And most likely the world," I added, given that I was in Costa Rica to investigate the possibility of a lab here.

"You're not here as a pre-med student?"

"I already have more than the equivalent of a pre-med degree from the boarding school I attended in Kentucky."

"With Lexi."

"Yes, with Lexi."

"Is she also a clone?"

"Yes. She's one of the original seven."

Raven seemed to be taking in the information in stride. *So far, so good.*

"My ability to get inside your head last night has to do with how I was cloned. There are many theories as to exactly why or how, but each of the original clones has a set of gifts, or supernatural powers—a result of the genetic manipulation by the doctors who did this to us."

"And you can speak to people's minds?"

"Yes. But it doesn't stop there." I grabbed her hands again. I thought she might jerk away again, but fortunately, she didn't. She let me hold her hands in mine. She actually gripped me a little tighter than before. "Whatever you were injected with last night knocked you unconscious. I was able to slip inside your head and control your body and mind enough to get you away from the dangerous situation and back to camp without Felipe or anyone else knowing what had happened. You heard my voice because I was talking to you, but you were also unconscious."

She narrowed her eyes. "Could you control me right now?"

tracked

I smiled. "No. Not unless I knock you out first. My supernatural powers only work when someone is unconscious or asleep. Lexi thinks I might be able to do more eventually. She seems to continuously discover new gifts, but I've been too busy... grieving, I guess... to hone any other abilities I may have."

"I don't know what to say. I'm glad you got me away from there last night. But..."

"It's weird. I know. I wish I could say that I've already told you everything."

She stared up at me, her eyes growing tired. "Why do I get the feeling you're saving the worst for last?"

I didn't answer that. "When I was inside your head, I took the opportunity to examine your injuries—the damage done by your concussions. And... while I was poking around, I discovered something at the base of your brain." I tried to keep all emotion from my voice. I didn't need her to know that what I was telling her was the worst possible news I could deliver to someone. Especially someone I... what? Cared about? Liked a lot? What did I feel for this beautiful creature sitting before me? I didn't know if my heart could take another heartbreak like the one I'd suffered with Dani. But as I looked into Raven's eyes, I knew I couldn't walk away either.

Raven's voice was insistent. "What did you see, Kyle?"

I flinched at the sound of my name on her lips. "You have what is called a 'tracker' at the base of your skull."

"A tracker?"

I swallowed hard, then held up my fingers and formed a circle with my thumb and forefinger. "A tracker is an electronic device about this big. The person who cloned me and my friends began creating these small devices as part of her operation."

"And you're saying I have one of these? Why? How? And you saw it?" The muscles in her hands stiffened beneath my fingers. I tightened my hold.

"I don't know why, but yes, I saw it."

"You've seen trackers before? Do you have one?"

"I don't have one. But yes, I've seen them." I thought of Dani.

"What is it? Is it something used to heal brain injuries? Could the doctor here have inserted it inside my head when I was injured last year? I remember so little about what happened afterwards." She looked away as if in deep thought. "Surely my parents would have told me if I had something like that inside my head..." She found my eyes again. "Wouldn't they?"

I held her gaze. "The tracker isn't a good thing; it's not in there to provide you with any kind of treatment. My guess is that it was inserted during the... incident last summer." I hated to bring that up, but it was the most likely explanation I could think of. "It's used to track your whereabouts. Someone wanted to keep tabs on you."

Raven's eyes widened. "Like a tap on a phone, but instead they... tapped my brain?" She suddenly stood. Her hands left mine and shot to the back of her neck. The stool she'd vacated slid backward, screeching along the floor. "What does that mean, Kyle? The person who killed Nicholas knows where I am at all times? And this person has *always* known this?" She backed slowly away. Her voice trembled. "Has the killer been inside my head all this time?"

tracked

I rushed to her and scooped her into my arms, holding her head next to my chest. "I'm not going to let anything happen to you. We're going to figure everything out. I've got help coming."

"What kind of help?" She pushed away from me. Her eyes flashed with anger. "From other cloned humans? How do I know you're not part of this operation started by the people who created you? I'm just supposed to trust you and this crazy story?"

I grabbed her arms and held them to her sides. "Listen to me. You trusted me ten minutes ago. Remember that. I'm not here to hurt you. I never would have told you any of this had I not seen the tracker inside your head. I wouldn't have brought you into this unfortunate world I live in if I didn't have to. I am so sorry."

"I... I think I need to be alone."

"Raven, listen to me. You're not safe. You ran from here this morning. I had no idea where you had gone. I can't help you if you run from me. If you're taken by these people, I don't know if I'll be able to find you in time."

"In time? What does *that* mean?" Her eyes twitched rapidly as they drilled into mine. "You think these people want to kill me? Because I saw that murder?"

Shit. Why did I say that? "No. Raven, they are not going to kill you. I will not let that happen." What was I saying? I couldn't promise her that.

She looked away. Beads of sweat formed along her forehead. Her arms felt clammy beneath my hands. She was having a panic attack, and there was nothing I could do to stop it.

"I need my medication."

"Medication?"

"I have medication in my cabin."

"For panic attacks?"

She nodded. Her breathing was suddenly coming out in short rasps.

"Let's go get it." I was not about to leave her alone.

Her hands gripped my forearms and squeezed. She stared into my eyes. "You won't leave me, will you? Please don't desert me." Her legs crumpled beneath her body, and I scooped her into my arms before she could slump to the floor. I just held her there, rocking her back and forth.

How could I go through this again? At the same time, how could I abandon her?

With the brush of my fingers, I pushed hair off Raven's cheek and behind her ear. I stared at her closed eyes, and I made a promise to both of us.

"I will see you through this. No matter what happens, you will not go through this alone."

TWENTY-SEVEN

Raven

When facing your worst fears and troubles, people often advise, "Go to bed. Everything will look better in the morning."

All of those people are assholes.

I lay awake, staring at the bottom of the bunk above me. It was almost five a.m. and still dark outside my window. The frog outside sounded like it was sitting on my pillow. I turned over and glanced at the neighboring bunk. Kyle's arm rested on his forehead, and I could tell by his breathing that he, too, was awake.

Without a word, I crawled out of bed. I grabbed some clothes and escaped to the bathroom. Staring back at me from the mirror was the shell of a girl I didn't recognize any longer. And it wasn't just the dark circles under my eyes or my physical appearance that tripped me up—it was how much I'd changed on the inside.

I no longer wanted the same things in life that I used to. Which was good, because most of those things—a top college education, a career in social work, a normal life with a boyfriend maybe—now seemed completely unattainable. I would always be the broken shell of a person looking back at me.

I quickly washed my face and brushed my teeth, then slipped into some running shorts and a tank top. When I exited the bathroom, Kyle was leaning against the door, blocking my exit.

He pushed off from the door. "Good morning."

I wasn't sure how Daniel and Eva would react if they found Kyle in my cabin, but I didn't care. I slept more peacefully knowing he was in the bunk beside me. At one point during the night, I almost climbed into bed with him and let him hold me. But there was an undeniable distance between us. And it was growing.

A few beats passed as I assessed his tousled hair and bloodshot eyes, neither of which took away from how gorgeous he was. Then I sat on my bunk and slipped on my running shoes. "I was going to go down to the rock by the river and meditate, but I think what I really need is a good hard run."

"Mind if I join you?"

Like I had a choice. "No."

Tension filled the air between us like a thick fog. Neither of us spoke as we made our way up the hill and past the pavilion. A bus was parked next to the pavilion and kitchen, evidence that Daniel and Eva had returned with the next group.

Daniel had gone easy on me so far this summer, not asking me to be too involved with the visiting groups, but I wasn't sure how long that would last. I knew I would have to engage in the group activities sooner or later. And just the thought of being around lots of people at one time sent my heart into hyperdrive.

Kyle and I hiked up the hill to the road. We hadn't even begun to run yet, and my pulse was already racing.

tracked

Kyle touched my arm. "You okay?" He was so attuned to everything about me, it seemed.

I rubbed the space over my heart and took a deep breath. "Yes. Let's run."

Kyle stared at me like he wanted to say something more, but decided against it. We ran in an uncomfortable silence, still battling the dense fog that divided us. My thoughts took me through every word of the conversation Kyle and I had had last night. They took me through the countless hours I'd spent on the couch of a psychiatrist over the past eleven months. And finally they took me to the moment, last June, when I ran scared from Costa Rica.

I ran because of an incident I had no memory of. I visited a psychiatrist because I suffered some sort of PTSD and had yet to face the actual event that made me shy away from social activities. And now, I had some foreign device in my skull, and bad people were using it to track my whereabouts and even influence my decisions.

We were about to the halfway point on a four-mile loop when I stopped abruptly. Kyle ran a few more steps before turning to stare at me. We both breathed heavily.

"Did you mean what you said?" I asked.

He let out a huge breath. "I've meant everything I've said to you. Which part are you referring to?"

"Will you and your friends help me?"

Kyle answered before my words were even fully out of my mouth. "Yes. I will do whatever I can to see you through this."

I nodded while glancing toward the volcano. "Why?"

"Why what?"

"Why are you willing to help me? This can't be safe for you or your friends."

"No, but we've seen what these people are capable of, and..." Kyle's voice trailed off. He was committed to helping me; I could hear that in his voice. But something had changed.

I remembered him cradling me last night as I suffered a panic attack. He somehow got me to my cabin and found my medication. And he stayed with me. But he was different this morning.

"I'm not quite summer fling material anymore, am I?" I said. He furrowed his brow, and I forced a weak smile. "Sorry. Bad joke."

He stepped over to me. He reached around and ran his fingers along my ponytail, letting his hand rest against my neck and tipping my head backward. "You are beautiful. And brave. I can see the fight in you this morning." His breath brushed across my face and smelled of spearmint. "You're going to need it. We both are. I just don't want either of us to be distracted as we do whatever we have to do to remove this tracker and find the people who put it there." He leaned in and kissed me softly on my forehead, the way a good friend or a father would.

I lowered my head and sighed. "We better get back. Daniel will expect us to help with the new group."

As we neared the camp again, I realized that the weight that had been sitting on my shoulders had lifted slightly, just from knowing that Kyle was going to help me. Even if he had no desire for any other kind of relationship with me, I felt safer knowing he was close.

Kyle entered the security code for the new gate he'd helped install last week. Just as we were about to enter the camp, we

tracked

heard the sound of something scurrying across the road behind us. We both turned toward the sound: a lizard darting under some ground cover.

Then I saw movement out of the corner of my eye. Kyle must have seen it as well, because he suddenly stepped forward toward the movement. A man darted from behind a tree and began running down the road. But Kyle was faster. He caught up to the man and tackled him to the ground.

The man fought him, but Kyle punched him, and the guy relented. He lifted his hands in front of his face. "Pascal sent me!" he screamed.

I jogged over to them. Kyle had his arm pulled back, about to hit the man again. That's when I saw the New York Yankees cap. "Kyle, wait." I stood over them. "Who are you? What do you mean, Pascal sent you?"

"I was just supposed to watch you and make sure nothing happened to you."

"You've been following me. You were at the waterfall last week."

"Yes. I'm sorry. I wasn't trying to scare you."

"Where is Pascal?" I asked.

"It's early. He's probably in bed."

"What's your name?"

"Pablo."

"Well, Pablo, call him."

"Pardon?"

"You have a phone?"

Pablo nodded.

"Then call Pascal and hand me the phone."

Pablo did as I asked. He had no choice, seeing as Kyle had him pinned to the ground. He handed me the phone as it began to ring.

"What's wrong?" Pascal asked when he answered. No "Hola," no sort of greeting.

"Get to the camp, now."

"Amagita?"

I ended the call and handed Pablo his phone.

~~~~~

"You had me followed?" I screamed when Pascal arrived.

Pablo was sitting in a chair in the back storage room. Kyle was standing behind him. Both watched me yell at Pascal.

Pascal pointed a finger at his minion in the Yankees cap. "You. You're fired."

Pablo winced, but nodded in understanding.

Pascal turned to me. "I was worried about you. You hadn't been back here since—"

I held up a hand. "I get it. But why not just ask me if I felt afraid? Everyone has assumed I need protection, but not a single person has asked me how I'm doing."

"Would you have told me?"

I crossed my arms. "I'd be feeling better if I wasn't having to look over my shoulder for people who may or may not be following me."

Before Pascal could respond, Daniel stepped into the room. "I'm the one who asked Pascal to hire Pablo," he said. All heads turned. "I didn't want to take any chances with you. And apparently it was a good move. Want to tell me what happened while we were away?" He eyed Kyle and Pascal. "One of you should have called me."

tracked

Kyle had no reaction whatsoever. Probably a good move.

I placed my hands on my head, as if I could stop it from exploding from the buildup of rage. "It was neither of their responsibilities to call you about me. I planned to tell you as soon as I saw you."

"Raven, honey," Daniel started.

"Don't 'Raven, honey' me. This having-me-followed business stops *now*. If you want to help me, you'll help me remember what happened last summer."

"Amagita." Pascal stood in front of me and grabbed my hand. Kyle shifted slightly behind him. "I'm not sure that's a good idea."

"Are you kidding?" I pulled my hand away. "A week ago, you wanted me to remember so badly that you called me in California and begged me to come to Costa Rica."

"You did what?" Daniel asked.

Pascal held up a hand apologetically. "That was before we discovered that the kidnappings were happening only to people from this camp. I didn't think Raven would be in danger if she came back. Come on, Daniel. Her parents were here. You're here. This is her home."

"Do you *hear* yourselves?" I asked. "You're talking about me like I'm not even here."

Daniel closed his eyes briefly. "Raven, I'm sorry, but your parents called. I had no choice but to tell them that you were attacked Friday night. You're booked on a flight at the end of the week to return to the States."

I couldn't believe what I was hearing. "Oh, well, how kind of you to make the arrangements. But why wait? Why not just take me today?" I raised my hands to my sides, then let them slam into my thighs.

"Good question," Pascal said. "I can take her to San Jose today."

"I'll take her Friday when this week's group is scheduled to return." Daniel pointed to Kyle. "And *you* will continue to look out for her."

"Unbelievable." I was being treated like a petulant child. "Look at you guys. My heroes." A hysterical laugh erupted from my mouth.

"Knock, knock." A female voice spoke softly behind me.

We all turned to face the doorway, where a girl four or five inches shorter than me stood. Her brown hair hung in smooth, straight strands, and her eyes were a vibrant shade of emerald. A man nearly a foot taller, with sandy blond hair, stood behind her.

"Lexi!" Kyle said. He crossed the room and scooped her into his arms. Then he turned to us hesitantly. "Daniel, Raven, this is Lexi Matthews and her boyfriend Jack DeWeese. They're my friends from Kentucky. They're here to help for the week."

Lexi's smile faltered slightly as she took in the situation before her. She glanced hesitantly up at Kyle before sticking out a hand to Daniel. "Nice to meet you," she said. "You'll find that I'm truly gifted at popping into a conversation at the worst possible time."

And Lexi would find that I was gifted at making lousy first impressions. I stormed right past Lexi, Jack, and Kyle, and didn't even pause when I heard Pascal and Kyle shout my name.

TWENTY-EIGHT

Kyle

"What the hell is going on, man?" Jack asked me as we stood by the river.

"She's pretty," Lexi added, nodding toward Raven.

I stared up toward the pavilion where Raven sat by herself talking on her cell phone. I was dying to know what was going on in that head of hers, but unfortunately, I couldn't mindread, and anytime I got close to her, she clammed up. I decided to give her some space—as long as I could keep her in my sight.

"She's beautiful," I agreed. I faced Lexi and Jack. "And she has a tracker. Plus enough damage from past concussions that she could possibly die if she knocks her head again."

"Any sign of IIA agents?" Lexi asked.

"Not sure, but I did witness Dr. Jeremy Porter practically shove Raven's mother into the back of a car."

"The man Jonas was cloned from?" Jack ran a hand through his hair. "What is he doing in Costa Rica?"

"Jonas thinks he stole, or was given, the shipment of trackers that went missing from the labs in Palmyra. We know that he left the United States shortly after he became wanted for questioning in the death of Marci McDaniel. Who knows how long any of these doctors have been working on some of this stuff we're just starting to learn about."

"What do they want with Raven?" Lexi asked.

"I'm guessing she witnessed more than just a murder last summer."

"Why didn't they just kill her?"

That was the very question I'd asked myself a thousand times since discovering the tracker. "I don't know. And I don't know what will stop them from doing just that if she becomes a liability."

"I'm sorry, Kyle." Lexi placed a comforting hand on my forearm.

"Me too."

"What now? What's the plan?" Jack asked.

"We need to get that tracker out of her head. You can do that, right?"

"Depends. Is it one of the older versions, or one of the newer?"

"I don't know." I scrubbed my face with my hands.

Lexi reached up and pulled my hands away. "We're here. We're going to figure this out."

"Any idea where the lab might be?"

"None. I was only just starting to get to know the town. I didn't really feel any sense of urgency until I saw Dr. Porter, and then Raven was attacked and I found the tracker inside her. Oh, and..." I cast a sideways glance at Lexi.

"What?"

"Dr. Porter recognized me. Or at least, he recognized that I was someone who knew Jonas, because he sent his regards."

tracked

Lexi considered this. "And yet you've seen no signs of IIA. And no one has shown you any unusual interest."

I shook my head.

"I did some research about La Fortuna." Jack pulled out his cell phone and began scrolling. "There are only clinics nearby. The closest hospital is fifty minutes away, and it's public. If Raven had major head trauma last year, I assume her American parents insisted that she be taken to one of three private hospitals in San Jose."

"True," I said, "but Jonas and I think the lab is probably off the grid—not tied to any of the hospitals."

"That would make sense," Lexi agreed.

"I think her friend Pascal knows more than he's saying," I said. "However, he probably has nothing to do with the tracker in her brain, or he wouldn't have hired someone to follow her."

"He's the dark, handsome character I met earlier?" Lexi asked, then shrugged when Jack cocked his head. "What? I'm not even allowed to look?"

Jack pulled Lexi close. "No, you're not. You're only allowed to have eyes for me."

She smiled and let him kiss her.

I acted like I was about to throw up. "Did you *both* have to come?"

"Yes," Jack said. "We did. We are all still at risk any time we're around these crazy doctors. Who knows what they're doing with this lab? If they're still trying to perfect the trackers, then they're still after Lexi, and quite possibly any of us who can crack the code on what Sandra's original intentions were with the entire cloning operation. Can you imagine what they might do if they find out three of the original clones are here at this camp?"

Lexi shuddered, but then snapped right back out of it. "So, what's going on with you and Raven? It's obvious you're smitten."

I arched a brow. "Smitten? Seriously, people use that word?"

"You're evading."

"I don't know." I shook my head, staring down at my feet. "This girl is so good. Has so much going for her. Well, she *had* so much going for her."

"What do you mean? Why past tense?" Lexi asked.

"Whatever happened to her last summer set off a chain of events that has led to her losing a lot. The only thing she feels like she has left is this camp, where she's practically grown up every summer."

"Did you tell her about Dani?"

"Yeah."

Lexi placed a hand on my shoulder. "We'll help you save her."

TWENTY-NINE

Raven

Thankfully, Daniel bought my excuse that I had a headache and let me skip out on the group's activities for the day. Eva was in the kitchen working on lunch and dinner. The scent of an Italian sauce drifted into the office where I pored through documents and searched the filing cabinet for any records Daniel may have kept from last summer.

But just as I'd feared, there was nothing about me. Not in the office, anyway. Where else could I look? My parents didn't have a house of their own here, but Daniel did. Perhaps he kept the more sensitive records in his house on the hill.

I reached under the desk for the small key that I knew was there—the one that unlocked the small key cabinet behind me. Then I retrieved the key to Daniel's house from the key cabinet, locked the cabinet back up, and returned the small key to its spot under the desk.

From the office door, I watched as Eva busied herself chopping vegetables for a salad. She had headphones on and was singing some sort of Spanish ballad. I smiled at how happy she seemed.

Outside the building, the camp was quiet again. Earlier that morning, the thirty or so volunteers from a medical group from New Mexico had been rushing about, preparing for the clinic they were opening for the week. They planned to offer vaccinations to the children in several of the villages—a different location each day. But now the camp was once again peaceful.

I walked along the driveway to the sidewalk that veered off toward Daniel and Eva's cabin. I glanced behind me. No one was around. I assumed everyone from the camp had gone with the group. I approached the back door, the door Daniel and Eva used most. The key turned easily, and I stepped into the living room of their modest home. I immediately felt bad, like I was breaking and entering. Because that was exactly what I was doing.

But I needed information about last summer.

Daniel and Eva lived in a simple two-bedroom home. They had converted the guest bedroom into a private office, because any time they had guests, they would simply give them an entire cabin to themselves.

I opened the bottom desk drawer—the only one big enough to hold file folders—and fanned through the contents. Most of the folders held financial reports for the camp, or personal records for Daniel and Eva. There were also a couple of folders on employees, and a set of folders for the groups that had visited recently.

A file labeled "Kyle Jones" caught my eye. I pulled it out and lay it across the desk. Did I dare open it? Was I invading his privacy?

"Why stop now, Raven? You've come this far," I said aloud.

I opened the file to find a copy of Kyle's passport, his birth certificate, an employment application, and several handwritten notes. The notes appeared to be from various phone conversa-

tracked

tions with..." "Lexi Matthews, President of Wellington Boarding School?"

I swiveled around in the desk chair and stared out the window that overlooked the camp below. "What is a girl younger than me doing as president of a prestigious boarding school?" Kyle was becoming more and more mysterious with every piece of information I discovered.

I turned back to the notes. Lexi had confirmed that Kyle graduated from Wellington in May. His parents died when he was young. He was scheduled to attend the University of Kentucky in the fall. He was a straight-A student with extensive knowledge in the area of pre-medicine.

Except, according to Kyle, he had a far more extensive knowledge of medicine than that.

I replaced Kyle's folder and continued my search through the other documents. But I found nothing concerning me.

I closed the drawer and looked around the room. In addition to serving as a private office for Daniel, the room had a nice little reading nook in one corner. A cozy bookshelf stood next to a chaise lounge with a blanket draped over it and a floor lamp standing behind it. On top of the blanket was a thick stack of papers fanned across an open manila file folder.

I stood slowly and crossed the room. The stack before me was more than just papers—it was newspaper clippings and photographs. I sat on the edge of the chaise, lifted one of the articles, and read the headline: *Local Man Murdered, Unidentified Witness in Stable Condition.*

I quickly flipped through the rest of the pile. There were more newspaper articles—about my soccer team's games in California. The entire folder was filled with information about *me*. I guessed it made some sense that Daniel and Eva were keeping track of my life, but: why was it spread out like this? Why was he reading through it *now*?

Underneath the newspaper articles were forms and papers. I picked up the first form—some sort of medical paperwork. And right there at the top of the page was the date I feared: the day last summer when my world was sent spinning out of control, altering the course of my life forever. I skimmed the information on the page. *Mild concussion and minor laceration to the forehead.*

I instinctively reached my hand to the scar that was hidden underneath my bangs—a reminder of that night that stared back at me from my bathroom mirror every day.

But I was also confused. I had memories of waking up after the incident in severe pain. I was in the hospital, but I was dazed, and most definitely drugged. I remembered my parents and Daniel and Eva visiting me in the hospital. I remembered Miguel and his mother visiting. I thought I even remembered Pascal's voice during one of the first nights in the hospital when I was barely lucid.

By the time I fully awoke, all of that just felt like a terrible nightmare, and physically, I was mostly fine. My parents packed me up and took me home. I never got the chance to talk to Pascal or Miguel or anyone other than Daniel and my parents.

At the bottom of the medical form was an illegible signature, but below that was the typed name: Dr. Jeremy Porter.

I searched the very few memories I had of my days in the hospital, and I didn't remember a Dr. Jeremy Porter. In fact, I didn't remember any of the doctors who'd taken care of me.

tracked

My phone buzzed with a text message. I was surprised to find that it was from Kyle. *You okay? Why didn't you come with the group?*

I'm fine. Surprised you noticed. A little melodramatic for me, but whatever. He'd been acting strange ever since my attack. Since he told me about his identity and about this "tracker" he claimed was inside my head. I had so many unanswered questions, and Kyle was too busy hanging with his newly arrived friends to give me any explanations.

I wanted to know who had put this tracker thing inside my head, what its purpose was, and why Kyle had gone noticeably pale when he'd explained it to me.

And why had none of my doctors noticed it this past year? Or, what if the doctors *had* seen it, and it was simply a device that was designed to heal my injuries? Perhaps my parents didn't tell me about it because they thought it would freak me out. *For good reason.*

I put the form back and glanced around Daniel's office, making sure everything was just as it had been when I entered.

My phone buzzed again. *Of course I noticed. Difficult to have a summer fling when the girl's not around.* He ended the text with a smiley face emoticon.

I smiled at that. At least we could still joke about the relationship we would never have. I slipped out the back door, making sure it was locked behind me. I turned toward the patio behind Daniel's house—and yelped at the sight of Lexi sitting in one of Daniel and Eva's deck chairs.

"What are you doing here?" I asked.

She stood, wiping her hands against her pants as if they were nervously sweating. "Kyle thought you could help me out."

"With what?" When I heard the shortness in my breath, I sighed. "I'm sorry. I don't mean to sound—"

"It's okay. I promise I understand. You can sound however you need to sound. I know as well as anyone how confused you must be. You must have so many questions. I'd like to help you with that."

"Oh, right. You're reading my mind."

She smiled apologetically. "The tracker inside your head gives me access to your thoughts."

I fingered the key against my palm. Maybe Lexi *could* help me. "Can you tell me about Dani?" I asked in a small voice.

"Yes."

~~~~~

Lexi and I found a sunny spot by the river to spread out a couple of towels. To most people, we probably looked like a couple of young women sunbathing. In reality, we were having a meeting of the minds—brainstorming solutions to a problem I didn't even know much about yet.

Filtered sun kissed our skin off and on, depending on how the wind blew the limbs and leaves above us and where the sun was positioned in the sky.

After removing my sundress to reveal a bright red crocheted bikini and to expose more skin, I leaned back on my elbows and listened to the water running over the rocks. It was a sound that had soothed my mind many times in the past, but it only roared between my ears today.

tracked

Lexi lay back completely. Her face looked calm, relaxed. *Lucky. Can't remember the last time I felt truly relaxed.*

"For making a trip on short notice, you came prepared," I said, eyeing her sporty bikini top and mismatched swim shorts. Lexi was very muscular, especially in her upper body—quite different from my own build. Though I was fit from years of soccer, most of my power was in my legs.

She opened one eye and smiled, and it was a smile filled with warmth. I imagined she would be a wonderful friend to those she let in. "Kyle and I swam together at Wellington. I don't go many places without a swimsuit."

I pushed my sunglasses farther up my nose. My oversized straw hat shielded my face—and hopefully hid the way I was scrutinizing Kyle's friend. I knew nothing about the girl beside me. Kyle had told me that she was a cloned human. Was that something I was supposed to talk about? If Kyle could get inside my head, what could she do... besides hear my thoughts?

"Why didn't you go with the group to set up the medical clinic today?" Lexi asked.

In years past, I would have been very involved with all of the humanitarian groups. And I would have loved it. But something about spending my days with a group of people I knew nothing about no longer appealed to me. I'd grown increasingly wary of putting myself in situations with large groups of people. My shrink had told me that that was normal for someone suffering from post-traumatic stress disorder. I recognized that, but so far I hadn't found a solution that worked for me.

But I decided I didn't need to get into all that with Lexi. "Well, since I'm apparently leaving Costa Rica on Friday, I didn't see the point." Besides, I had other things I needed to do— like finding the doctor who had treated me.

"Kyle tells me you've spent most of your summers helping your parents run this camp. You must know a lot about La Fortuna and the surrounding area."

"Sure. This is my home. I've planned the social activities for our visiting teams for years now." Which was ironic, seeing as I had no desire to subject myself to those activities any longer. I'd been no help to anyone so far this year, but Daniel obviously wasn't counting on me this time around.

"Have you noticed any new construction in La Fortuna in recent years? Any large buildings?"

That was a weird question. "What kind of buildings?"

"We're not sure what we're looking for. But a building big enough to be a large laboratory. It might not look like anything on the outside, but on the inside, it will be a sleek and modern, state-of-the-art medical lab."

"No, nothing comes to mind."

"I don't know how much Kyle told you. We came here to help you, but we also came here in search of some missing trackers. We're scared that these trackers are being mass-produced in a lab somewhere. And, as I'm sure you can imagine, we're concerned with how they'll be used."

Lexi and I remained on our backs, our faces pointed toward the sun. I massaged the back of my neck where Kyle had indicated the tracker had been inserted. "What does it mean that I have one of these trackers?"

I felt Lexi shift beside me. When I opened my eyes, she was sitting criss-cross, facing me. I followed suit and mirrored her

tracked

position. Her emerald-green eyes glowed with the intensity of a story bursting to get out.

"Well, the short version is: I don't know."

"And the long version?"

"Like I said, I'm not sure how much Kyle told you, but he, Jack and I, and some others... we were 'created' by a few doctors who thought they could advance medicine decades through the cloning of humans and the genetic manipulation of our DNA."

I picked at the grass in front of me. "He told me this. It's starting to sink in. I can't say that I'm surprised that the technology exists to do this, but—"

"Why would they do such a thing and risk horrible consequences?" Lexi asked, reading my mind. "That's a question I continue to wrestle with." She reached for her phone and scrolled while she spoke. "A few of these doctors... actually, one in particular—she took her experiments beyond the level of insane." Lexi laughed, but there was no humor in it. "Sandra Whitmeyer. She's responsible for everything evil surrounding the genetic modification experiments, especially the creation of the trackers."

"What exactly *are* the trackers? And why were they created?" Kyle had told me a little, but I wanted the perspective of someone who wasn't overprotecting me.

"At first these devices were created as a way to keep tabs on the clones that Sandra had control of, plus any others she discovered. But then she began to program the trackers to imitate supernatural powers she was finding in the original human clones."

"What sort of supernatural powers?"

"Well, when I met a second clone of Jack's DNA—his name was Lin—he was able to talk to me and hear my thoughts the same way Jack can." Lexi twisted her hands in her lap. She was leaving part of the explanation out, probably for my benefit.

"A clone of Jack? Like, he looked just like him?"

Lexi nodded. "Identical."

"That had to have been weird."

"Very." A sadness touched her eyes. "Lin's tracker gave him some powers, but Sandra was unable to re-create many of the powers of the original clones—our various abilities to heal, for instance, among other things. And that pissed her off. She put a lot of people through a great deal of pain trying to get at our minds so that she could replicate these powers and place them inside trackers."

"You have the ability to heal? Like, with your mind?"

"Yep. Jack once healed my broken arm just by touching it."

I stared at Lexi, trying to process what that meant. "Can Kyle do that too? Heal broken bones?"

"He's still learning how to use his powers, but it doesn't appear so."

"Do I have some sort of supernatural powers inside my tracker?"

"I have no idea." Lexi smiled, but it didn't travel past her lips. "Raven, I'd like to examine your tracker, if you don't mind. I have the ability to get inside people's heads and other areas of the body. Literally. I can examine brain damage and other injuries and illnesses. I can also move things around and heal... and I've been known to extract *some* trackers."

"Only some?"

tracked

"Unfortunately, Sandra improved her technology very quickly. She discovered ways to make the trackers more difficult to remove."

Maybe I didn't have supernatural powers, but I knew when someone was leaving out a huge portion of a story. And I got the strong feeling that by "more difficult" she meant "impossible."

"What happens if you can't remove mine?" I asked.

Lexi looked away and stared off into the direction of the river.

I touched her leg to bring her attention back to me. "Lexi, I need to know what I'm up against. Daniel thinks he's sending me back to California at the end of the week. My parents don't know that I've lost my scholarship. They don't realize that I have nowhere to go. This is the only home I have, and I need to know... I don't even know *what* I need to know. But I'd like to start by understanding this *thing* that's inside me."

"I can examine it now if you'd like."

"Here?"

"If that's okay. It'll take less than a minute."

"Okay," I whispered.

"Just relax. It's just going to look like I'm staring intently at you."

Her hands relaxed in her lap, and her eyes looked past mine, like she was seeing straight through me. But I knew she wasn't. She was seeing *inside* me. And I wasn't sure if she could read my thoughts while she was poking around in there. If she could, she'd know that I was terrified of her—and of this entire situation I was in. I didn't understand any of it, and I was sure that I was in some sort of trouble that no one could help me with.

I'd lost so much since last summer, and I was tired. And I didn't know where to begin to turn it all around. Did I go back to Stanford and try to work out some sort of work-study and financial aid to make up for the scholarships I'd lost? Did I confess to my parents that I'd lost the scholarships, then spend the next semester looking for another school that I could afford? If such a school even existed.

Did I fight to stay here in Costa Rica? Would I be taking my life into my own hands by doing that? Was Nicholas's murderer just waiting for the right opportunity to take me out?

Then again, maybe that wasn't the answer at all. Maybe I needed to go back to the beginning—to what had started me on this horrible bumpy road. But how? The psychiatrist had done nothing to help me remember that horrible night.

A pain shot through the back of my head like a meteor entering the earth's atmosphere. I screamed out. My hands locked across the base of my neck, and I rolled to the ground, writhing in pain.

"Raven! Raven, can you hear me?"

I could hear Lexi's voice, but she was far away, and I couldn't make my mouth form words in response.

"Raven, look at me. You're okay. I'm sorry. I'm so sorry."

My eyes fluttered open, and Lexi was staring down at me.

"There you are," she said. "I'm so sorry. I shouldn't have tried to move the tracker at all. I knew better than that."

I took several deep breaths as the pain slowly subsided. When it had, I sat up and glared at Lexi. "Surely with that kind of pain, you at least figured out a way to remove it?"

tracked

"I'm afraid not. It's locked in there tight. And it's not going anywhere any time soon." She scooted back on her towel. "I'm sorry."

"Yeah, so you keep telling me. So I guess I'm stuck with this thing?" A breeze picked up, and I felt like it was carrying all my hope away into the rainforest.

"We have other ways to make sure the tracker doesn't hurt you. We're going to do everything we can, okay?" Lexi touched a warm hand to my forearm.

I nodded, but what I really wanted to do was curl up in a ball and cry. "Will you tell me about Dani?" I asked, finally able to breathe more easily.

Lexi's lips tugged downward. This conversation was obviously just as hard for her as it was for Kyle. "Before we knew about trackers and what they did, Sandra inserted one into my best friend's head just to punish me."

"What happened?"

"Sandra killed her."

My hand covered my stomach; I felt like the air had been knocked out of me. When I managed to take in another breath, I asked, "She died because of the tracker?"

Lexi's brows tilted inward. "She died because Sandra Whitmeyer is a monster." She closed her eyes briefly. "But yes, the tracker was used to kill her."

"Is it like a bomb?" My voice cracked and my hands began to shake. "If I move a certain way, will it detonate?"

Lexi grabbed one of my hands. "No." She moved closer and sat on her knees with her legs tucked under her body. She looked directly into my eyes. "Kyle, Jack, and I are going to do everything we can to remove this tracker—or find the server that controls it and deactivate it. I promise we're going to help you."

"And this is why Kyle suddenly wants nothing to do with me." It was finally starting to make sense. I reached for my sundress and slipped it back over my bikini. I stood and gathered my towel.

Lexi jumped to her feet. "Raven," she said, pinning me with a hard stare and stopping me from stuffing the towel in my bag.

Was she about to use her supernatural mind powers on me? I wanted to scream at her, *Go for it, and while you're at it knock me unconscious until this is all over with.* If there *is* an ending to this madness. But I managed to suppress that reaction.

Her face softened, and the warm smile she'd had when we'd first arrived by the river returned. "I never thought I would see Kyle have feelings for another woman. But I heard it in his voice the first time he spoke of you over the phone, and now that I'm here..."

She angled her head up toward the sun. I waited for her to continue.

"Kyle's in love with you, Raven. He might not know it yet, but there's no mistaking the look in his eyes when he sees you or when he talks about you. It's just that—he's terrified of losing someone again. He's worried he can't save you. But that doesn't mean he's not going to fight like hell trying. And Jack and I are going to help."

Kyle, in love with me? My heart misses several beats as I process the possiblity. But—I couldn't think about that now. No distractions. "Why would you do this for me?" I asked. "You don't even know me. None of you do."

tracked

"You'll have to ask Kyle and Jack their reasons, but as for me... well, apparently it's my life's mission to destroy everything in this world that Sandra Whitmeyer has ever touched."

"Does that include me?" Lexi and I both jumped at the sound of a man's voice.

We turned just as a dark-haired man stepped out from behind a tree and approached us slowly, the way a tiger stalked prey. He was dressed in khaki pants and a white linen shirt with sleeves rolled to his elbows. The muscles that stretched his shirt, the slight five-o'clock shadow, and his expensive sunglasses screamed trouble in so many ways. He was part hot model, part beach bum—with a dash of badass that some girls would swoon over.

"Jonas!" Lexi screamed. She ran and leapt into his arms. He didn't even stumble as his arms circled her. He buried his face into the crook of her neck.

"Glad to see me?" he asked with a muffled voice.

"You came," Lexi practically whispered.

"You know me. I'm a sucker for a damsel in distress."

Lexi pulled back, and he let her slide down to her feet. He was much taller than her.

"Jonas," Lexi said with a hand sweep toward me, "I'd like you to meet Raven MacMillan."

Jonas stepped around Lexi and reached out a hand. "A very pretty damsel." When I gave him my hand, he bowed and kissed the tops of my fingers.

I pulled my hand away. "Another clone?"

Jonas eyed Lexi. "And she knows secret stuff."

"We're slowly filling her in."

I finished stuffing my towel in my bag. "Welcome to Costa Rica, Jonas. I'm going to let Lexi get you up to speed. I need a little time alone right now. I'll see you both later."

"Raven," Lexi said. "We could really use your help filling in the gaps. We're not here to conduct some secret mission. This involves you. I think you can help us find this lab."

"When Kyle and Jack get back this afternoon, come find me. We can all talk then." I turned and headed for my cabin, hoping to get there before I let out the sobs I was holding in. Sobs for the death sentence this tracker had given me. Sobs for meeting someone I was falling for, but who now wouldn't even look at me for fear of watching me die the same way his last girlfriend did. And sobs for knowing what I had to do next.

I was going to have to face the one night in my life I had hoped I would never have to remember.

"I think I'm in love," Jonas said before I was out of earshot.

"You say that about every pretty girl you meet. This one is already spoken for, so back off."

How could Lexi speak so casually after the conversation she and I had just had? Had she and Kyle and their friends truly seen so much of this that this was just another day to them?

Maybe it was best that Kyle kept his distance from me. It would make it so much easier for me when I finally found a way to admit that his world was not one I wished to be a part of.

THIRTY

Kyle

"Tell me exactly what you told her!"

Lexi flinched at my booming voice. Jack jumped down from the top bunk and moved to shield her. In all the years I'd known Lexi, I had never yelled at her. Then again, she'd never given me reason to like she had now.

Jonas lingered on the opposite top bunk, his head propped on his elbow and a smirk plastered on his face. "She's quite the looker, this Raven," he said.

I pointed a finger at him. "You. Shut up. If you weren't planning to help, why did you even come?"

Jonas raised two fingers and pretended to zip his lips closed.

I turned back to Lexi. "Well? What did you say?"

She was breathing hard and glaring at me with those green eyes that could melt ice. Before I could block it, her presence slipped into my head and took control of my mind. *You need to relax. Take a breath. We can't do something productive when you're this worked up.*

Almost instantly, I began breathing easier. My pulse slowed.

Jack mindspoke next. *And for the record, you yell at my girl like that again, I'll give you a pretty broken nose to go with that pretty face of yours.* He smiled sardonically.

Jonas laughed. *Just like old times. The gang's together. Some of us, anyway.*

"Where is Bree, anyway?" I asked, now that Lexi had successfully forced me to relax. "She finally wise up?"

Jonas and Briana—another of the seven original clones—*thought* they had started some sort of secret relationship over the past several months. But when Briana announced she was traveling to Palmyra for the summer, no one was surprised. We all had bets on how long "Joana" could last.

"Maybe," Jonas said. "We got in a fight when I told her I didn't want her to come here."

"Why did you tell her that?" Lexi asked.

"No." I stopped them, regaining control of my thoughts. "We aren't talking about Jonas's girlfriend. She'll be fine. Back to Raven."

"Are you ready to listen?" Lexi asked. "Your yelling is going to do nothing but get us kicked out of this camp."

She was right. Daniel was probably already starting to suspect that Lexi and the others weren't here for purely humanitarian reasons.

"Getting kicked out of this camp would probably be a good thing," Jonas said. "Not the safest of places. Any asshole can waltz in here unnoticed."

Lexi gestured toward Jonas. "Case in point."

"Please," I said, "just tell me what you told Raven today that would make her bolt out of here before I got back."

tracked

"I don't know. I told her about the trackers, about us, about Sandra Whitmeyer."

"Well, that's enough to make anyone run," Jack said.

"You obviously went way beyond what *I* told her," I said. I'd only given her small pieces of information. I hadn't wanted to scare her to death without some sort of plan. And now that I had reinforcements, we could hopefully formulate exactly that. "What did she say when you explained the trackers to her?"

Lexi's face paled slightly. "Well, there was one thing."

"Here it comes," Jonas said.

"What one thing?" I asked.

"You told me you'd told her about Dani."

"I did. I told her—" My back stiffened. "Shit! You told her Dani died from the tracker in her neck?"

Lexi nodded. "I'm sorry. If it makes you feel better, I regretted it immediately."

I ran my hands through my hair. I had to think. What could possibly be going through Raven's mind right now? My heart felt tight, like it might implode. We had shared such great times together before I'd discovered the lethal tracker in her head.

Jack crossed to me and put a hand on my shoulder. *You'll share those moments with her again, if that's what you want. Let's concentrate on disabling her tracker first, okay?*

I shook my head, staring at my shoes and letting out a frustrated chuckle. "Will I ever get you guys out of my head?"

"Oh, come on. You love us in there." Lexi smiled.

"Sounds like we're finally ready to get down to business." Jonas jumped down from the bunk. "So, where is the reason for my existence—this Jeremy Porter?"

Lexi and Jack sat on one of the lower bunks, and Jonas and I sat on the other, facing them.

"I've only seen Dr. Porter the one time," I said. "I think we start by going to the hot springs tonight. That's where Daniel thinks Raven's gone."

"With all due respect, man, I'd like to see your girl in a bikini again, too, but—"

"Jonas, I *will* beat the shit out of you." I faced Lexi and Jack, trying to keep my focus despite Jonas's needling. "Pascal is some sort of friend to Raven. He knows more about the night she witnessed a murder than anyone, I suspect. It was his father who was murdered, and his brother told us the first day I was here that Pascal was obsessed with finding the truth. Also, that had to have been the night the tracker was implanted in her brain, which means the murder had something to do with whatever Jonas figures was happening here all along."

"And Raven was the only eyewitness, right?" Jonas asked.

I nodded.

"What else did the articles say? What do the cops here say was the motive?" Jack asked.

"They have no clue who could have committed the murder, and they have no idea why," Jonas said. "This stuff would be way over their heads. Of course, I could be wrong." He shrugged.

"That's big of you to admit," Lexi quipped. "So, we go to the hot springs. Can I wear my bikini?"

"No," Jack and I said at the same time.

"Look, I've finally found some peace with being the weirdos that we are. I'm wearing my bikini. If there's even a small window of time to relax, I'm doing it." Lexi smiled and curtsied at her declaration.

"We need to be ready for anything at any time," I said. "If Jonas's DNA donor is running around, there's bound to be others who will recognize any one of us." I turned to Jonas. "You need to keep your cool around Pascal. You and he are a lot alike, and that can't produce happy results."

"What is that supposed to mean? I'm offended." Jonas grabbed his chest, feigning having been stabbed in the heart.

"Take it as a compliment. Raven seems to adore him."

Jonas smiled at that.

"What do we do once we're at the hot springs?" Lexi asked.

"We'll find Raven. See what she's up to. She's a smart girl. I don't imagine she's wallowing in a corner." That was actually what worried me. She was pissed at me, and she was looking for answers before Daniel forced her to fly back to the States. Not a good combination.

"Yeah, Raven strikes me as someone who might get herself into trouble so fast she won't even realize it's happening until it's too late," Lexi said.

"Sounds like someone else I know." Jack pulled Lexi in and placed a swift kiss on her lips.

"After we find Raven and make sure she's okay, I'll find a way to introduce you to Pascal," I said. "And if possible, we'll locate another shady character I've met, a guy named Felipe. His father took over Navos Hot Springs and Resort after Pascal's father was murdered. I like this Felipe guy even less than Pascal."

"Well, we all know the drill," Lexi said. "Keep your minds open so we can hear each other's thoughts. I'll pass information to Kyle since he can't hear our thoughts unless they're directed at him." It was like having our own internal walkie-talkies.

"And keep your eyes open for IIA," I reminded them—as if I needed to. I wasn't sure any of us would ever stop looking over our shoulders for men in suits with guns aimed at our heads.

Fortunately, all of us were trained in a variety of martial arts and self-defense tactics. And to make up for her size, Lexi wore a ring on her finger that contained a substance that could paralyze a two-hundred-pound man in two seconds flat.

Jack and Lexi stepped toward the door, but I stopped Jonas with a touch to his arm. "One last thing." I bent down and lifted my mattress. Underneath it was the syringe from the night Raven was attacked. "What do you make of this?"

Lexi and Jack paused in the doorway as Jonas held the syringe up. "Did it glow more when you first found it, like was it fluorescent?"

"Yeah. It did."

"Was this injected into Raven?"

"It knocked her unconscious."

"Then something was mixed in with it."

"What is it? What did they do to her?"

"It's an activation serum," Jonas said. "According to the lab tech I kept on at Palmyra after I cleaned up Sandra's mess, some of the latest trackers were designed to be inserted but not fully activated until this substance was injected into the body. The activation serum is meant to help the body adjust to whatever the tracker is designed to do."

"What does that mean?"

tracked

"It means they're getting closer to fully activating her tracker."

Lexi stepped back inside. "I did examine her tracker today. It's not like one I've seen before. And when I tried to move it—"

"You did *what*?" Jonas asked. "Bad move, Matthews."

Lexi punched Jonas in the stomach.

"Why? What happened?" Panic ballooned in my stomach.

"That must've stung like hell," Jonas answered for Lexi, and I could tell by the look on Lexi's face he was right.

"It just means we'll have to find a way to deactivate the tracker, or at least gain control of it," she said.

I looked at their faces. They were three of my best friends. If it was possible to beat this, I knew I had the right team of people on my side.

"One piece of good news," Lexi said. "I also was able to examine the damage to Lexi's brain from her concussions."

"Did you heal the damage?"

"Well... that's the thing."

I narrowed my gaze. "What?"

"She didn't have any brain damage that I could see. I saw no signs of a concussion, recent or otherwise."

THIRTY-ONE

Raven

The hot springs were bustling when I arrived. It was dinnertime, and I knew I had very little time before the group from camp joined me for the evening. I hadn't asked Daniel's permission to meet Pascal for dinner at Navos, but when Pascal's driver pulled into Puro Cielo's driveway, I climbed into the dark sedan and left without so much as a glance at Kyle.

Pascal greeted me with a kiss to my cheek. A friendly kiss, nothing more. At least that's what I told myself. "Dinner first, Amagita?"

"Aren't you working?"

"I can entertain one of our best customers for a couple of hours."

I smiled. "Lead the way, then."

Pascal reached down and wrapped his fingers around mine. He pulled me through the crowded restaurant like he owned the place, to a booth near the back that was somewhat secluded but allowed us a decent view of the activity in the bar area.

When we were seated, a waitress in a very short black skirt, a low-cut black top, and a small black apron arrived and set glasses of water in front of us. She handed us menus, and her fingers lingered longer than necessary on Pascal's when he took his. "Can I get either of you anything else to drink?" She stared at Pascal as she asked the question.

Pascal looked at me and raised an eyebrow. When I shook my head, he answered, "Water is fine, Ricca. Give us a few minutes."

"Sí. Very good, sir."

I watched her slink away. "Friend of yours?"

"Yes, as a matter of fact, she is. But not like you mean. She might like to be, but I've made it clear I'm not interested. I don't date people I work with." Pascal leaned in and clasped his hands. "So, tell me, what brings you running to me this evening?"

"I'm not running anywhere."

"Please." Pascal sat back in his chair and took a drink of water. "You've been fleeing every difficult situation since the day I met you. What now, this Kyle person?"

I looked away from Pascal toward the bar. I hated when he was right. He knew me too well, and I hated that too. "I'm not running from Kyle." Not exactly.

"Okay, then what?" He crossed his ankle to his opposite knee. He seemed so relaxed, yet I was anything but, and the pills the doctor had given me for anxiety were barely helping.

"Why did you have me followed?" I asked. "Seems like a stupid waste of your money."

If I hadn't been watching for it, I would have missed the way Pascal moved his jaw back and forth, an attempt to loosen his mounting anxiety. He let his foot fall to the floor in front of him and leaned in toward the table again. "I have the money. And you've been away from the country for a while. Can't it just be because I was concerned?"

tracked

"No. You wouldn't have gone to that trouble without a good reason."

"*You* are a good reason."

"Cut the bull, Pascal. Stop acting like I don't know that something sketchy is happening here in La Fortuna. And I don't think it has anything to do with these fake kidnappings and the threat to close Puro Cielo."

Pascal took in a breath. The gold specks in his hazel eyes seemed to flare. "You're right. These kidnappings, at least the ones prior to the attempts on your mother and you, may have been nothing more than scare tactics. Someone didn't want you back in La Fortuna."

"*Who* didn't want me back here?"

Pascal broke eye contact. Before I could demand more information, Ricca returned to take our orders. I didn't even look down at the menu.

"Do you trust me?" Pascal raised a brow while holding the closed menu.

Did I trust Pascal? "With my life," I whispered, and Pascal narrowed his gaze at me. I didn't trust him not to lie to me, and he was definitely bad about withholding information and dropping off the face of the earth for a year. But he would never hurt me. And he could definitely order a stupid dinner.

Without looking at the waitress, he rattled off a list of food items in Spanish, took my menu from me, and dismissed Ricca. "You don't play fair, Amagita."

"I'm not playing games, Pascal. Why did you have me followed?"

He rubbed his fingers across his lips before folding his hands on the table between us. "I've been doing my own... shall we say... investigative work."

"Into what? Your father's murder?"

"No. Not exactly."

"Then what?"

"Not what. Who." Pascal traced the condensation streaming down his water glass. When he looked at me again, worry had edged out all other emotions from his expression. "My new boss and his son."

"Felipe and his father?"

He nodded. "Felipe and Leonardo Rojas. Dr. Leonardo Rojas."

"Doctor?"

Pascal nodded. "Some sort of molecular biologist."

"Then what is he doing here?"

"Career change?" Pascal asked, but I could tell he didn't actually believe it.

A chill skipped across the back of my neck as I remembered how familiar Felipe had looked to me that day in town, when we first met. Only it wasn't him. It was his eyes. "Eva said they were from Venezuela?"

"*Sí*, yet I've found very little information about them on the internet other than Dr. Rojas's previous profession. And my friend at the police department says the same thing, but adds that they've been extremely charitable within our community and with the schools."

"And they came to La Fortuna for the first time last summer?"

Pascal nodded.

tracked

"What does this have to do with having me followed?"

"I overheard a conversation Leo was having the day after you arrived. I don't know who he was talking to or what he was talking about, but he mentioned your name." Pascal reached across the table and grabbed my hand. "Amagita, I don't think I've gotten a good night of sleep since. Please don't fight Daniel and me about going home on Friday."

I pulled my hand from him. "You've told me nothing. What am I even running from if I get on a plane for the States? What could this stranger from Venezuela possibly want with me unless you think he had something to do with Nicholas?" Or could Leonardo Rojas have something to do with the people that Kyle and his friend were looking for? "Besides, if they're interested in me, what's to stop them from finding me in California?"

"I don't know," Pascal breathed. "But I promise I'm going to find out. I've got people working on it. I just need you to go back home. You'll at least be a little safer there. I promise to call you when I've figured out what's happening."

"I can't."

"You can't what?"

"I can't go back to California. I have nothing to return to."

"What do you mean? Of course you do."

"No, I don't, Pascal. How would you know anyway? Until this past week, you've had zero contact with me in a year. You have no idea what's going on in my life."

"Please enlighten me then." Though his tone was sarcastic, I could sense his frustration at not having control of this situation, or of me. "I'm sorry. Why do you think you need to be here in Costa Rica?"

"Puro Cielo is the only home I have left. It's my family's passion." I took a large drink of water, hoping to relieve my dry mouth. "And I'm not returning to Stanford. I lost my scholarships."

"What? Daniel didn't tell me this."

"He doesn't know. When you called me, I had just received the news that I couldn't return to school. That's why I came. Mom and Dad sold our California house, and I no longer have a school to attend. I never got the chance to even tell my parents."

"And now we're pushing you away from here."

"This is the only place I have left. It's always been my home away from home. Now it's my *only* home."

"We'll figure something out. I'll help you."

"No. *We* won't. I don't want that kind of help from you."

"Then what *do* you want from me? You weren't all that happy to see me when you got here."

"I wasn't ready. But now I am."

"Ready for what?"

"I want you to help me remember."

The color drained from Pascal's face. He lifted his glass, but it was already empty. "Amagita," he whispered. "I..."

"Well, isn't this cozy?"

Pascal and I jumped and looked up at Felipe, who had sidled up to our table without me noticing. His grin revealed perfectly straight and unnaturally bleached teeth.

"How are you doing, Raven? I hope the unfortunate incident the other night didn't scare you too badly."

"Not much rattles me," I said. I barely even looked up at Felipe. The smell of his cologne was asphyxiating.

tracked

"Really." He turned to Pascal, who looked like he might explode. "Quite the lady of strength you've got there."

My fingers curled against the black tablecloth. I tucked them into my palm, forming a tight fist.

Pascal shot me a look of warning. "She sure is. What can I do for you, Felipe?"

"Well, one of the back pools is getting strange pH readings, and I need you to look into it."

"I'll get right on that." Pascal's voice was all business, hiding any sign of animosity he had for the boss's son—and any apprehension he might have felt after my request.

"Raven, I hope you're going to stay and enjoy the springs tonight." Felipe's eyes roamed from my face to my chest to my legs under the table, and he made no attempt to hide it. Pascal shifted nervously. I wished I could calm him.

"The group from the camp should be here soon," I said. "So, yes, I plan to." But I would be on high alert tonight with Felipe roaming the facility.

"Well, I'll let you enjoy your dinner." He turned back to Pascal, and his expression turned serious. "Don't forget to check out that problem."

When Felipe was gone, I let out a breath. "What was that about?"

"Power trip." Pascal grabbed my hand again. "Listen to me. Do not get caught alone with him, okay?"

I shook my head. "I won't."

Our dinner arrived: hummus and pita bread, fish tacos, and the signature black beans Costa Rica was known for. The atmosphere around the bar shifted into a more festive atmosphere despite the tension growing between Pascal and me over a night we'd avoided for so long. A bachelorette party was getting rowdy in one corner, and in another section, a group of tourists was slamming shots.

"Why do you want to remember now?" Pascal didn't even look at me as he spoke.

Neither of us touched the food in front of us.

How did I tell him that I had this thing in my skull—that someone could control my mind and my actions with the flip of a switch? Or that I could be killed just as easily?

I knew that this tracker had to have been placed in my head the night of the murder—the night I had no memories of.

"Because remembering is the only way I'll take back control of my life."

~~~~~

The rest of dinner was filled with forced light conversation while a tension hung between us like a dark storm cloud. When at last Pascal was called away to deal with some urgent problem, I escaped to relax in the hot springs.

I kicked off my flip-flops and slipped out of my dress beside my two favorite pools at Navos. Steam rose from the water as I walked down the steps and immersed myself in the soothing heat of one of the warmer hot springs. Fortunately, because this was one of the smaller, more secluded pools, it wasn't crowded.

I swam over to the bench below a waterfall and let the water pound into the tight muscles in my shoulders. As the water hit a knot in my neck, I closed my eyes tight and thought about the conversation I'd had with Pascal. Before I'd arrived in Costa Rica, he had been hell-bent on me remembering the night of

tracked

Nicholas's murder. And now? He insisted on more time to think about it.

I got it. I did. He was worried about who Felipe and Leonardo Rojas really were and what they were doing in La Fortuna, and about the strange kidnappings.

And I was worried about the tracker lodged in my brain. I still didn't know why I wasn't in a constant state of panic over everything I had learned in the last forty-eight hours. As the water poured over me, I found just as much therapy in the gushing sound of the water as I did the massaging affects of the force.

"I don't know where Raven is. She's enjoying the hot springs, I suppose."

My eyes flew open at the sound of Pascal's voice. It was as if he were standing right next to me in a quiet room, not under a roaring cascade.

"When was the last time you saw her?" Kyle asked.

I looked around. The only other people in the pool were two separate couples at either end. And no one stood by the lounge chairs where I had left my things. Not to mention, I shouldn't have been able to hear anything while beneath the waterfall.

Raven.

This time a voice that sounded vaguely familiar was inside my head. My pulse spiked. I could still hear Pascal and Kyle arguing, but suddenly Jonas's voice was inside my head over top of the arguing.

It's Jonas, Raven. Can you hear me? He sounded like he was playing with a two-way radio out in the middle of the sea, searching for the right channel.

I slid my hand around to the back of my neck and massaged the base of my skull. Water splashed off my hand and neck and ran down the front of my body in an all-consuming sort of way, a sensation that normally relaxed me. *Jonas? As in Lexi's friend?*

Had I just spoken with my mind?

That's right. "Guys, shhh. I've got her."

"What do you mean you've got her?" Lexi asked.

Raven, are you okay? Jonas again.

I'm fine. Relatively speaking. How is it that I can hear you?

Because I have a stronger ability to mindspeak than the rest of these losers. And I can read people's thoughts.

No, I mean, where are you? I can hear Kyle and Pascal arguing, and you and Lexi speaking.

What?

"What's wrong? What is she saying?" Lexi asked.

"She says she can hear us talking." This time when Jonas spoke, his voice sounded strained, hesitant, like he was trying to solve a riddle by speaking in a slow monotone.

"Where is she? I don't see her. Did you tell Kyle yet?" Lexi asked.

"I did. He's on his way." Jack's voice.

Raven, where exactly are you in relation to the front entrance? Jonas asked.

Almost as far away as you can get. And I'm underneath a waterfall.

"Well, whaddaya know!" It almost sounded like Jonas was laughing.

"What?" Lexi asked.

"She's got bionic hearing," Jonas answered, practically laughing as he said 'bionic hearing' like it was some joke.

"What do you mean? What's she saying?"

tracked

"Stop pulling on me, Lexi. She needs help, and I can't help her with you yanking my arm." I couldn't help but think that Jonas and Lexi acted like a brother and sister, fights and all. "Find Kyle and get him away from Pascal. Raven's not going to want any of her normal friends to see her after the first time she's used a tracker. I'm not sure I want to see this. I'm going to go in search of her."

My heart beat so fast, I was sure it would explode beneath the thundering waterfall. *I shouldn't be able to hear your conversations, should I? What does this mean?*

I was scared to move. What if moving caused the kind of pain that Lexi had inflicted earlier when she said she'd nudged my tracker? I had no idea what was happening. And now other conversations were starting to buzz inside my head. The couple at the end of the pool were talking about their ziplining adventure from earlier that day. The other couple was talking about... sex... and in a way that I could never unhear.

I swam away from the waterfall. The water's temperature felt warmer than it had a few minutes ago. I started breathing harder, like I'd been swimming laps. And though I was in water, I was sweating.

My head spun. The wall in front of me came in and out of focus. As I reached my hand for it, I misjudged the distance and my hand slapped back into the water.

Raven, calm down. It's going to be okay.

It's too hot. I've got to move to a cooler pool.

I found my footing on the bottom of the pool and placed a hand on the wall in front of me. I drilled the heel of my other palm into my chest and massaged where panic was setting in.

I'm coming to you, but you're going to have to help me.

"Jonas, where is she?" Kyle asked.

Kyle? Using both hands, I lifted myself up and climbed over the small ledge that separated the warmer pool from the cooler one. I immediately felt relief as I lowered myself into cooler water.

"She can hear you speak. Keep talking."

"Raven, which pool are you in? I'm in front of the main offices. They're to my left, and the in-pool bar is on my right."

Keep walking. Pass the large pool on the right. The words in my head were coming out more slowly than they had been. *There's a... small walkway... with foliage and flowers.*

"Keep walking. There. Go that way." Jonas was directing someone. Kyle, maybe.

I'm so tired. I leaned my head back against the side of the hot spring. A couple of teenagers jumped in the pool beside me and swam to the other side. My eyes closed briefly. So many conversations were buzzing in my ears now—a low, constant roar of noise that was almost soothing when I didn't try to pick out individual exchanges or voices. *I can't keep my eyes open...*

Raven? Stay awake. We're almost there. To someone else: "She's falling asleep."

Kyle's voice again. "Raven, do not *go to sleep*. Do you hear me? Is she in a pool right now?"

I'm trying, I said, but I...

THIRTY-TWO

Kyle

"Where is she? I don't see her!"

Steam rose from the pool in front of us like a thick fog. I raced around the edge, almost falling in twice.

"This must be where she started," Jonas said. "She was under a waterfall in a warmer pool but got overheated and moved to a cooler one."

"There!" I shouted, darting to the next pool.

Raven was lying on the bottom of the pool, lifeless.

I jumped in, not even bothering to remove my shoes. Raven's body was limp as I gathered her in my arms. When I stood, she immediately began coughing against my chest. With Jonas's help, I lay her on the edge of the pool on her side. She coughed up water and took in a labored breath.

A member of the hot springs' staff approached. "Everything okay?"

I traded glances with Jonas. "Yeah, she just got a little overheated."

The staff member lifted a two-way radio from his belt. "I've got a female, teenager, overheated by number nine."

Jonas stood in front of the staff member. "Look, she's fine. No need to call in reinforcements."

"I'm sorry, sir, but it's policy."

Jonas zeroed in on the poor guy in front of him, and I knew the fellow didn't have a chance against Jonas's mind tricks. "You will call whoever that was back and tell them it was a false alarm. Then you will walk away and forget you saw us."

The entranced employee raised his radio to his mouth. "Uh... sorry, false alarm. Everything's fine here." Then he turned and continued his rounds of the pools.

We returned our attention to a barely conscious Raven. "What happened?" I asked.

"Dude..." Jonas said. "I tapped into her brain. She *heard* me. We conversed. And..." He shook his head and laughed.

"What?" I said. "Her tracker is allowing her to talk with you?"

Raven scrunched up her face, then slipped back into an unconscious state. But she was breathing.

"Yes, but that's not all." Jonas sat on the edge of a nearby lounge chair. "She's got some sort of hypersensitive hearing. She said she could hear you and Pascal at the same time she was hearing Lexi and me talk out loud. Plus I was mindspeaking... inside her head."

I held up a hand. "I know what mindspeaking is. So you're saying..."

"Her tracker has been activated. And my guess? She just passed out because she was overwhelmed by a deluge of senses when all of these voices came at her at once."

I stared down at an unconscious Raven. Strands of her black hair stuck to her face. Her almost unnaturally dark eyelashes fanned at the edges of her closed eyes. She was so beautiful and brave. I didn't want this life for her.

tracked

"Kyle, as much as I'm enjoying seeing your girlfriend lying here in a bikini, we've got to move her before someone else discovers us."

I angled my head at him in warning. He held his hand up with a smirk. He was right, though. We had to move her. I was either going to have to carry her out of here, or I'd have to control her mind again.

"Jack and Lexi are near Daniel," Jonas said. "What should I have them tell him?"

"Tell him Raven has a headache and we're taking her back to camp." With Raven's history, he'd believe that.

When I slipped into Raven's mind, she was so peaceful I hated to disturb her slumber. But I had no choice.

Raven, I mindspoke.

Her eyes fluttered open. "Hi," she said. A smile stretched across her face before realization darkened her features. "What happened?"

"You're unconscious. I've got control of you."

She narrowed her gaze. "Voices. They were all around me."

I brushed my fingers along her cheek, pushing the wet strands of hair off her face. "I know. We'll talk about it later. Right now I need you to stand and lead us to where your things are. If anyone stops us, just say you have a headache and you're going back to camp to turn in early."

"Okay," she said. She was completely within my control. I had no idea how long it would last or what obstacles her newly activated tracker might add to the experience.

I ordered her to show me where she'd left her clothes. I needed her to cover her bikini and as much of her skin as possible before either Jonas's eyes popped out of his head or I slammed a fist into his jaw.

We'd nearly made it to the front entrance when Raven stopped so suddenly that I plowed into her. Jonas was in the lead and didn't notice; he continued forward and joined Lexi and Jack beside the exit.

"Why did you stop?" I asked.

Raven's face was angled toward the restaurant.

"Who are you looking at? Raven, what is it?"

"Shh. I'm listening. They're talking about me."

"Who is?" I looked back toward the restaurant. It was past the prime dinner hours. A group of men in suits sat around a large table in the center of the restaurant, drinking and smoking cigars. "Those guys? What are they saying?"

Raven walked closer to the restaurant. I was afraid that if she got much closer, she'd draw attention to herself.

Raven, you will stop and listen to me. We are leaving. I want you to turn and walk toward the exit. Toward Lexi.

She refused my commands, and I could feel my control slipping slowly away.

I glanced frantically toward the others. If I lost control of Raven, I would go blind, and I would have no one there to help me. Not to mention, Raven would collapse.

Kyle, do you see the gentleman at the far end of the table, facing us? Raven was now mindspeaking back to me.

Yeah. What about him? I moved closer to her.

I think that was my doctor last summer. Dr. Porter, I think?

I narrowed my eyes. *Crap. We have to get out of here.* But I didn't act quickly enough.

tracked

Jonas sidled up beside Raven at the same time that his DNA donor lifted his head and spotted us. Dr. Porter started to rise, but hesitated when a man with his back to us at the opposite end of the long table turned. I immediately recognized him as an older version of Felipe.

"It's him," Raven said, staring directly at Felipe's father. "That's the man..."

Before I could stop it, Raven collapsed, and my world went black. "Jonas, I'm blind. We have to get out of here, and fast."

"I'm on it," Jonas said.

Though I couldn't see her, Lexi was beside me. "I'll redirect the men's attention long enough for us to get out of here."

"Well, I guess everyone knows we're here now," Jack said. "I've got Kyle."

"Raven?" I asked.

"I've got her," Jonas said. "And let me tell you, if I wasn't already infatuated with a certain ginger..."

"Jonas, I'm only going to warn you this one last time. Next time you make a quip about my girl—"

"Oh, are you ready to own that?"

"Are you two finished?" Jack asked. "We're starting to attract attention."

With that, Jack led me out the front entrance. Thankfully, Jonas had rented a car when he arrived in San Jose. With Jack behind the wheel, we made a grand exit—from whatever *that* was.

THIRTY-THREE

Raven

His eyes appeared from behind a tree on the path ahead. I couldn't make out his body, or even his head, but his eyes glowed, staring straight at me. When I turned and tried to run, arms grabbed me, and again, I stared into those familiar eyes.

And heard familiar voices.

I heard my name over and over. From Pascal. From Kyle. From Daniel. From Dr. Jeremy Porter. From...

From the man with familiar eyes.

I had to run. I had to get away, but I couldn't. Arms encircled me and lifted. I kicked my legs and tried to wriggle free.

When I finally gave up and settled into the hold of a man behind me, I saw another figure.

Nicholas Centeno stared up at me with eyes of glass. His head was cocked to the side, awkward and unnatural against the large tree trunk. I wanted to help him.

I took a step forward, toward Nicholas, but cool fingers encircled my forearm and pulled gently. "You can't help him. He's gone."

I turned slowly. "Kyle. You're here." I smiled, but felt immediately shy.

He lifted a hand and traced the line of my hair all the way to the spot just above my heart. He flattened his hand on my chest so that his fingers lightly grazed my collarbone. "I'm here." He looked around while letting his hand drift around my body, grazing my arm, to my back. "Where is *here*?" he asked.

"You're inside my nightmare."

Eyes the color of glossy chestnut, dark and mysterious, found mine. "This isn't a nightmare. Look around again."

Kyle turned my body with one hand while letting his other hand slide along my back around to my stomach. His thumb and forefinger reached just shy of my breasts. I could feel the warmth of his palm through the thin fabric of my white nightgown. My stomach tightened in response to his touch.

Everywhere I looked, candles flickered: along the forest bed, in candelabras nestled in the trees, even in midair. Kyle pulled me closer, my back against his chest, and his arms enveloped me in a shield of comfort and security.

"This is not my nightmare," I whispered. "But it's not real."

"I'm real. You're real. The memory of this will be real."

My body stiffened at his words—and at the way the warmth of his breath caressed my skin.

He turned me to face him again, and while he let the back of his hand brush against my bare arm, he said, "This is anything you want it to be. Even though we're technically inside our own heads, we don't have to do anything you don't want to do. This is not a fantasy—a dream to be forgotten when you wake." He touched a finger to my chin and leaned his head down, running his nose along the set of my jaw and breathing in my scent. He let his lips brush against mine. "What we do inside our thoughts will live as memories in our minds."

tracked

"You've done this before," I said—and immediately regretted it when sadness touched his eyes. "I'm sorry."

He pressed a finger to my lips. "Don't be sorry. Yes, I shared moments with Dani, but you and she are different people. A part of me died when she died, but..." He took in a deep breath before continuing. "An even larger part of me awakened when I met you."

I draped an arm around his neck and urged him closer. I buried my face into the crook of his neck. His scent intoxicated me in this already dreamy state, and my legs weakened as his hand roamed the curve of my waist.

As my mind moved further and further away from the nightmare that was Nicholas's murder, I settled into a dream I hoped to never wake from.

THIRTY-FOUR

Kyle

Raven deserved more than my fantasies being lived out inside our dreams. What I had told her—that what we did inside these dreams was real, and that we would have lasting memories of it—was all true. But I didn't want the first time we did anything to be an event that didn't actually take place physically.

And I wanted her physically—and emotionally, and however else I could have her. But I would wait until she was fully ready and the timing was right. Or at least until the timing was better.

For now, I would enjoy this moment for however long we could make it last.

We lay on a large quilt in the middle of the forest. The candlelight glimmered on her exposed skin, casting a golden glow across her face and arms. The sparkle in her eye as she licked her lips about did me in.

Lying on my side facing her, I let my hand skim her rib cage and settle into the curve of her waist. "You're beautiful."

Her eyes darted over my right shoulder when I spoke. She looked anywhere but at me.

"Don't shy away," I said.

Her eyes found mine again, and she nibbled at her bottom lip.

"I'm sorry I didn't tell you about Dani," I said. "But this is a very different situation from the one she was in, and I'm not going to let anything happen to you." At least, I would fight like hell to keep her safe.

"I believe you."

"When we wake up, we're going to have to face a lot of hard realities that you're not able to remember inside this dream." Small lines formed between her eyes, and I attempted to erase them with my finger. I smiled. "Stop thinking so hard. It won't work." I pointed to my temple. "I can control where your mind goes while you're sleeping, remember?"

She returned my smile. "That could come in handy."

"If you want, I can even help you remember what happened that night." I didn't want to, but we might not have a choice.

She sucked in a heavy breath. "When I came back here, I had no intention of remembering. But now I feel like a part of me is missing. And..." She glanced down to where she was drawing figure eights on my chest.

"And what?"

"I owe it to Pascal. And to Lucia and Miguel. They need closure—to lay Nicholas to rest once and for all."

"Okay. Then I'll help you. But for now... sleep."

I leaned in and kissed her softly, then pulled her closer. She rolled over in my arms and burrowed her back into my chest. I released her mind into a peaceful sleep, and we lay there in the bottom bunk of her cabin until I drifted off into darkness.

~~~~~

I woke to the strangest of whimpers.

tracked

It was still dark, and I was alone in the bed. My eyes adjusted slowly to very little light. I could barely make out the outline of a body on the floor next to me, rolled into a tight ball.

"Raven?" I crawled out of bed onto my knees beside her. I hovered my hands over her body, scared to touch her for fear that she was in pain and I would make it worse. She was still dressed in a thin white gown. I gently grazed her arm. It was clammy and cool.

She flinched. Her head snapped up, and she scrambled into my lap like a small child might. "Make the voices stop," she cried. Tears ran down her face. "I can't take them anymore." Her arm snaked around my neck and held tight. Her face burrowed into my chest.

I rocked her back and forth while I searched my mind for ideas. "Shh. It's going to be okay," I reassured her, but it fell flat, because I hadn't a clue how to help her. Yet I knew who might. "Raven, I want you to climb into bed. I'll be right back."

"Where are you going?"

"Not far. I'm just going next door to get Lexi. I think she can help."

Raven did as I instructed. She looked like a little girl, curled up with her hands over her ears, though I was fairly certain that covering her ears did nothing to shut out the noise.

I hurried outside. The sky was a dark shade of azure, and birds sang out as the first signs of light appeared on the horizon. I used my key to let myself into my cabin. Jack and Jonas had taken the two top bunks.

Lexi rose to her elbows on the bottom bunk when she heard me enter. "What's wrong?"

"I need you to come with me."

She didn't ask questions; she just grabbed Jack's button-down shirt, put it over her tank and pajama shorts, and followed me back to Raven's cabin.

I shut the door behind us. Lexi looked at Raven, who cried softly, and then back at me. "How long has she been like this?"

"I don't know." My voice sounded panicked even to me. "I woke up to her like this."

Lexi knelt beside Raven. "Raven, honey, can you hear me?"

Raven's head popped up. Her eyes shot to Lexi's, then to mine, and then she seemed to retreat into herself. She swung her legs around to the edge of the bed and let her feet touch the floor. She just stared at her feet while she wiggled her toes.

Lexi turned and eyed me. I could only shrug.

I stepped closer and knelt beside Lexi. "Raven, tell us how to—"

"They've stopped. The voices. They're not there." Raven searched both Lexi's face and my own, as if she hoped we would tell her that the voices were gone forever. I think we all knew the likelihood of that. Then she stopped and cocked her head.

"Wait. It's Daniel. He's talking to Eva. What time is it?"

"Five thirty," I said.

"She's coming down to make breakfast."

"Daniel and Eva live in the house at the top of the hill?" Lexi asked.

"Yes," Raven answered. "Eva's mad at Daniel. Some people woke them up this morning with bad news. They were fighting. And I think it was about me. At least, that's what woke me up. I heard my name, and then these male voices were just arguing, and it was too much all at once."

tracked

"Last night, when you first heard voices in your head... Was Jonas the first one you heard?" Lexi asked.

"No." Raven looked toward me. "I heard Kyle ask Pascal where I was. And then I could hear Jonas—both inside my head, and when he was talking to you." She nodded at Lexi.

"Well, obviously your tracker has been activated. And you've been given some supernatural hearing ability. So far, it sounds like hearing your name triggered a deluge of voices both times. And this morning the haze of sleepiness probably made it hard for you to concentrate and make out the conversation."

Raven thought about that, then nodded.

"What we have to do is find a way to tame the voices so that you hear only the ones you wish to."

"I don't want to hear any of them."

Lexi tilted her head to the side. "We could use this ability to our advantage."

"You want me to eavesdrop on people's conversations?" Raven gnawed on her bottom lip.

"It might help us find the lab where your tracker is being controlled. We can't disable the function of your tracker unless we find the server where it's being programmed."

Lexi and I traded glances. I didn't like bringing Raven into this world; this should have simply been a summer fling. However—and I had to continuously remind myself of this fact—I wasn't the one who had brought her into this world. I wasn't even around when that tracker was placed in her head. It was *that* person who had brought her into my world.

And now that she was here, I wasn't sure I could let her go.

There was a knock at the door. Lexi and I both flinched.

"It's Jonas and Jack," Raven whispered.

I went to the door and threw it open. Jonas and Jack stood in the doorway. I swung around to face Raven. "How did you know that?"

Raven looked just as surprised by her knowledge as Lexi and I were. She seemed to consider the question before replying. "I knew Jack and Jonas were at the door the same way I know that Briana is in Portland, Oregon, Georgia's hiking the Grand Canyon, and Fred is in Lexington, Kentucky."

THIRTY-FIVE

Raven

I stood and faced the group of human clones gathered in my cabin. "Who are those people? How did I know all that?"

Jack grabbed Lexi's hand and pulled her closer to him. Kyle stuffed his hands in the front pockets of his jeans, staring at the floor in front of him.

Jonas stepped forward; his eyes narrowed in on mine as he pulled a phone from his pocket and tapped it a few times. He raised the phone to his ear. "I know, and I'm sorry... Yes, it *is* early... Bree, calm down. Listen to me... You're right, I have *some* nerve..." Jonas ran a hand through his dark hair and blew out a sigh. This Bree person was obviously crazy-angry. "And I want to talk about all that. I do. Just not now. We have a situation... I'm with Kyle, Jack, and Lexi. We need to know your location."

He pulled the phone away and turned to the rest of us. "She's in Portland."

"She hang up on you?" Lexi asked.

Jonas offered her a blank stare, suggesting he wasn't getting into it.

Kyle pulled his hands back out of his pocket and seemed to wake up from his deep thoughts. "Is it possible that Raven's tracker is programmed to know where we're located?"

"Who? As in the seven original clones?" Jack asked.

They all traded glances. I barely understood what was happening. All I knew was that I was hearing bits and pieces of conversations, some louder than others, and they were growing in number as it got later in the morning. And on top of the voices, I was also seeing flashes of people I'd never met and a clear vision of where they were in the world. Somehow, I just *knew*—almost to the exact latitude and longitude.

Jack, Lexi, Jonas, and Kyle began speaking in low voices. It was a conversation about me, of course, but not once did they include me in the discussion. I let my focus wander. And as their voices grew quieter, others, in my mind, strengthened.

"They know." Two words from Daniel stood out among other morning conversations I was overhearing.

"I warned you that if you allowed her to come back to La Fortuna, they'd find her and come after her. I told you I could only keep her safe for so long. The information she holds is too valuable." The voice sounded very familiar, but I couldn't place it.

I had no idea if I was listening to a phone conversation or what. I knew where the clones were, but I didn't know where Daniel was. I could only assume he was still in his house.

"What do I do now?" Daniel asked.

"There's nothing you can do. IIA agents are coming for her. I only came to warn you. If you want the guests of your camp to remain safe, you'll hand her over."

"Hand her over? Over my dead body."

tracked

"Daniel, they don't care about you. They don't even care that you lied to them. But if you get in their way, they will kill you." There was a brief silence, and in that silence I feared for Daniel and Eva. They'd been like parents to me—and now Daniel was willing to die for me. "What did you expect? As soon as they discovered her in La Fortuna, you knew they would activate the tracker stored in her brain. They've always known where she was. But now she's attracted the attention of the others that these people are after."

I jerked my head toward Kyle. The voice was talking about Kyle and his friends. Of course the doctors who were creating these supernatural powers would want the original cloned humans; these were the only ones whose powers weren't dependent upon the help of the trackers. And I—or my tracker—apparently held information about the whereabouts of all of them.

I crossed the room slowly and began pulling on a pair of pants under my gown. I slipped into the restroom to finish dressing. I had to get away from here before innocent people died because of me. I couldn't let Daniel sacrifice himself because I had refused to see the truth of that night last summer. If only I had faced the reality of who had killed Nicholas sooner, I might have remembered who'd put the tracker inside my skull. I might never have returned here.

When I exited the bathroom, Kyle was waiting for me. He was dressed in long pants and a T-shirt. "What's going on, Raven?"

"Nothing. Why?" I grabbed my backpack from the floor and began filling it with a few necessary items, including a change of clothes. "Where'd everybody go?" I kept my voice calm, pretending it was any other morning.

"They went next door. Where are you going?"

I lifted my head. "What do you mean? It's almost time for breakfast."

He stepped closer, forcing me to stand and face him. "I might not be able to read your mind, but Jonas can. You can't face this alone. We are here to help you."

My back stiffened, and I suddenly couldn't breathe. "What am I supposed to do? They're coming for me, Kyle. You didn't ask for this. I won't be the reason you and our friends are captured, or whatever it is these people have planned."

"You ever think you're in this mess *because* of me?" he asked.

"No. You didn't even know me when someone began tracking me. I don't know if I just happened to be in the wrong place at the wrong time, but I know I can't just sit back and hope for the best any longer."

My door opened. "Ready?" Jonas had a backpack slung over his shoulder, and Jack was tucking a gun into the back of his pants.

I suddenly realized I had no idea what I was involved in.

"Raven," Kyle said, "it's taken the four of us a while to learn to work together and figure out how to handle the doctors and IIA agents who are behind these experiments. It would help us a lot if you would trust us and not try to act on your own, no matter what happens."

I examined each of their faces. All eyes were on me. I had known that my mind was messed up; I had realized that strange things had occurred soon after I'd run from Costa Rica last summer. But running from these problems had only landed me smack dab in the middle of the situation I was in now.

tracked

"Okay," I said finally.

As I said the word, the screeching of tires rang out from the main road that ran above the camp. Immediately I heard a voice from that direction. *"She's still here. Let's go in slowly. The element of surprise is on our side. Maybe, as her doctor, I can get her to leave with me under the pretense of needing an examination."*

"My doctor is here," I said. "I don't think they know I can hear their conversations."

"What do you mean? Who's your doctor?" Kyle asked.

"I found records in Daniel's house the other day. A man named Dr. Jeremy Porter was my doctor in the hospital last summer. Now that I think about it, Daniel told me that Dr. Porter also referred me to my doctors in California."

"Well, that explains how she was hospitalized and no one discovered that she had a piece of metal lodged in her brain," Jonas said. "But now I'm even more surprised that Raven is still alive."

"*Jonas*," Kyle warned.

"It's okay," I said.

"We don't have time for this," Lexi warned. "There are very few ways to exit this camp without going out the main gate. And we don't have Briana to alter our appearances. So what's the plan?"

"There *is* another way, but we'll have to get wet," I said. Kyle didn't look excited about this, but he nodded. I reached out and squeezed both of his hands while we locked eyes. "This is where you're going to have to trust *me*." When Kyle let go of my hands, I pulled out my phone and sent a text message to Pascal.

"Where is she, Daniel?" Dr. Porter asked. *"I have ten IIA agents at the top of the drive ready to search your entire camp."*

"There are ten agents here," I said.

"Then we better hurry." Jack pulled on the straps of his pack. "I, for one, have no intention of getting caught in their web again."

~~~~~

I led the way from my cabin to the river. We had to pass by several of the camp guests who were meditating near my favorite spot.

"Someone was looking for you," one of the guests said. He craned his neck as if the person looking for me had just left. "Hey, she's right here!" he yelled.

"Shh. Don't yell."

The guest looked at me funny.

"This is a place of quiet and solitude." I gestured toward the two women beside him sitting in lotus positions with their eyes closed. "I'm on my way up to breakfast. I'll see whoever was looking for me there."

He seemed to buy it.

But as I glanced up the hill toward the pavilion, I saw him: a man with dark hair and dark eyes. Even from this distance I recognized the doctor—and I could see who this man resembled.

I turned to Jonas.

He shrugged. "We told you we were cloned humans. Meet my clone daddy."

"Stop!" Dr. Porter shouted. He turned and called behind him. "They're down here!"

"Let's go." I turned and pointed to the path.

tracked

We sprinted along the river. When we reached the large rock where Kyle and I had swum days before—which now seemed like a lifetime ago—I pointed at the rope that hung low against a shallow, rocky area. "Grab the rope and try to stay on your feet as you cross the rocks," I said. "It'll be slippery. If you fall, the rapids will carry you down the river. If you make it across the river, follow the path off to the right until you run into the road."

Jack grabbed the rope first; Lexi followed close behind.

"You next," Kyle said.

I didn't argue. I was halfway across the river when a shot rang out. I instinctively ducked.

"They won't shoot us," Jonas said.

"How the hell do you know that?" Why even fire if they didn't mean to kill us? If they thought I was getting close to knowing who murdered Nicholas, the murderer would no doubt be happy to shut me up with a bullet.

Jack and Lexi were safely on the riverbank and waiting for us when a second shot rang out and hit a tree trunk directly to Lexi's right. She yelped, and she and Jack immediately took cover in the forest.

"Asshole, don't hit them!" Dr. Porter screamed at someone.

"I have my orders to shoot anyone other than the black-haired female," one of the agents said.

Another shot rang out, and this time it hit the rope directly between Kyle and Jonas. The tension in the rope changed, and I lost my footing. I landed in the rushing water, knocking my hip and left arm against a rock, and then I slipped into the deeper rapids and was swept down the river.

Kyle and Jonas were both thrown into the rapids after me.

Jack and Lexi yelled something about catching up with us farther down the river. Despite being wet, we realized we were getting away much faster this way.

Kyle, the strongest swimmer, quickly made his way across the rapids to shore. Jonas made it to the riverbank next. I kicked and pushed at the water with my arms, but the rapids were carrying me away at a fast clip, and I was struggling to keep a hold on my backpack.

"Swim, Raven! Kick like hell!"

I did, and I reached out for a low-hanging tree branch, but I missed and continued downstream.

Kyle and Jack must have sprinted ahead of me, because next thing I knew, Kyle was there, swinging out into the river while hanging on to Jack's arm. He stretched his body out as far as he could and locked his arm with mine. He snatched me up out of the water, embracing me briefly.

When we were all safely on the riverbank, he cupped the sides of my face. "You okay? You didn't get hit, did you?" He surveyed the length of my body, looking for injuries.

"No." But I was going to have a nice bruise on my hip. And my arm throbbed.

"Jack, Lex," Jonas called. "I'm going to need a little help here." Jonas was making his way down the riverbank toward us. Blood streamed down his arm and dripped from his fingers. His face had turned a ghostly shade of white. I could just make out the jagged point of a bone emerging from the skin of his forearm.

Lexi ran to Jonas's side. "How did you manage—"

"I hit a rock when I fell."

tracked

Jack held Jonas's arm up in front of him. "This is going to hurt you way more than it's going to hurt me." Jack smiled, and Lexi nudged him.

"Cut it out," she said.

Something told me that though Jonas was probably a big softie on the inside, he got as good as he dished out.

While Jack placed both of his hands over Jonas's injury, Lexi stared intently at Jack's temple.

"What's happening?" I asked.

"Jack can heal broken bones and other injuries," Kyle explained. "But the consequence of his healing ability is severe nausea, and sometimes he passes out, depending on the severity of the injury."

I stiffened and glanced back toward the camp. "If he passes out—"

"He won't. Lexi can lessen the side effects."

We could do nothing but watch as Lexi and Jack did their thing. A low growl reverberated from deep within Jonas's throat as the bone sticking out of his arm slowly disappeared into his skin. After several minutes, the only evidence of the compound fracture was the dried spider web of blood along his arm.

When Jack and Lexi stepped back, Jonas held his arm up in front of his face. He opened and closed his hand, twisting and turning it as he tested its mobility. "Great job, guys." He picked up his pack and secured it to his back again. "Let's go. They're going to be hot on our trail."

Was this a new normal for me? To watch this group of strangers perform unnatural healing and mind control acts with casual indifference?

Jonas slowed and looked over his shoulder at me. "You'll get used to our craziness." He was obviously reading my mind.

I pushed ahead of the four of them so that I could show them the way out of the forest. Hopefully, Pascal would be waiting like I had asked. Although I had no idea how I would explain any of this.

"Where exactly do we think we're going to run that we won't be followed?" I asked. "If they can trace my tracker, how can I hide?"

"So far, it seems that the cell connection and even the satellite service in Costa Rica is spotty, at best," Kyle said. "So, as long as we find a place to stay that has little to no cell service and where the tree canopy is thick..."

"There's no cell service in the Navos Resort Cottages surrounding Arenal Volcano," I said, "and it's close to where all of this began."

THIRTY-SIX

Kyle

"Tell me what they're discussing."

Raven had been talking with Pascal beside his car for thirty minutes—ever since he'd saved us from the pursuit of the IIA agents and brought us to one of his resort's cabins. Standing about thirty yards away, she'd looked back at me exactly seven times so far.

"Do you really want to know?" Jonas leaned back in a chair on the porch of one of Navos Resort's guest cottages with his feet propped up on a railing. He flicked a lighter repeatedly. He had been a smoker several months ago, back when he was tangled up in Sandra's web of deceit, but he had since quit.

"Yes."

"You know she can hear our conversation. She'll know what I'm telling you. Shouldn't you just wait for *her* to tell you?" Jonas wasn't usually one to care so much.

"Fine. Tell me this. What happened between you and Briana?"

He shrugged. "She wanted more than I could give her."

I laughed. "Seriously?"

"What? Why is that funny?"

"Briana is the only person I've ever met who could even come close to giving you exactly what you need and deserve."

A smirk twitched at the corners of Jonas's lips. "Possibly." The grin didn't last long before his lips tugged downward again. "But don't you ever wonder if we're just destined to watch each other get hurt over and over?"

I turned and eyed Raven's back. Her arms were in full motion as she discussed something with Pascal. "I thought exactly that same thing when I watched Lexi cry over Jack's lifeless body last year. I was already grieving for Dani, and I was pretty certain Jack was going to die and leave Lexi in shreds."

Jonas flicked the light again, cocking his head while staring at the flame. "I don't want Bree to hurt like that. Hell, I don't think I could ever watch her suffer. And we all just seem to find pain when we're together."

"So instead, you sent her away heartbroken and alone so that you could protect your own feelings? And how is that working out for you? Your heart all warm and fuzzy inside?"

He let the flame die and glared at me. "You're an asshole, you know that?"

"Takes one to know one." I looked at Raven again. "I just want to keep her safe." I raked my hands over my face. I was exhausted, and I knew that any second IIA agents could find us. "I feel helpless. Raven doesn't deserve this. And I don't understand how she just happened into a tracker at the base of her skull."

"None of us deserved to be born into the world Sandra created."

"Which is exactly why we should stick together, not alienate each other." I bumped his foot and almost knocked it off the railing, commanding his attention. "Thanks for coming to Costa Rica. I'd like to think that if Briana needed you, you'd—"

tracked

"Of course, I'd lay down my own life for that sexy hothead."

I smiled. "She is that. Always has been." I placed my hands on the porch railing, my knuckles turning white as I stared at Raven, willing her to turn and come back to me. "I need a plan. I can't tap into some phantom lab's computer system and disarm her tracker unless we figure out where this lab is. And we have zero leads."

"Well," Jonas said, "that's not entirely true."

"What do you mean?"

He nodded toward Raven. She was finally walking back toward us. Pascal still leaned against the car that had rescued us.

I straightened. Raven's eyes looked sad, tired. She glanced toward Jonas. "You heard everything?"

Jonas nodded. "It's the only option we have."

"Will someone tell me what's going on?" I grabbed Raven's hand and laced my fingers with hers.

She peered up at me with those blue eyes that I didn't think I would ever be able to say goodbye to. I hoped I wouldn't ever have to.

"I remembered part of what happened last night while I was unconscious. I saw Felipe's father, Leonardo Rojas. And it wasn't the first time I'd seen him—though at first I wasn't certain how that could be, since even Pascal didn't meet him until well after I had returned to California. But then I thought, since he was having drinks with Dr. Jeremy Porter, my doctor—"

"And my clone daddy," Jonas added.

"I think I must have seen Dr. Rojas the night of Nicholas's murder." Raven picked up my other hand and squeezed both of my hands tightly. "So Pascal is going to walk me through that night and see if we can jog some of my memories."

Holding Raven's hands, I searched her eyes. "Why are you so determined to remember that night? Why now?"

Raven turned her head away and blinked back tears welling in her eyes. "Daniel wasn't surprised at all when Dr. Porter showed up at the camp this morning with a team of IIA agents." She swallowed hard before she continued. "My life has fallen apart, and now I can't trust the one person who was supposed to be watching after me."

The pain on Raven's face about did me in. I wanted to scoop her up and run from this place, but I knew that as long as she had an active tracker in her brain, that wouldn't be possible. Not to mention, Pascal still leaned against a car a hundred feet away, obviously waiting on her.

"What can I do to help?" I smoothed a strand of hair behind her ear.

Jonas stood behind me. "I'll be inside Raven's head the entire time Pascal walks her through the details of that night. I'll see anything she remembers. I might even be able to help her see whatever her mind is blocking."

I thought about Raven's nightmares—and how they always included someone hiding behind a tree. I had never sensed danger from that person, but someone had obviously died that night, so I didn't dare discount the possibility that the murderer may have invaded her dreams in order to keep tabs on her memories. Pascal might be able to draw that person out.

"While we're doing that," Jonas said to me, "you, Jack, and Lexi are going exploring. I picked up on something from Pascal while he and Raven were talking. His father, Nicholas, ran the

tracked

resort at the time he was killed. He had rented out a portion of the maintenance shed at the base of the volcano behind the resort, and he agreed to allow the renters to perform some sort of overhaul on the structure."

"Why is this significant?" I asked.

"The renovation bothered Pascal because the barn was only a couple of years old, and its purpose was to store maintenance equipment. We're talking about a barn to house tractors and backhoes. Why would there be a need for an overhaul?"

"So... why has Pascal never checked it out?"

"He has. Nothing looks different or out of place, except one added door in the back of the barn. The door was locked when he checked, and it didn't seem worth bothering with. It's in a tight spot in the very back, so he assumes it's just some closet."

"So I'm supposed to go check out a closet in an old storage shed, and you're going to help my girl?"

Jonas nodded. But Raven hooked a finger in my belt loop and pulled me closer. "Your girl?" She smiled.

I brushed my fingers along her hairline and traced an imaginary line down the side of her face then around to the back of her neck. "It's going to kill me to let you go off with Jonas and Pascal. I don't know Pascal very well, but he seems a bit too much like Jonas—reckless."

"I resemble that remark," Jonas said, and laughed.

I ignored Jonas and continued to hold Raven's gaze. "If anything happens to you, I will never forgive Jonas or Pascal."

"Nothing is going to happen to me," Raven said. "If these people wanted to kill me, they would have done it already. It's not like I've been in hiding ever since I got here."

That was true. But that wasn't what scared me. There was a reason they'd allowed her to live and be free so far. *That* was what frightened the hell out of me.

THIRTY-SEVEN

Raven

Pascal and I entered the hot springs through the employee entrance in the back. Jonas followed, trying to stay out of our way as I mustered up the courage to allow Pascal to lead me everywhere he knew I'd been that night.

"Do you hear voices or conversations right now?" Pascal whispered. He'd taken the news of my new supernatural ability better than I'd expected. But I assumed he was whispering in an attempt to keep Jonas from hearing. So while he'd heard me say that Kyle and his friends had certain abilities, he didn't quite understand that whispering wasn't going to keep them from hearing.

I shook my head. "It seems that a conversation has to be *about* me in order to trigger my ability to hear it." But once the ability was triggered, I could hear any and all conversations around me. It was too new and strange for me to understand.

And to be honest, I wasn't sure I *wanted* to understand it. What I wanted was to have this stupid thing out of my head and for Kyle not to look at me like I was a bomb about to detonate.

I stopped in front of a lounge chair beside one of the hot springs. "I remember talking to Daniel and Eva right here. We brought a small group from Puro Cielo."

"What did you talk about?" Pascal asked.

"We talked about you. And your dad. How someone was going to purchase the resort." I faced Pascal. "That must have been Leonardo Rojas. But I don't think Daniel ever told me the name. It wouldn't have meant anything to me if he had."

I turned back to the chairs. "Typically, I would have enjoyed the springs with the group at that point."

"But you didn't that night?"

I shook my head. "No. I wanted to find you."

"You and I had fought the night before." Pascal spoke like a person who had relived every moment surrounding that night a thousand times.

"That's right. I was so angry at you."

Pascal smiled, but it didn't even come close to reaching the rest of his face. "That you were. Do you remember why?"

"I wanted you to take me on a real date. You refused. You said I was too young. And that my future was attending Stanford." I thought a little deeper. "And that we were simply in two very different stages of our lives."

Pascal pulled in a deep breath and let it out slowly. "I've thought about that argument every day for the past year."

"Why did you turn me down?" I asked. "*Really.*"

He glanced over his shoulder at Jonas. "Because I knew that a date with you would only bring us closer. And if I fell harder for you, I would have done everything I could to convince you to stay in Costa Rica instead of going back to California. It

tracked

would have been stupid and selfish of me to try to keep you here."

I tilted my head. "You let me believe that you had no feelings for me. That I was just a kid."

"I know. And I've regretted it ever since. I've asked myself: what if I had given in to your request? Maybe we would have been on a date, and nothing would've ever happened that night."

"We both knew I was going to Stanford in the fall no matter what happened over the summer." And though Pascal and I had loved each other, we weren't in love with each other in the love-can-conquer-all sort of way. "And you and I both know that your dad's murder had nothing to do with you and me. Our choices might not have been capable of changing anything."

"But if I could have kept you from witnessing whatever it was you saw…" Pascal ran a hand down my bare arm, leaving goose bumps in his wake.

I thought back to that night again. "I went looking for you, but I couldn't find you anywhere. No one was in the offices. The restaurant wasn't very busy that night. And the staff working the front entrance hadn't seen you. I remember the place being really quiet compared to most nights."

"So what did you do?"

"I headed back to where I'd left Eva and Daniel. And that's usually where my memories cut off." I'd discussed this precise moment with my doctor in California many times over the past year. I never remembered anything beyond this point, other than the nightmares of being in the forest, with eyes all around me.

"Should I take you to the spot where you were found?" Pascal asked.

I touched Pascal's arm. "In a minute."

Jonas had been standing off to the side, away from Pascal and me. He had promised he wouldn't interfere unless he thought he could help—but he was observing every move I made. So when he slipped inside my mind, his presence didn't surprise me.

You said Daniel was aware that the resort was being sold, Jonas mindspoke. *How did Daniel feel about that?*

Pascal watched me with confused eyes as I turned to Jonas. "He and Eva were very tense." I thought back to the conversation. "I remember not understanding how the future of the resort could possibly affect the camp. And why did Eva care so much?"

Pascal looked between Jonas and me. "Is he speaking inside your head right now?" Though Pascal had accepted—on the surface anyway—most of what I'd shared with him, the look on his face now told me he was struggling to believe in the whole mind communication thing.

"Yes," Jonas answered for me. "I'm trying to help Raven's mind go completely back to that night."

Jonas slipped inside my head again. *Where exactly did you go? Show me.*

I led Jonas and Pascal to the offices and showed them the route I'd taken to the front entrance when I'd found no one in the offices. And I talked about what was going through my mind. "At that point, I was focused solely on Pascal. Even if he and I never shared another romantic moment, I didn't want to lose him as a friend."

tracked

"You would never..."

"I know. It's okay." I smiled.

As we walked back toward the chairs, I paused in front of the pathway that led to the offices, restrooms, and locker rooms.

"Wait." I stopped. I stared at a dark corner near the entrance to the men's locker room. "Daniel and Nicholas argued that night."

"What? You saw my father?"

"I guess I did." I cocked my head as I eyed the spot where they had stood. "They got in each other's faces. They spoke in loud whispers. I had never seen Daniel act like that before. I thought they were going to throw punches."

"Try to imagine you're back on that day," Jonas ordered. "Close your eyes if you have to. Can you hear what they're saying?"

I closed my eyes. "I—I ducked behind a tree. I was eavesdropping." So unlike me.

What are they saying?

I thought back. "Daniel is asking Nicholas what he plans to do. Telling him that the offer he'd received on the resort was a good one. This confused me. Until that moment, I had thought Daniel was against Nicholas selling."

"My father wouldn't have sold Navos without a really good reason," Pascal said.

"What else, Raven?" Jonas asked.

"Nicholas claimed that he didn't trust the buyers. That he'd intercepted a delivery."

"What kind of delivery?" Pascal asked.

"It was supposed to go to the maintenance shed. It was addressed to Dr. Leonardo Rojas." I squeezed my eyes tighter. "Daniel looked nervous. He questioned Nicholas about the package. I didn't understand why he cared so much."

"Did he say what was in the package?" Jonas asked.

"No, only that he was taking it up to the maintenance shed right then. Said he scheduled a meeting with the buyers there. He wanted to know what was going on inside the shed before he went any further with the deal. But he had a bad feeling. Said there was no way he was selling his resort to these people if anything shady was happening on his property. He wouldn't do that to the people of La Fortuna."

"He was that close to closing on the deal?" Pascal's voice held the same surprise I felt. There had been no talk around town of the resort and hot springs changing ownership. Nicholas must have kept it very quiet. "What happened next?"

I gave my head a little shake. "That's all I remember." I opened my eyes. The corner by the men's locker room was now bare, and it was lit up, not dark.

"Why didn't he tell me any of this? I was already working for the hot springs."

Jonas held up a hand to silence Pascal, and Pascal's right hand curled into a fist.

"Did you speak to Daniel then?" Jonas asked.

I could feel Jonas's presence winding in and around my thoughts. "No." I closed my eyes again. I was remembering more at that moment than I'd remembered during the hundreds of hours in the psychiatrist's office. "I stayed hidden. Daniel and Nicholas argued a few minutes longer, then after

tracked

agreeing to let Daniel attend the meeting, they left in the direction of the front entrance."

"What did you do?"

"I followed them." I shrugged. "I was worried about Daniel. I didn't understand why he was so concerned about the camp and what that had to do with the sale of the resort. I was also worried about my parents. They're part owners of the camp. The camp and La Fortuna are *my* home, too, in many ways. And a small part of me wondered if Nicholas would lead me to Pascal."

Pascal shifted beside me.

"Trouble." Jonas said beside me. He nodded toward the front entrance. "The IIA is here. I see four agents. Maybe a couple more dressed undercover."

Several men dressed in dark suits spoke into their wrists. Could they be any more obvious? Behind them were a couple of men dressed in Hawaiian shirts—also obvious, because Ticos didn't dress in clichéd floral button-downs. There were so many of them, they didn't really even have to sneak around. They could have simply surrounded us fairly quickly.

"What do we do?" I asked, unable to hide the panic in my voice.

"I'll delay them with some mind tricks, if Pascal can get us out of here," Jonas said.

"This way." Pascal led us to the back of the resort and out the back entrance, where the car was waiting for us.

As we approached the car, the sound of a voice stopped us. "Pascal, where do you think you're going?"

We turned. Felipe was standing there with the man who had attacked me last week—the one with hair that reminded me of a horse's mane. I stiffened and grabbed Pascal's arm.

Pascal looked down at me with a raised brow, then up at Felipe. "I'm not on duty, so it's actually none of your business."

"It is if you're taking a resort vehicle."

I took a few steps forward and stopped directly in front of Felipe. "Who is this?" I nodded toward the guy beside him. "Why is the man who attacked me last week with you? I should call the police."

"But you're not going to, are you? Because if you do, the police will discover a lot of secrets hidden inside your head about the crimes at your precious camp."

"You really think I care about that?"

"Yes, I think you do." A grin tipped the corners of his mouth. "Besides, my father pretty much owns the police."

What did that mean? Was Leonardo Rojas that influential?

"Where are you going to go if the camp shuts down?" Felipe continued. "You flunked out of college. Your parents are in Africa. They sold your childhood home in California."

How did he know so much about me? I moved closer, in no way matching his size, and rotated my shoulders back. "I have an American passport that says I can go almost anywhere in the world I wish to go."

Felipe looked down on me, his hot breath practically suffocating me. "They will find you wherever you go. You can't hide."

I stumbled back. Jonas suddenly rushed Felipe, pulled a gun from his waistband, and shoved the point into the big man's chest while holding a fist full of his shirt with his other hand.

tracked

"What do you know about the people looking for her?" he demanded.

Horse Mane pulled his own gun and pointed it at Jonas. Jonas turned his head and smiled. "You don't want to point that thing at me, pal."

Felipe laughed. "It's okay, Eddie. They're not going to shoot me."

Horse Mane—Eddie—didn't lower his weapon.

"Tell me why not." Jonas smirked.

Pascal pulled me backward, closer to the car.

"Because I'm one of you," Felipe said.

Jonas straightened and seemed to grow next to Felipe. "You have fifteen seconds to tell me what the hell you mean."

Felipe stuck his chest out, matching Jonas's macho stance. "I am a cloned replica of my father, Dr. Leonardo Rojas. And you're a clone of Dr. Jeremy Porter."

Pascal swallowed hard, and my mouth dropped open. What kind of world had I fallen into?

Jonas held Felipe a little tighter before shoving him backward. "Why are you telling me this? You could have called the IIA agents out here already, but you haven't."

"Because I need your help. I know that you were raised by Sandra Whitmeyer. And I want to find her." Felipe glanced nervously behind him. "She has something of mine. I need it. And I think you'll help me."

Jonas stared at Felipe for what seemed like an eternity, while my pulse raced with fear that agents would burst through the back doors at any second.

Suddenly, Eddie aimed his gun at Felipe. *Jonas is controlling him*, I thought.

"You both will go back inside and distract the IIA agents." Jonas ordered. "Don't let them find us, and I'll think about what you've said."

Felipe nodded slowly, then turned and looked at me. "Eddie was under orders to inject you with the serum that activated your tracker the minute you stepped back onto Costa Rica soil. He has a tracker of his own, and he couldn't disobey his orders. I stopped him from kidnapping you that night, but I won't be able to help you as much now that your tracker is active."

Felipe and Eddie both turned and headed back inside the hot springs.

I stared after them, repeating Felipe's warning in my head. I had no idea what he meant.

"What was that?" Pascal asked.

"No idea." I turned to Jonas. "Do you believe him?" I pulled open the car door.

"We don't have time to figure out if Felipe is telling the truth right now. You're remembering things, and I think whatever is locked inside your head will tell us who else is involved."

~~~~~

"Pascal, you're scaring me," I said.

Pascal led me through the jungle, holding my hand a little too tightly. It was starting to get dark, and the lights of Navos Resort blinked in the distance like fireflies. Arenal Volcano sat behind us, quiet so far tonight. I remembered a time when lava had flowed at the top, glowing partway down the mountainside. But not tonight. Arenal Volcano was in an "intermediate resting phase," according to the experts. That meant that lava

tracked

shifted deep within the volcano, but nowhere near the surface. Not at all like my life, which was a raging inferno toward disaster.

Jonas followed us closely, but he remained quiet. I was certain Felipe had thrown him off with his confession about being another clone.

Pascal stopped. He let go of my hand and turned to face me.

My pulse quickened. I turned in a circle, looking from tree to tree. "This is where it happened, isn't it?" It was dark, and shadows lurked. The river rapids swished in the distance, a sound that normally relaxed me. I closed my eyes, praying the sounds of the river would calm the knots twisting in my belly. But when I opened my eyes, the underbrush hissed from the summer breeze at the base of the trees, and the shadows grew.

A feeling of intense darkness washed over me. An act of evil had taken place here, and the memories of it swirled around my limbs like elusive black smoke.

"Are you sure you want to remember?" Pascal's voice was gruff. "Are you sure you're ready to face your worst nightmare?" He stood on a tree root, making him tower over me even more. "I could just drive you to the airport right now. You could leave all of this... these clones with weird supernatural powers... and go back to your life. You deserve better. I want you to have better." He swallowed hard.

I turned away. Unfortunately, he was wrong about that. Thanks to the object in my head, I couldn't run from this.

I wandered around, taking in the surroundings. Monkeys cried out in the distance and owls hooted above.

Pascal knelt and ran his fingers through the underbrush. "I found you right here." He cleared his throat to mask the slight cracking of his voice. "I thought you were dead."

I flinched. "What are you talking about? *You* found me?" Why had no one ever told me that?

"Someone left me an anonymous message at the resort. Said you were in trouble and told me where to find you." Pascal's hands shook. He stretched his fingers out wide, then closed them tightly. "I've never been as scared as I was the moment I saw you motionless on the ground and my father dead just a few feet away." Standing next to me now, he raised a hand to the scar on my temple. "There was so much blood. It was matted in your hair. And you didn't move. You were so still, I was sure you were dead, too."

I wiped my sweating palms on my pants. Taking a deep breath and letting it out, I attempted to slow the blood racing through my veins. I still couldn't picture the scene, but I could *feel* some of what I had felt that night: the clean breeze of the rainforest against my cheeks; the warm, moist ground against my back.

"Where was your father?"

Pascal pointed to a spot next to a large tree trunk a few yards away.

I tilted my head, imagining Nicholas's face. And as I did, I saw a vision of him. "His head was angled awkwardly against the tree. His eyes wide." I closed my own eyes tight. I fell to my knees and ran my hands through the air above the spot where Nicholas's body had lain. I pushed myself back up. "What else did you find?"

"Amagita, you're bleeding."

tracked

I followed Pascal's line of sight to my arm. I had scraped my elbow when I fell into the river earlier; the wound must have reopened.

"We need to clean that." Pascal grabbed my hand and led me toward the river, which was closer than I had expected. The moon reflected off the water, casting a glow on Pascal's face as he helped me sit against a tree. He rolled my sleeve up to my elbow, revealing a superficial wound. Then he removed his outer long-sleeved shirt, dipped it in the water, and used it to clean the wound.

"What else did you find?" I repeated. I eyed the curves of Pascal's muscles beneath a tightly fitted T-shirt, then slowly lifted my head and studied the lines in his face, the sadness in his eyes as he dabbed at the blood.

"Nothing. I found nothing else."

"Did you see anyone?"

He shook his head. "And the police kept any details they may have discovered out of the newspapers."

I placed my hand over his. His eyes found mine. "Do you think Felipe or Leo had something to do with Nicholas's death?" I asked.

He blew out a deep breath. "I didn't think they were even in Costa Rica at the time of the murder."

"But now?"

"After everything you've shared with me, and what I've witnessed in the last several hours, I'd believe anything." He pulled me to my feet, then reached down and cupped my cheek. "I just want you to be safe. It's starting to look like my father was killed because of something he knew or witnessed. And now you're telling me they did something to you that night, too. Besides beating you to near-death. I just don't know."

I covered my face with my hands and rubbed my forehead with the pads of my fingers. "How have I remembered parts of the evening, but not the whole evening?" Why was I blocking so much?

Jonas approached me slowly. *It's time that I help you remember.*

I took Pascal's hands into mine. "I have to remember. Even if the truth is painful, we need to know what happened. Jonas thinks he can lead me to my suppressed memories. I need you to let him."

Though it pained Pascal, he nodded and backed away from Jonas and me.

Jonas stepped in front of me. "I will force you past whatever it is that's blocking your memories. I would have done it already, but I promised Kyle I would let you go at your own pace. We're running out of time, though."

I was willing to bet that Jonas wasn't always this considerate. "Help me remember. I can handle it. I have to."

He slipped inside my head, and I was instantly taken back in time to that night one year ago.

THIRTY-EIGHT

Kyle

We waited until twilight to make the short hike up the mountain to the maintenance building. We passed several signs warning us that we were entering a restricted area because of the volcano, yet we were miles from the opening, and it was a "resting" volcano.

The building was located on a plateau. Dense trees surrounded it on two sides, and a tiny access road led directly to its large main doors.

"I don't get it," Jack said. "It just looks like a barn."

Before checking the main doors for access, we decided to walk around the entire perimeter.

"I don't know." Lexi practically walked on Jack's heel, hovering at his back. "Something doesn't feel right."

"I agree," I said. "And I don't understand why this building is located in the restricted area, yet people work up here every day."

"You guys are paranoid," Jack said. "It's dark and the sounds of the forest are just getting to you." He eased up and peered around the corner before motioning for us to follow. He did that three more times before we were back to the front. For someone who called us paranoid, he was being super-cautious.

Jack tried the smaller door at the front of the barn with no luck. I tugged on the handle of one of the larger doors, and it slid open just enough for the three of us to squeeze through.

Inside the barn was exactly what one would expect to find in a resort maintenance shed: tractors and equipment for maintaining the grounds of Navos. I pointed a flashlight at each piece of equipment, then shined it all around. I motioned for Jack and Lexi to follow me. "Jonas said the mysterious door was in the back."

Sure enough, there was a metal door in the back that couldn't possibly lead anywhere except maybe to a small closet. Its shiny silver was out of place inside this large wooden structure meant to house oversized lawnmowers.

I wiggled the knob. Locked. I tapped my knuckles against the cool metal. It sounded thick and solid, and it echoed against the quiet of the increasingly dark night.

"Kyle," Lexi said behind me, "Jonas is getting ready to go inside Raven's head. He says he can clearly see what's blocking her memories, and he plans to strip it."

My stomach knotted up. "Where are they?"

"They're not far from here, actually."

"Tell him we're headed that way." I didn't see what else we could do here. It was a locked closet door, as Pascal had said. This had been a wasted trip.

But before I could express that thought aloud, Lexi and Jack both straightened and stared at the door behind me. "What is it?" I asked.

Something beeped above my head. I turned and looked up—and saw what appeared to be a camera with a red flashing light.

tracked

I'm hearing voices or thoughts from people beyond that door, Lexi mindspoke.

I hear them too, Jack said. *Can you see if they're from cloned humans?*

Lexi gave her head a little shake. I didn't know if that meant she couldn't see, or if the people they'd heard weren't clones, and I didn't have time to ask because just then the door opened so quickly we didn't even have time to back away.

A man and woman dressed in blue surgical scrubs pointed guns at our heads.

"We've been waiting for you."

THIRTY-NINE

Raven

Pascal was leaning against a tree near where he had found me lying bloody and injured. Jonas had instructed Pascal to say nothing while he tried to extract my memories, and by the way Jonas was wringing his hands, he was struggling to get a clear vision.

Where did you go after following Daniel and Nicholas out of the hot springs? Jonas asked.

I closed my eyes and tried to concentrate on the memories that were coming back one by one. "Daniel and Nicholas left through the back. They took a golf cart along the access road up to the maintenance shed."

"How did you follow them?"

"Pascal had bikes at the resort. I grabbed one and pedaled up the mountain after they were out of sight. The moon was full, so there was plenty of light to follow the path. And I could see lights from the hot springs and the resort cottages in the distance."

Jonas continued to coax out my recollections. "What happened next?"

"There were other cars outside the maintenance building, but I didn't see anyone. Nicholas and Daniel were out in front, talking. I went around through the trees and parked my bike on the far side of the barn, hoping they wouldn't see me. I remember having a bad feeling about all of it. It didn't make sense that they would meet outside a big ugly barn. When I peered around the side of the building, I saw Nicholas holding a small metal object in his hand."

Jonas's eyes went wide. "A tracker?"

"I don't know. I guess. It was..."

Jonas did something in my mind, and suddenly the memory was crystal clear.

"Do you know what it is?" Daniel asked, taking the device, which looked like an oversized beetle or a spider, and holding it between his thumb and forefinger.

"No, but a large case of these arrived yesterday ahead of the men who want to purchase Navos. That one you're holding must be special because it was inside its own little box with a handwritten note: 'This one is programmed to your specifications. Love, Sandra.'"

"Interesting." Daniel turned the object over in his hand.

"Sandra?" Jonas asked out loud. "Are you sure that's what he said?"

"Yes. I remember his words exactly. And it was strange the way Daniel held the tracker. Like he knew what it was but had never seen one." I gave my head a shake. "I don't know... just a feeling I got."

"Keep going."

"Headlights! Someone's coming," Nicholas said. They both turned toward the approaching car. "They're here."

tracked

Daniel pocketed the tracker and stood behind Nicholas as a car pulled around the access road and stopped in front of the large barn doors. A man climbed out of the driver seat. "Good evening, brother."

"Leo." Daniel stepped around Nicholas and shook hands with Leonardo Rojas, while another man climbed out of the passenger side. "Good evening, Felipe," Daniel called to him. Felipe looked younger, though it was only a year ago, and even from a distance, I could see that his eyes were strikingly similar to his father's.

I turned to Pascal. "Why would Leo call Daniel 'brother'?" He already knew Leo and Felipe.

Pascal shrugged. "I have no idea."

Focus, Raven, Jonas warned. His voice inside my head was becoming urgent, bordering on hostile.

I closed my eyes again and tried to picture Daniel shaking Leo's hand.

"Do you have the shipment that arrived here yesterday?" Leo asked Nicholas.

Nicholas nodded and wandered over to the golf cart. He lifted a box. "Yes, but I want to see exactly what you're doing up here before we go any further with our negotiations."

Leo clasped his hands together. "Great. Let's go inside."

Nicholas hesitated. He swiveled his head like he was looking for someone. He seemed unsure, nervous. But he entered anyway.

"They all went inside?" Jonas asked.

The memory went fuzzy. "Yes... No... I'm not sure. Wait! No. Felipe started to enter, but he stopped. He turned and stared in my direction. I ducked further into the shadows."

"Did he see you?"

"I didn't think so, because he turned back around and entered the barn, closing the large doors behind him."

I eased along the barn until I was next to the main doors. I no longer heard voices. They had vanished deep inside. When I peeked through the crack between the doors, I saw no one, so I squeezed through quietly.

That's when I heard the faint sound of their disappearing voices. I followed the sound until I saw Felipe passing through a strange door. It was metal, and looked out of place inside this simple structure. Felipe paused with his hand on the door, almost as if he were holding it open for someone behind him, but then he let it go. The door closed slowly, and I sprinted forward and caught it just before it closed and latched.

"Did you go inside?" Pascal asked, bringing me out of my semi-trance.

"Pascal, please," Jonas groaned. *Did you go past the door? What was there?*

I once again pictured the door, Felipe's disappearing back, and Daniel holding the spider-like object in his hand. "I did." I cocked my head, staring at what was behind the door inside my mind. "Stairs."

"Stairs? To what?"

"They led down. I started to follow, but—"

My eyes sprang open and I turned to Jonas. "Something's wrong."

Jonas narrowed his eyes at me, giving nothing away. "What do you mean?"

tracked

"Something's wrong with Kyle. What's happened? You're hiding something from me."

"Nothing's wrong. They're fine. Let's keep going." He worked the hard edges of his jaw back and forth. He was fighting against something.

"You're lying." *Kyle, Lexi, where are you? What's happening?*

Pascal was at my side. "Why do you think something's wrong?"

"Jonas, why aren't they answering me?"

"They can't. They were forced inside some lab. But they're fine."

"They went through that same metal door, didn't they?"

"It appears so. But they can take care of themselves." Jonas's eyes and the lines that formed across his forehead did not exude confidence.

"Did you believe Felipe when he said he was a clone?" I asked Jonas. "Do you think he would hurt any one of you? Or me?"

"I'm not sure. Why?"

Because I can sense his presence the same way I can sense all of yours. He's about thirty yards away, and he's heading straight for us.

Jonas grabbed me and pinned me with a hard stare. *I don't know if Felipe is good or bad. But he is the reason you aren't remembering the details of that night.*

What do you mean? I asked.

I mean, he's all over your memories. Kyle told me that when he would get inside your dreams, another person was always there. He couldn't see that person, but he could tell it wasn't a memory of a person—but an actual person. He entered your dreams the same way Kyle did. Kyle couldn't see who it was, but I can see Felipe clearly inside your memories, and he's preventing me from unblocking your memories all at once.

That's why his eyes were so familiar to me! He was there that night. Did he kill Nicholas? Did he hurt me? My body trembled.

"Hello," Felipe said, breaking through the trees. "It's nice to see you again, Raven."

I walked slowly toward him. *How many times have you been inside my head?*

Often. It's a lovely place to visit. His Venezuelan accent slipped in and around my mind, and it felt so familiar.

He turned toward Jonas. *Jonas, Pascal, you two boys will go back to the resort. Daniel should be there soon. He's worried about Raven, and he definitely needs to be here when Raven remembers everything.*

Without a single word or an ounce of fight, Jonas and Pascal turned and left, trance-like. Seeing Jonas like that sent a chill down my spine.

I turned slowly back toward Felipe, and though he terrified me, I rotated my shoulders back and took a step closer to him. "I'm not scared of you," I lied.

"Yes you are, but you've no reason to be." He grabbed my arm and pulled me forward, positioning me in front of him, my back to his chest. He faced me toward the spot where Pascal had told me Nicholas was murdered. He snaked an arm around my body so that it rested across my stomach and held me firmly in place.

Now, it's time that you remember everything.

FORTY

Kyle

"What is this?" We were being led down a set of stairs beyond the mysterious door. It all made sense now. This wasn't a small closet or storeroom; it was an entrance into something much bigger.

As I stepped off the last step, I found myself facing the very lab Jonas had sent me to look for.

Directly in front of me were several stainless steel worktables covered in equipment I didn't recognize. A glass partition separated this part of the room from an area that housed a dozen or so cots, and off to the side was a small chamber with steel walls and a glass door.

"It looks like a smaller version of one of Sandra's labs," Lexi said, looking around. Even though a woman had a gun pointed at Lexi's back, Lexi remained calm.

The woman picked up a phone receiver. "We have three of them... Yes, sir... Will do, sir." She replaced the receiver. "This way."

She shoved Lexi forward, toward the small chamber with the solid glass door. The man gestured with his gun for me and Jack to follow.

I scanned the room and traded glances with Jack and Lexi.

There's no one else here, Lexi mindspoke.

I'm looking for some kind of catch, but I can't seem to find one, Jack added.

"Get in," the woman ordered when we reached the chamber.

The man beside her drilled his gun into Jack's back. Jack flinched, but managed to keep his cool. At least I thought he did, until—

"I don't think so." Jack whipped around, grabbed the man's wrist, and lifted it into the air. The gun went off, and the bullet ricocheted off the glass partition—it was obviously bulletproof. We all ducked at the sound of the gunshot, but the woman didn't duck fast enough.

She dropped her gun and stumbled backward, holding her stomach, then fell to the ground.

The man scrambled over to her; she had curled into a fetal position. "Oh, no! You're okay. You're okay." He looked up at us, his eyes pleading. "Help her. You can help her."

Lexi stared down at him. "Who are you? Why did you say you were waiting for us?"

"I'll tell you anything—just please help my wife."

Jack walked over and lifted the man by his lab coat. "What is this place? What are they doing in here?"

I walked through a door in the partition to the area with the cots. They were all empty, but one of the beds had a pile of clothes on the end of it. I picked up a shirt and pair of pants, then turned to Lexi. "These belong to a small child."

Lexi knelt beside the whimpering woman. Blood seeped through her fingers where she was holding her wound. "What is this place used for?" Lexi asked.

tracked

The man pushed the woman's bangs off her forehead. "It's going to be all right. You can tell them. We only did what Dr. Porter asked."

The woman rolled onto her back. She winced in pain. "We give children from the nearby village purpose and meaning." Her answer sounded memorized and rehearsed.

Lexi shuddered. "What kind of purpose?"

"Dr. Porter and Dr. Rojas place trackers in their brains and provide them with knowledge and skill. Then they send the children to other countries to be used for good."

I closed my fingers into fists. "What kind of 'good'?" I asked in horror. I was positive their definition of "good" differed from mine.

"They work for governments—to gather information. And in return, Dr. Porter and Dr. Rojas send money to the children's families."

Lexi plopped onto the floor beside the woman. "I thought this would have ended when I put Sandra out of commission."

"I think this is what Jonas feared," I said. "Someone has been sending him videos of people in trances. They look similar to how Dani looked when Sandra had complete control of her mind." I tried to recall everything Jonas had told me. "He said two containers of trackers went missing from Palmyra. One went missing a year ago. And one back in October, just before we arrived on the island."

"Are you going to help my wife?" the man asked again. "We told you all we know."

Lexi gazed directly at the man, then redirected her hard stare to his wife. Her eyes widened. "They both have trackers," she announced.

"Dr. Porter has been very good to us," the man said. "He gave us jobs when there was no work."

"I'm sure he did." Lexi placed a hand over the woman's stomach. The woman was losing a lot of blood. "This is going to hurt. I'm sorry." As Lexi focused her mental powers on repairing the woman's injury, the woman cried out as if she were giving birth. The healing process took less than two minutes.

"You're going to be fine," Lexi said when she was done. She turned to the man. "You can take your wife to that chamber to recover." She pointed to the very chamber where the woman had ordered us initially.

Without a word, and under Lexi's control, the man picked up his wife and carried her inside. Lexi closed the door behind them and locked it.

"Now what?" Jack asked.

But before any of us could answer, the man inside the chamber turned. A look of pure horror passed over his face.

A moment later, a substance began spewing from the top of the chamber.

Lexi ran to the door and tried to open it. She began screaming and pulling on the handle. She punched on the electronic panel to the right of the door, but nothing happened.

The man sat down on the floor, cradling his wife. He leaned in and kissed her gently on the lips, then leaned back against the back wall. Within moments, he was still—his eyes open but not seeing.

Lexi backed slowly away from the chamber. When she bumped into Jack, she turned and buried her face into his chest, grasping his shirt with her fists. "I killed them. I ordered them inside that chamber, and I killed them!"

Jack smoothed her hair. "No, you didn't. You are *not* responsible for that. And remember, they were trying to get *us* into that room. If they had, we'd be dead."

The discussion was interrupted by Jonas's voice, booming in our heads. *Kyle! That asshole Felipe is a clone with mental powers. He sent me away from Raven.*

My heart rate began a fast climb. If Felipe was a clone with supernatural abilities like us, and if he was in any way involved with what was going on here inside this lab, what was he doing to Raven? I would kill him if he hurt her.

Where's Raven now? I asked.

We were at the spot where Pascal's father was murdered and Raven was attacked. It's actually not that far down the hill from the maintenance shed. Maybe a half-mile or so, by the river. Daniel is with me now, and he says Felipe won't hurt her.

Do you believe him? I was halfway back up the stairs to the maintenance shed before the question was even out of my mouth.

No idea. The fact that Felipe got inside my head doesn't make me one of his biggest fans right now. He is an identical clone of Leo Rojas, though, so who knows what he's after. I'm afraid that he's been inside Raven's head all along. And since Daniel was around on the night that Raven's trying to remember, I'm not exactly trusting him either.

Lexi, didn't you say you saw no evidence of Raven's head injuries? I asked.

None, Lexi confirmed. She and Jack were right behind me.

Could Felipe be a healer as well? Jonas, where are you now? I asked.

Pascal and I just tied Daniel to a chair in Pascal's office. You were wrong. I kinda like this Pascal character. As soon as I told him that you all suspected Daniel and Leo of trafficking children from Costa Rica to other countries, he pulled out some heavy duty rope and made a call to a friend of his at the police station. Now I'm on my way back to Raven. And I'm going to hurt Felipe. I'm punching first, asking questions later.

We'll meet you there.

FORTY-ONE

Raven

Felipe placed his hands just below my shoulders and held me firmly in place, facing my worst nightmare. "You know that Nicholas was found right over there." He pointed with his right hand. "And you know that you were found here." He pointed to my left.

I shivered at the thought. "I don't remember how I got here, though."

"Let's back up. Do you remember the inside of the lab?"

"I remember Nicholas yelling when I was only halfway down the stairs."

"I won't be a part of whatever this is. And there's no way I'm selling my resort to you!"

"Nick, these kids wouldn't have had a chance without Leo's generosity," Daniel argued.

"Generosity?" Nicholas gasped.

With one hand on the wall, I eased down the stairs until I could crouch down and see inside the lab at the bottom—a large room with white concrete walls. To the back of the room was a large glass partition, separating Leo, Felipe, Nicholas, and Daniel from...

"Kids!" I said. "A dozen or so kids were behind a glass wall, playing and sitting on cots. They were dressed in hospital gowns and matching pants." I turned and looked up at Felipe. "What were those kids doing there?"

"Focus on what happened next," he said.

Leo explained the operation of the lab to Nicholas in a cool, calm voice: that the children were orphans who needed food and a place to live. He didn't seem to care that Nicholas looked as if he might puke.

Daniel was pleading with Nicholas, telling him that he couldn't tell anyone about the lab, or everything would end badly—for all of them. Nicholas was backing away, toward the stairs. No one had noticed me there yet. I got scared, so I turned and ran.

I shoved through the door at the top of the stairs like a bullet, and I didn't stop running. But then I heard my name. Nicholas had spotted me. He caught up to me and told me to keep running and to hide in the forest.

Daniel shouted after Nicholas. I wasn't sure if he had seen me or not. I was so out of breath I couldn't run anymore, so I ducked behind a tree and peeked back around. Nicholas had stopped and was facing Daniel.

"Look, Nick," Daniel said. "This operation is part of something huge. The International Intelligence Agency is helping the people of Costa Rica. They're bringing more money into our beloved country than we could in a hundred years."

"This is not your country, Daniel," Nicholas spat. "And these people are helping themselves. Those are innocent kids locked up down there. What are they doing to them?"

Daniel held up the metal object he had pocketed. "They're placing these devices into their heads and giving them the opportunity to be a

tracked

part of something bigger. Those kids will work for the IIA or for their country's military. They'll have a chance at a real life—a life these orphans could otherwise never have hoped for."

"Are you listening to yourself?" Nicholas replied. "You've served the people of La Fortuna for years. Did you ask those kids if they wanted to be part of some government experiment? The Rojas aren't even from Costa Rica." Nicholas stepped closer to Daniel. "Who are they? And why are you so involved with this?"

Daniel lowered his head. "Leo is Eva's brother," he said. "I had no choice."

"They have something on you."

Daniel looked up, his eyes pleading.

"This was a setup." Nicholas straightened. "There is only one way this is going to end."

"Nicholas." Leo walked out from behind a tree, followed by Felipe. "The transaction for me to take ownership of Navos Resort and Spa and Navos Hot Springs has already been expedited. The documents have been signed by you, notarized, and filed with the appropriate offices."

"You forged my signature!" Fear quivered in Nicholas's voice.

"You will need to leave town. Felipe here has one of our devices... for you." Leo pulled out a knife and waved his son forward.

I turned to Felipe. "You... you hesitated. You were terrified." I had never imagined Felipe scared, but he had looked so young in my memory.

Felipe forced me back into the past again. *You were there. What were you feeling as you watched?*

I trembled at the sound of his voice inside my head. *I've heard your voice in my mind before.*

Of course you have. Now focus. What happened next?

"You hesitated a moment longer, and your dad pushed you aside. He grabbed the knife and shoved you into that tree over there. And then he marched toward Nicholas."

Thoughts of Pascal flashed through my mind. Then and now. Nicholas stood taller, and he faced Leo head on. My heart constricted, knowing what was coming.

Daniel darted in between Leo and Nicholas. "Leo, man. He'll be fine. He's excited to bring money to his family and to the people of La Fortuna."

"I can speak for myself, Daniel," Nicholas said. "You might be a complete traitor to the people you serve, but I will not sell out my family and friends to this group of barbarians. And I will not sell my resort to this Venezuelan con artist." He faced Leo. "But you knew this."

Leo tilted his head side to side. "It's unlucky that you received the shipment of trackers. And it's unfortunate that you had to see what we were doing at the maintenance shed. I would have preferred to have avoided that. But it was you who insisted."

Daniel grabbed the knife and the small tracker from Leo. "Let me talk to him. Give us some time alone." He was nearly begging. He turned back to Nicholas. "I told Leo that you would be on board with the deal. That you just wanted to sell the resort so you could retire and spend time with your family."

"Well, you were wrong. And—why the resort, anyway?"

Leo smiled. "Why not? The IIA needed a business front for the operation. Eva and Daniel mentioned the hot springs. It's a perfect business. And undeveloped land comes with it."

Nicholas turned to Daniel. "What's in it for you? How could you do this to the MacMillans?"

tracked

"I'm doing this for William and Bennett. The camp's been losing money. We almost had to shut down last year."

"So this is about money?"

"Nick, please just let me insert one of these trackers in your neck."

"Why on earth would I let you do that?" Nicholas's voice had lowered into a calm, fearless tone.

"Because this tracker will erase your memories of this event. You'll be able to go back to business as usual—to the moment before you received the shipment of trackers yesterday. Please. I'm trying to help you. This is the only way."

"Daniel wanted to take Nicholas's memories away," I said.

"That would have eased his conscience, I guess. Daniel had been hoping Nicholas would sell the hot springs, retire, and not question what the new residents of La Fortuna planned to do underneath the maintenance building."

"You won't be putting anything inside of me," Nicholas said. "We'll just sort this all out with the local authorities." He started to turn.

"I can't let you leave." Leo pointed a gun at Nicholas. "You've seen too much. As has Raven. Come on out, honey."

I turned to Felipe. "They saw me." Panic reverberated through my words. "They were going to kill Nicholas. And me."

"Yet you're here. You can face this. You're *ready* to remember." Something about the confidence in Felipe's voice gave me the strength to go forward.

I stepped out from behind the tree. Tears formed in my eyes. "Please don't hurt Nicholas," I pleaded. "He and I won't say anything about whatever is going on here. I don't even understand what you're doing."

Leo marched over to me and smacked my face with the back of his hand—the one holding the gun. Fire erupted in my jaw, and my temple stung where the gun had made a large gash way too close to my eye.

I writhed on the ground, holding my head.

"No!" Daniel yelled. He darted in front of Leo. "Don't hurt her. I can handle Raven. She'll want your help in saving Puro Cielo." He looked down at me, and I could have sworn I saw tears in his eyes. Then he turned to Nicholas. "You have to let me insert this tracker. He will kill you."

"You're kidding yourself," Nicholas said. "Look at Raven. She's like a daughter to you, and look at what he just did to her!" Nicholas made a step to help me, but Daniel blocked his path. Nicholas straightened. "You'll have to kill me if you think you're going to put that thing inside me."

"It's not going to hurt you," Daniel said. "I've seen the procedure. It only takes a tiny incision. Think of Pascal and Miguel. Think of your beautiful wife, Lucia."

Daniel was holding the knife at his side. Nicholas darted at him, clawing at the hand that held the knife, but Daniel held tight. So Nicholas punched Daniel in the jaw. Daniel stumbled backward. His face reddened.

"Daniel, stop!" I yelled from the ground. "Nicholas is our friend."

Suddenly I felt the pain of a kick to my side, and another to the back of my head.

Barely clinging to consciousness, I rolled side to side. My temple burned and a stabbing pain erupted behind my right eye. Shadows moving at the base of the trees made me flinch.

tracked

Daniel and Nicholas continued to argue twenty feet away, but they drifted in and out of focus. Their muffled voices were a confusing crescendo of sound, their bodies merging into a single figure. Suddenly, one man separated from the other. Nicholas clutched his chest and collapsed backward against a tree before sliding down to rest at my eye level.

His eyes were wide, glassy. Nicholas was dead. "Oh Pascal. I am so sorry." A sob escaped my throat.

I raised a hand and pressed it against my aching temple, where my fingers met with sticky hair. When I pulled my hand away, it was dark and wet. I gagged at the metallic smell of blood.

I rolled onto my back. My body trembled. I wanted to get up, but the throbbing pain in my rib cage glued me to the thick foliage. I glanced down the length of my body. Fire ignited in places I hadn't thought possible. My eyes burned.

Time passed before I heard voices discussing my fate. "Don't kill her. I'll do anything," Daniel pleaded.

"You will do everything I tell you."

"Yes."

"I will save your camp for the sake of my sister, and you will answer to me." Leo held out his hand. "Now give me the tracker."

Daniel held out his palm; the tracker lay flat in the middle of his hand.

"Not that one. The one you hid in your pocket when we arrived. The one meant for my son."

Daniel pulled the other tracker from his pocket and placed it in Leo's hand.

My spine stiffened, and I turned to Felipe. "Leo gave the tracker to you, though. You inserted the tracker into my neck."

"I did. I knew the tracker would save your life."

"How could you be so sure?"

"Because that was my tracker—the tracker designed especially for me, sent here by Sandra Whitmeyer."

"You were supposed to receive a tracker that gave you the power to know where other cloned humans were?"

"Among other gifts."

"And I'm supposed to believe that you gave me that tracker in order to save my life?"

"It wasn't a completely unselfish move."

Leo handed Felipe the tracker. "You know what to do... before anything else goes wrong."

Felipe pulled a knife from a sheath at his ankle, then fell forward to his knees. He raised his arms and reached around to the back of his neck. But before making an incision in his own neck, he looked down at me. Tears were streaming from my eyes. I was shaking from the shock of everything that had happened.

Suddenly, Felipe forced my head forward. His fingers brushed my hair off the back of my neck. My body shook; I was defenseless. I felt a sudden pinch to the skin just below my hairline and above my spine, the coolness of metal—and then a searing pain and pressure I couldn't identify.

I wailed and gnashed my teeth, writhing from the burn of whatever he had just done.

He stood, and the pain subsided slightly. Leo's voice boomed behind him just before Felipe was shoved out of my eyesight.

"What have you done?" he screamed at his son. Where Felipe had been, Leo now stood, staring down at me with chilling hatred. "Looks like you're going to get your wish, Daniel. For now, anyway." He bent

tracked

down and whispered, "You will return to California. Forget what you've seen."

Felipe's voice entered my head, but his lips remained motionless. "I'll see you in your dreams."

"Why did you give me the tracker?" I stared into Felipe's eyes—eyes that were much more gentle than the stone-cold loathing I remembered from Leo.

"I refused to have my whereabouts tracked by my father and Dr. Porter. I agreed to accept a tracker from Sandra, but I wanted one without the tracking capabilities. They knew this, but they refused."

"So this was some act of rebellion? At my expense?"

"My father would have killed you if I hadn't embedded that tracker inside you."

"How did Daniel know about the tracker?"

"Father told him about it while drunk one night. The only reason Father has allowed Daniel to live so far is because his only sister is in love with him."

Tears burned my eyes. I'd never felt so betrayed. How had Daniel managed to keep so much from my parents? From me?

"I know it might not seem like it, but I've been protecting you. That's also why I've been in your dreams. My father assured Daniel that you could live, as long as you remembered nothing about this night. It became my job to make sure you didn't remember."

I turned back to the empty forest, where an incredible crime had taken place. "But now I *do* remember. Daniel killed Pascal's father." I wrapped my arms around my stomach in a hug, but nothing was going to make me feel better about this.

The man who was like a father to me had killed someone. And he had lied to me, had let me suffer.

"Yes. Now that you know, what are you going to do?"

I faced Felipe, studying his eyes. "The real questions is: what are *you* going to do? What will your father do when he finds out I know the truth? And that I now have the knowledge that this tracker provides?" I backed away from Felipe. My hands shook at my sides, so I closed them into fists to hide the trembling.

"You really think I protected you for the past year only to let my father kill you now?"

"I don't know."

"I've done nothing but protect you and the knowledge your tracker holds."

"What does that mean?"

"Because of the tracker, my father and Dr. Porter always knew where you were. And when you returned to Costa Rica, it made them nervous—they feared that you might remember Nicholas's murder and blow their cover."

"So, what? Am I supposed to pretend I haven't remembered?"

"It won't matter. The IIA has set a trap to kill most of your friends, if they're not already dead."

I knew that wasn't true, because I could sense the presence of Kyle, Lexi, and Jack just to the north of me. But I could tell that Felipe believed it.

"The IIA can't kill you without also killing the information the tracker feeds you. They know that you now hold the whereabouts of every cloned human in existence—and even more information once the rest of the tracker is activated and

tracked

you learn how to use it. That's why they've left you alone so far. But you won't make it off of this mountain tonight." *Not unless you let me help you.* Felipe mindspoke the last words.

I narrowed my eyes, but decided to let the mindspeak go for now. "You said 'even more.' What else can this tracker do?"

Another voice interrupted us. "I'm not sure we need to worry about that."

Felipe and I turned. Leo marched toward us with the same look I remembered from the night when he nearly beat me to death.

"I'll be taking Raven's tracker from her now," Leo said.

Having seen that look before, I should have reacted faster, but I froze when Leo raised his knife and drove it fast and hard into my chest.

FORTY-TWO

Kyle

I heard Raven's bloodcurdling scream inside my mind. The way Lexi and Jack whipped around told me they'd heard it as well.

We ran through the dense forest toward the river, tripping over tree roots and slipping on moist underbrush. As we neared Raven, her semi-unconscious mind came in and out of focus. I couldn't get inside though; something had happened to her. *She might be in shock,* I told Lexi and Jack.

From somewhere up ahead, I heard Felipe's voice. He was screaming at his father. "Why did you do that? You'll kill her!"

My heart pounded inside my head. History was repeating itself, and I simply didn't know if I could get over losing another person I cared deeply about.

We slowed, approaching quietly. We stopped just short of breaking through the trees that separated us from Raven.

Leo was crouched beside Raven. "I'm not killing her—yet." His calm voice made the little hairs on the back of my neck stand at attention. He pulled something from his pocket, rolled Raven onto her side, then shone a light to the back of her neck.

What is he doing? What is that thing?

I don't know, Lexi answered.

Felipe turned in our direction, possibly hearing our mindspeak. But Leo continued to talk. "I'm getting back the tracker that should have been yours."

My heart practically stopped. I would have burst through the trees, but Lexi's hand to my arm stopped me.

"If she dies, the tracker dies with her," Felipe said. Then he mindspoke to us: *IIA agents are almost here. They've been ordered to shoot you on Leo's command. I've already knocked out Jonas to save him from himself.*

Lexi, Jack, and I traded panicked looks. Without Jonas's ability to control minds, we were severely limited.

Where's Jonas? Why would you knock him out? Why wouldn't Felipe just kill Jonas if he wanted him out of the picture?

He's just beyond those trees. Felipe pointed in the opposite direction from where we stood. *I don't want him dead. I need his help when we're done here.*

"As she nears death," Leo explained to Felipe, "the tracker will loosen its grip on the surrounding tissue, and we'll be able to extract it without damaging it."

What did he do to her? Jack asked.

She has a deep stab wound to her chest, Felipe said. *It nicked her heart. She has maybe five minutes before the point of no return.*

I put my hand on a tree trunk and inhaled deeply. I was losing her. I loved her, and I was losing her.

Lexi faced Jack and me. *I can't control Leo's mind* and *try to heal Raven's wound. Jack and I need to be closer than this anyway to even attempt the healing. Raven, can you hear me? You hang on, you hear me? We're here.*

Lexi then grabbed hold of my arms. "Don't you dare give up on her," she whispered.

tracked

Kyle. The faintest of whispers entered my head. *I love you, too.* She was answering something I hadn't said out loud. She had heard my thoughts.

Don't you dare die on me, you hear me? I mindspoke through what sounded like gritted teeth.

I'm sorry, but I think it's too late. I can see the wound to my heart, and it's bad. I'm losing so much blood. I'm not sure how much longer I can stay conscious.

At the sound of Raven choking, I placed a hand over my mouth to suppress a sob.

Raven. It's me, Lexi. You can see the wound? Lexi looked at me. "That's odd."

Yes. It's bad, Raven said. *The blood is seeping out everywhere.*

"If she can see the internal wound, then maybe that tracker has given her more than just supernatural hearing." *Raven, I want you to ignore everything else around you and focus on the spot where the knife nicked your heart.*

Okay. I can see it.

Now, I want you to imagine pinching the wound closed. Imagine bringing the tissue together and closing off the spot where the blood is leaking out.

"Her heart rate is slowing," Leo announced. "The tracker is starting to retract its hold on her spinal nerves. Soon, Felipe, we will have the knowledge and power that Sandra Whitmeyer meant for us to have."

"You mean the power *I* was meant to have, don't you, Father?"

Raven, can you hear me? What are you seeing now? Lexi asked.

I was holding my breath, sliding in and around Raven's mind. Even as she was losing consciousness, I could see what she was seeing. I could see her wound.

Lexi, I can see the wound, I mindspoke. *She's doing it! She's smoothing out the tissue of her heart. She's closed it. But she's lost so much blood.*

Jack placed his hand on my head. *I can see the wounds now as well. The heart is intact.*

Good. You both keep working on her wound, Lexi mindspoke. *I'm going after Leo.*

Lexi slipped out into the open. Leo looked up from his place beside Raven. "Oh, my. If it isn't the infamous Sarah."

"If I'm that infamous, you know that I don't answer to that name."

"It doesn't matter. Now that I'm finally getting this tracker back, you're no longer needed—by any of us. And after what you did to your clone mother, everyone will crown me as king when they hear that I've killed you." Leo flashed a hand into his waistband, pulled out a gun, and shot Lexi.

"No!" Jack screamed, bolting toward Leo, and before Leo could get another shot off, Jack tackled him to the ground, punching him repeatedly in the head. Felipe finally pulled him off and shoved him away.

With Leo reeling, Jack scrambled to Lexi's side to assess her wound. She lay flat on her back. No sound was coming from her.

Though my heart constricted at the thought of losing Lexi, I couldn't turn my mind away from Raven at that moment without the risk of losing her. Jack was on his own for now.

tracked

I turned my attention back to Raven. Her main wound was closed, and her other wounds seemed to be mostly mended. I slipped inside her head, but Felipe was already there.

You were helping to heal her, weren't you? I asked.

She was healing herself. I'm not the one with healing abilities.

I cocked my head. *What are you saying?*

Her tracker holds all the abilities that all of you have, except maybe some of Lexi's and some of Jonas's, but she also has a few that none of you will ever have. I can just sometimes help her use them.

Like when she received the concussion at her soccer game? I asked.

And like last year when my father nearly killed her right here in this forest.

Are you saying that Sandra figured out a way to get the power of healing inside a tracker?

She thought she had, but then the trackers went missing, and this tracker ended up inside Raven. My father never told Sandra where it ended up, so to her, its capabilities were unproven. But I knew. I knew a year ago, when I slipped inside Raven's head after inserting the tracker. I helped her heal several broken ribs, a severe concussion, brain swelling, and internal bleeding in her abdomen. Once her tracker is fully active, she'll be able to access those powers on her own.

"What's happening?" Leo screamed. He had recovered from Jack's attack and was crawling toward Raven. Blood dripped from his nose, and his eye was already swelling. "Why won't you *die?*"

He raised his knife in the air and pointed it directly at Raven's chest.

Leo was going to kill Raven if I didn't do something. My pulse raced. As if time stood still, I was rushed by a deluge of senses and knowledge of the gifts given to me through DNA manipulation and the cloning process. I stumbled out from behind the cover of the trees that had protected me moments before while I was attempting to help Raven heal.

Felipe remained fixated on Raven—continuing to aid her, I hoped.

Leo saw me, his arms still raised high above his head, white-knuckling the knife aimed at Raven. For a moment his gaze drifted toward the gun several feet away from where he knelt, and then he looked back to Raven.

I raised a shaky hand out in front of me as if I could shoot lasers from my palm at the murderer in front of me. *You will stand and back away from Raven, right now!* I ordered Leo.

Miraculously, Leo stood and took several steps backward. He remained motionless and completely in my control. I let out a breath now that Raven was out of immediate danger. But she still had not moved.

I walked over and knelt beside her. I placed my fingers on her neck. No pulse. I leaned in close. "She's not breathing," I whispered.

All around me my friends were in various states of brokenness, and I was about to see the second person I loved die at the hands of evil.

A slow burn started in the pit of my stomach, erupting into a raging inferno of fury that flowed through my bloodstream. It touched my heart, then exploded inside my mind.

I still hung on to Leo's mind.

Felipe appeared to be in a complete trance as he stared, unmovingly, at Raven. "The damage was too great," he said softly. His eyes lifted and locked with mine. But then he gave his head a shake and stared intently back at Raven.

tracked

A rage I'd only experienced once before—when Dani died—exploded in my mind.

Not only did I possess the power to reach into Leo's mind, I could also clearly see into the minds of the IIA agents who were about to reach the clearing. The sensation was equal parts exhilarating and horrifying. I felt anger for what was happening to Raven and Lexi—and I was overwhelmed by a mad thirst for justice over the murder of Dani. I wanted these people to suffer, to hurt. Like *I* had hurt after losing Dani. Like Raven had hurt over witnessing Nicholas's murder.

"Not again!" I roared. An incredible pulse of pure energy shot from my body, focused like laser beams in a myriad of directions. As the IIA agents burst into the clearing, the pulses instantly dropped them in their tracks.

And I was left with only one mind to control: Leo Rojas.

~~~~~

Leo was holding his head with both hands and grunting in pain. His eyes were squeezed tightly closed, and I had complete control of his mind. My entire body buzzed with electricity, even though the projection of the pulse had left me exhausted.

I approached him slowly. *Pick up your knife.*

He let go of his head and did as I ordered, then returned to stand in front of me. *I want you to drive that knife into your own—*

"Let me." Felipe touched my arm. I looked at him, and he nodded to the ground beside me. Raven was moaning, turning her head side to side. Her face was wrinkled in pain.

I let out a gasp.

"Go to her. I've got this one." Felipe held out a hand. A tracker lay in the middle of his palm. "I think my dear father could use a taste of his own medicine. Since I know how to control the trackers, I'd like to let him suffer the way he's made others. We'll make sure he spends the rest of his life behind bars."

As I looked down at Raven, I suddenly remembered what was really important in my life. I realized I no longer cared what Felipe did to his father. The rage that had coursed through my blood like lava only moments before had already begun to cool. I was not that person who wanted to kill these evil doctors—but I was happy to do my part to destroy their ability to hurt others.

I took two quick steps and fell to my knees on the ground beside Raven. I slipped inside her mind, much more easily this time, even though she wasn't completely unconscious. *Can you hear me?*

She licked her lips, but she still didn't answer. Her shirt was covered with blood. I peeled it up and examined the skin underneath. The wound was closed. I tore the shirt up the middle and pulled the soaked garment away. Then I removed my own shirt and covered her body with it.

Lexi, Jack, give me a status update, I demanded.

Leo sat on a log; he appeared to be in a trance. Felipe was examining the back of his father's neck.

Jack. Lexi. Talk to me.

I heard moaning. *Jonas?*

Yeah. Jonas stumbled through the trees toward me.

"I need you to check on Jack and Lexi."

"You okay?" he asked.

"She's lost a lot of blood." I looked down at Raven. I traced the line of her bangs along her forehead as I slipped inside her head again. *Please don't die.* I'd do anything, even if it meant I had to let her go. I didn't care if she chose to return to California or wherever. I just didn't want her to die. I scooped her up, careful to keep her covered with my shirt.

She swallowed hard. *And why would you have to do that? Haven't you and I lost enough for one year?*

I pulled her closer to me and laughed. She was hearing my thoughts, even the ones I thought I had kept to myself. *Yes, we have.* I stared at her closed eyes, willing them to open. *You realize you just heard my mindspeak?* That was new to me. *How are you feeling?*

Pretty crappy. How're the others?

Jonas's voice cut in. *Everyone's good,* he said, and I let out a breath. *A little battered, and Jack reeks of puke* (a lovely side effect to Jack's healing abilities), *but we'll all live to see another day.*

I pushed hair off Raven's face. Her eyes fluttered open, and I was nearly lost when I saw the warm inviting blue of her irises. "Did you remember everything?"

Her eyes welled up and she swallowed hard as she nodded.

I didn't dare tell her everything would be all right. I still wasn't fully healed from everything I'd suffered since discovering this world she'd been dragged into. But I held her tightly, knowing I would fight like hell to help her.

"I can hear Pascal speaking to the La Fortuna policia. Daniel has been taken into custody. Jonas explained to Pascal everything that I remembered earlier and everything that you, Jack, and Lexi learned tonight. The police have been so confused over the dozens of children who have gone missing in the past year. He left out the part about the trackers, though." Raven turned her face into my chest. A sob escaped. "So many children have been hurt. And Nicholas," she cried. "My friends lost their father."

"I know. I'm sorry."

FORTY-THREE

Raven

Navos Resort & Spa and Hot Springs was closed to the public the next morning, but after checking my passport, a police officer allowed me to pass inside.

As I passed by the different pools, the sound of the waterfalls drowned out the nervous voices in my head. I was conflicted about what I would say to Pascal, who had lost so much a year ago and was finally getting some closure. Neither of us could pretend that knowing the truth made everything better. But at least we could start the healing process.

I knocked softly on Pascal's office door. It was open a crack, so I pushed gently.

Pascal had been staring at the springs outside his window, but he turned when he heard me enter. He stood and closed the distance between us, scooping me into his arms. "I am so sorry. I would have come to the camp, but I..." He set me back down.

"It's okay. I don't blame you for not wanting to see the camp."

Pascal grabbed my hand and pulled me to the sofa against the wall. We sat facing each other. I set my backpack on the floor and wrung my hands in my lap. "Have you spoken to Felipe?"

He nodded. "Briefly. I'm so mad at him. It's going to take some time for me to sort through everything that we've learned."

"Yes, it is." I stood and paced in front of him. "If it helps, Jonas examined Felipe's head and has been tracking his thoughts. Jonas thinks that Felipe has simply been a victim of his father's and Dr. Porter's plan. And apparently he has saved my life multiple times now."

"What will you do?"

I walked over and stared out the window at the hot spring outside his office. "I don't know. Mom and Dad are on their way home. They had so many questions that I finally just handed the phone to Kyle and let him explain the bare minimum."

"Did you tell them that you have super hearing?"

I faced him, laughing a little. "No." Nor did I tell them—or Pascal—about any of the other abilities I appeared to have. "What a nightmare for them. They'll never be able to talk about me with any privacy anymore."

"Are you going to stay in Costa Rica?" He looked down at his feet, then raised his gaze to meet mine. "I want you to. I want the chance to heal our friendship."

"Nothing's wrong with our friendship."

"Maybe I just want you near while I heal. I'm not ready to say goodbye to you."

I could only nod.

"I like that Kyle person."

I smiled. "Just Kyle."

"Well, 'Just Kyle' is pretty cool. I think he kind of likes you. Maybe more."

tracked

"I think I more than like 'Just Kyle' too."

He stood and crossed to me. "You know I'll always love you, right?"

I nodded.

"And we will both heal from this. I will always be here for you. Whether you stay in Costa Rica or return to the States, I will not let another year go by without speaking with you."

"I will hold you to it!" I reached my arms up and circled them around his back while laying my head against his chest. "I'm here for you, too."

"You've brought me closure from a year filled with nothing but questions and pain. They weren't the answers I expected or would ever have wanted—but knowing is always better than living in that darkness."

I wiped a tear from my cheek and sniffed.

"I'm sorry, Amagita. I know Daniel was like a father to you."

I pushed away. "What's going to happen to him and Eva?"

"My contact tells me that Daniel's being held on a murder charge. But as the police learn more, they'll most likely add human trafficking to the list. As for Eva, unless they can prove she was directly involved, they'll most likely send her back to Venezuela and revoke her passport."

I struggled to reconcile my love for Daniel and Eva with the crimes against them. It would take time to understand why Daniel did what he did. "Where's Leo?"

"Also in jail, along with several International Intelligence agents, who apparently had the most mysterious, debilitating headaches when they were arrested. Leo's list of charges is extensive. And the IIA claims that these agents simply went rogue and will be dealt with."

I nodded. It brought me some comfort to know that these people were in jail, but I doubted that would stop me from looking over my shoulder.

"I have one last surprise for you," I said. I reached down and pulled a thick envelope out of my backpack. "This is from Felipe. He wanted to deliver it himself, but he knows you're angry with him. And I think he's trying to reconcile a few things of his own."

Pascal cocked his head before opening the packet of paperwork. His eyes grew wide. "This is the deed to the resort."

"It should have been yours when your father died. Instead of trying to sort through the falsified documents that would prove that you should own the property, Felipe had Leo's attorney draw up documents to transfer the Navos to you, and Felipe forced his father to sign them."

"How did he manage that?"

I raised a hand to massage the back of my neck. "Let's just say Felipe has quite the hold over his father now."

FORTY-FOUR

Kyle

"I'm starting to like summer flings," Raven said as she leaned back in the water. She wore my favorite white bikini. Her jet-black hair spread out in the water like silk waves.

I placed my hand on her bare stomach and guided her over to me. *Stop calling this a fling,* I mindspoke.

She tilted her head backward and flashed me an upside-down smile. For the first time in days, the smile actually touched her eyes. She nestled in closer to me. My arms encircled her, holding her close. I leaned in and kissed her neck softly. I had no idea what would happen next, but I knew I had been given second chances—a second chance at love and a second chance with Raven. A chill moved through my body as I thought about how I'd almost lost her.

She drew figure eights on my arm, and we were so lost in our own thoughts that we didn't even hear or see the others until Jonas came flying through the air to land right in front of us, spraying us with water.

Jack and Lexi stood on a rock, laughing.

Raven dove under the water like a mermaid while Jonas and I stared after her.

"Eyes on me," I said.

Jonas smiled at me. "You've got nothing to worry about. It doesn't matter how many times I check, she's not looking at anyone but you."

Lexi and Jack joined us.

"Everyone feeling okay?" I asked.

"Never better," Jack responded while Jonas and Lexi nodded in agreement. "How's Raven?"

"Physically, I think she's doing okay. Mentally, she needs time."

"We can remove her tracker. It won't be easy, but we can do it."

"You mean take her to near death again so that the tracker will loosen its grip?" Raven surfaced and treaded water twenty yards away from us. She smiled when our eyes met.

"Yes. We could do it with Seth's help, back at Wellington." Seth was a neurosurgeon, and brother to that evil bitch Sandra Whitmeyer, but a friend to us. He'd been a huge help to all of us as we'd learned about our abilities and mind powers.

I opened my mouth to respond, but Raven stopped me with mindspeak. *No. I'll keep the tracker for now.*

"How will I ever remember that she can hear our conversations?" I asked. The others laughed.

Raven, you will be hunted by IIA agents and the doctors who are still at large, Lexi reminded her. *We don't even know where Dr. Porter ran off to.*

Yeah, Jonas agreed. *He seems to disappear any time trouble gets close to him.*

They'll try to kill you, Lexi continued.

My heart constricted—and not in a good way—at the thought that Raven would forever be tied to my world with

tracked

that tracker in her neck. That she could be hunted like the rest of us. At the same time, I couldn't imagine her not in my life—and I couldn't imagine risking her life by taking her to near death just to get the tracker out.

Raven swam over. "I understand the risks on both sides. I'll continue to think about it."

"She has the time to consider her options," Jonas added. "I have control of the trackers, so no harm will come to Raven from the tracker. Felipe was kind enough to show me everything and hand over access to the computer server."

"Wow," Lexi said. "Just like that?"

Jonas eyed Lexi. "No. Not just like that." A silent conversation seemed to transpire between them. I decided to let it go for now.

Lexi turned back to Raven. "What are you going to do next?"

I tried not to look like I desperately wanted to know the answer, while silently hoping she would declare that she planned to follow me to the ends of the earth.

"First I'm going to spend some time with my parents. There's still a lot I haven't told them. Like the fact that I don't have a school to go to in the fall."

"You could always join us in Kentucky." Lexi smiled, then sang: "Just sayin'!"

I wanted to knock Lexi off her rock for being so obvious.

Heat spread across Raven's face. "I was actually thinking I would call UK's admissions office and ask about the transfer. It might be too late for next semester, but—"

Jonas spoke up. "That would give you time to let me train you to use the abilities inside your tracker." He winked at me. He and Lexi were both about to get thrown in the water.

"How about the three of you give Raven and me a minute?" I said.

Lexi, Jack, and Raven all traded looks before laughing. "We like it here beside these lovely waterfalls," Lexi said for all three of them.

I glared at them. "Fine." I pushed off in the water and grabbed Raven's waist. I leaned in and kissed her on the lips, and then lifted my head to motion for her to follow me. We swam away from the others and found our own private spot in the water.

Raven threw her arms around my neck. "I was thinking."

"Oh yeah?"

"My parents are going to need help processing through the mess of things Daniel has made of Puro Cielo, and I'd like to help locate as many of the children that Leo planted trackers in as I can, but after that..." She smiled, then dipped her head below the surface of the water. When she resurfaced, she refused to make eye contact with me.

"You're killing me, MacMillan. Why are you acting so shy around me?" I pulled her closer, forcing her to look at me while my hands roamed her back.

"How would you feel about having me in Kentucky?" she said.

"Are you kidding?" I swung her around in the water. "I would love it." I leaned in and planted a soft kiss across her lips, then I tried to reel in my excitement. "But I don't want to

tracked

add pressure to your life. I want you to find who you are. Even if that means going back to school in California."

"I think I'd like to take a semester off. You know, to get used to a new normal. Maybe apply to a few schools for spring semester." She shrugged. "I need to figure things out. Including what having this tracker means. And I need to learn how to shut off the conversations when I don't want to hear them."

"We can help you with that." Apparently, I was still learning about my own supernatural gifts. No one mentioned how my abilities had exploded out of control on that mountain. The power I had felt when I took control of Leo's mind frightened me. And I was now able to converse by mindspeaking more than I'd been capable of in the past.

"Then it's settled. After I spend some time with my parents, I'll make plans to join you in Kentucky." She smiled. *Who knows? Maybe our summer fling will turn into more.*

Definitely. I kissed her again, this time letting my lips explore hers a little further before pulling away and memorizing the happy look on her face.

"I also think I can help with finding more of the clones," she said. "There are quite a few around the world. Did you know that?"

I glanced toward the others. Jonas was staring straight at us, his look severe.

Suddenly, Lexi and Jack sat up straighter and turned slowly toward us. I could sense the tension radiating off of each of them.

"Am I missing something?" I asked, obviously not hearing the same thoughts they were hearing.

"I don't know," Raven said. "I was just thinking about the many clones and their whereabouts. One clone in particular popped into my mind. Addison? Who is she?"

My head snapped toward Lexi's. "Addison is trouble. Do you know where she is?"

"Portland, Oregon."

My eyes met Jonas's. "But isn't that where Briana is?"

Jonas turned his questioning gaze on Raven.

"Yes, Briana is still in Portland," Raven confirmed. "Will Addison hurt her?"

Lexi and Jonas were already climbing out of the watering hole.

I wrapped my arms around Raven, pulling her in close and kissing her hair. "Looks like some of us are leaving for Portland."

A Note From the Author

Thank you for spending time with the characters of the *Mindspeak* series. I hope you enjoyed Raven's and Kyle's story. It's only the beginning for Raven's and Kyle's adventure...

To stay up to date with what's next in my little world of writing, subscribe to my free monthly newsletter, "A Piece of My Mind" on my website, heathersunseri.com. I send out news monthly, and I will never share your contact information. Subscribers to my newsletter receive exclusive free content, are entered to win monthly giveaways, and are guaranteed to hear the latest news about any of my books, including cover reveals and when new stories are available.

Now that you've finished reading the *Tracked*, please consider recommending it to a friend or leaving a review on any of the bookseller sites. Word-of-mouth and reviews are the greatest ways to help other readers discover new books. I would truly appreciate it. If you do review any of my books, please send me an email at heather@heathersunseri.com so that I can personally thank you.

Happy Reading!
Heather

Also by Heather Sunseri

The *Mindspeak* Series

Mindspeak
Mindsiege
Mindsurge
Tracked

The *Emerge* Series

Emerge
"The Meeting" (An *Emerge* short story)

ACKNOWLEDGEMENTS

1 Peter 4:10 Thank you, God, for the gifts you've given me. Thank you for leading me when I ventured into the villages of Costa Rica to talk about the love You have for all of Your children.

So many people make it possible for me to write the stories I write. From the many people I observe doing extraordinary things in the world down to the cooks at my local restaurants who feed me when I'm on deadline.

To the most amazing readers and book lovers in the world who make my job the most fantastic way to spend my days. With each Facebook post, Instagram, and tweet you share, you inspire me to do my job even faster. I write for all of you.

To the people directly and indirectly responsible for helping me create the best novels I can and for inspiring me to keep learning the publishing business in new and different ways every single day (in no particular order): David Gatewood (my amazing editor), Kathleen Brooks, Jessica Patch, Connie Boyce, Robyn Peterman, Kris Calvert, Laura Pauling, Chris Counts, J.M. Madden, Melissa Bybee-Fields, Donna McDonald, and Katie Ganshert.

To Mike Sunseri for too many things to list here, but specifically for encouraging me to turn the second book I ever wrote, a book that was lost deep within the files of my computer, into Raven and Kyle's story.

ABOUT THE AUTHOR

Heather Sunseri was raised on a tiny farm in one of the smallest towns in thoroughbred horse country near Lexington, Kentucky. After high school, she attended Furman University in Greenville, South Carolina, and later graduated from the University of Kentucky with a degree in accounting. Always torn between a passion for fantasy and a mind for the rational, it only made sense to combine her career in accounting with a novel-writing dream.

Heather now lives in a different small town on the other side of Lexington with her two children and her husband, Mike, the biggest Oregon Duck fan in the universe. She is a recovering CPA, and when she's not writing, she spends her time tormenting her daughter's cat, Olivia, and loving on her son's Golden Retriever, Jenny.

Heather loves to hear from readers. Please sign up for her newsletter—*A Piece of My Mind*—to hear when future novels are released by following this link: http://heathersunseri.com/newsletter. You can also connect with her in several other ways:

Heather Sunseri
P.O. Box 1264
Versailles, KY 40383

Web site: http://heathersunseri.com
Blog: http://heathersunseri.com/blog/
Email: heather@heathersunseri.com
Facebook: http://www.facebook.com/heathersunseri.writer
Twitter: @HeatherSunseri

Photo by Candace Sword

Made in the USA
Monee, IL
28 April 2026

49137068R00204